JOURNEY

Mark Joseph Mongilutz

ISBN: 0692747176
ISBN 13: 9780692747179
Library of Congress Control Number: 2016910469
Mark Joseph Mongilutz, Scottsdale, AZ

PREFACE

Journey is a work of historical fiction that draws narrative fuel from human experiences both real and imagined. The story imagines conversational, political, and violent encounters between fictional characters (or historical characters pressed into the service of our tale) whose respective cultures did, in fact, intersect to varying degrees throughout the sixteenth century. I have taken a number of liberties with the historical record, though respect for the past was present in my mind throughout the writing process. My aim is to encourage the reader's mental acquaintanceship with a time not so distant from our own, with an era of considerable significance to our modern world, and with ways of life that, despite their faint echoes in the present, have largely succumbed to our species' ongoing march of progress.

Where my trespasses may most rankle the sensibilities of those who know better is in my somewhat adventurous employment of foreign language in packages including key nouns (proper and otherwise), the occasional adjective, and perhaps a choice verb here and there. The unique contextual, grammatical, and syntactical properties of a given language's terms almost invariably suffer under such circumstances. A given noun in a given language may, for instance, require preceding articles, which would only serve to disrupt the flow of an English sentence, and are thus herein sacrificed in service to the reading experience. Tenses are also, while we're on the subject, vulnerable to the sacrificial altar, though these I have preserved wherever possible. I trust all such sacrifices will yield for the reader a fluid reading experience.

As *Journey* is a tale of polyglot adventurers moseying about Europe, Japan, and the vast waters in between, the inclusion of carefully selected foreign words is intended to enrich the storytelling process, to incite the sensation of engaging with peoples of many spoken tongues, and to consider the ways in which mid-sixteenth-century travelers might have fused in clever ways languages both familiar and exotic to their own ears. Though I have vetted this aspect of the work as best as am I able to, mistakes may well persist herein. They are mine alone.

Do enjoy the read…

…and I will see you in the afterword.

—MJM

1

PORTUGAL, 1568 (LATE SPRING)

Watch Tower

It certainly wasn't an unusual dawn, not to the watchman's trained eye, and he typically had a good sense of such things. His duty at this time of day (at any time of day) was fairly simple but of some importance to the town's safety and well-being. He kept his eyes to the south, to the endless sea. Ocean commerce was the lifeblood of Sesimbra, a Portuguese port town through which large quantities of goods, traders, and the occasional explorer passed on a daily basis. Though not a particularly large town, Sesimbra was home to well over one hundred sailing, merchant, and laboring families, a garrison of sixty soldiers, and a natural harbor capable of housing several sizable vessels. And while at least two anchorages were reserved for cannon-armed caravels, Sesimbra was by no means impervious to the ever-present threat of seaborne raiding.

And so the watchman kept his eyes to the south while the rest of Sesimbra slept. Well, *most* of Sesimbra, anyway; the watchman liked to imagine himself the town's sole guardian during these lonely nights. A vigilant gargoyle whose eyes would see all and whose lungs would bellow forth the lifesaving warning cry for which his towns-folk would one day be endlessly grateful. The odds were seemingly in his favor on this front, as the last significant trespass against safety had taken place well after the midnight hour of an early summer's morning almost two years past. A dark-sailed ship housing what was, to be sure, a large battery of long-range cannon had appeared seemingly out of nowhere, or so *that* watchman had insisted back in the Year of our Lord 1566. The ship let loose several (four, it would later be determined) volleys of cannon fire upon the harbor, causing no small amount of damage in the process, then, oddly, retracted its larboard guns and made sail for the west-by-northwest as quickly as it had arrived.

The following morning, several men reported their homes having been robbed to one degree or another either during or shortly after the bizarre attack. For his part, the stony garrison commander, *Capitão* Marius, concluded the attack to have been an effective distraction, keeping all eyes to the harbor while a land detachment belonging to the ship's crew had done its foul deed on shore.

"They surely made their way west immediately after hearing the final salvo," Marius determined, "which explains our missing horses. Travel a bit west and you may find one or two of them yet."

Only after realizing that the garrison headquarters had not been left unscathed during the night's round of thievery did Marius take aggressive action. Documents of some importance, a hereditary sword, and an official seal were among the items liberated from Marius's own chambers while he was doubtless making his way to the frenzied harbor. Whatever was contained in those documents, Marius was visibly distraught over their having left his possession. Mounted search parties were sent miles to the east, to the west, and even half a day's ride north (opposite the shore) in hopes of finding some trace, any trace, of the admittedly efficient and capable bandits. Several dispatches were sent to neighboring harbor towns, to a nearby fleet, to the captain of a mercenary vessel with whom Marius had contracted during his time at sea, and to the Crown itself in hopes of securing the resources he needed to track down the dark ship and its band of thieving villains.

But no such tracking down was ever to be. What quickly became known as the *Djinn* (for whatever reason) had somehow gone entirely unseen up, down, and beyond the Portuguese coast. Had at least one credible sighting made its way to the Royal Fleet, to Marius's mercenary connection, or to the Crown itself, a nominal hunt might surely have been materialized. Instead, Sesimbra was forced to recover from the larcenous transgression in the absence of any outside help. And while the wronged citizens quickly placed that ungodly business behind them, *Capitão* Marius was often seen staring to the south as if willing the *Djinn* to return for a long-awaited settling of scores.

"What they took from me," he was heard to have said shortly after the search party returned, perhaps to himself, "may come to haunt us all. Sooner or later..."

But all that business was the better part of two years past, and the watchman, Duarte, would not allow for any such evil to be visited upon Sesimbra while its peaceful townsfolk were under his protection.

A stream of consciousness very much along those lines was running laps within the watchman's active mind when something disrupted his mental stride. The horizon, which in the early morning hours had assumed a soft blue veneer, was no longer perfectly flat from north to south. What had been a supremely straight line against which the sun itself, emerging to the watchman's left, could have shaven its glowing face was now slowly opening up more or less in the center. Something of considerable size and curious shape was minute by minute making its way steadily toward Sesimbra.

"Is that..." the watchman began to say aloud before pausing as though to choose carefully, for an audience of none, his next few syllables, "...is that...*one*?"

Indeed, the growing shape could very well have been a flotilla of smaller ships, though if so they were moving in miraculously tight formation. And as not a sliver of horizon was visible anywhere within the shape's larboard/starboard limits, Duarte was compelled to embrace an unlikely truth.

"That ship...it's enormous."

Then, remembering the solemn duty that was his charge, the watchman went to work.

"Afonso! Afonso!"

A dozing guard leaning some thirty feet from the watchtower's base slowly emerged from his state of half slumber.

Looking around himself then up to the watchman, clearly irritated, the guard said, "What in God's name is it, Duarte? I was enjoying my rest, for once."

"Forget your bloody rest, Miguel. Go get *Capitão* Marius, and hurry. There's a vessel on pace to reach our harbor within the next hour or so. Hurry!"

"A vessel? We're a harbor town, Duarte. Why should one vessel…?"

"I think it's one. Can't be sure. Please get the *capitão*; he'll want to see this."

Afonso's face assumed a look of sheer confusion as he took inventory of all he had just heard. Arranging his response in deliberate fashion, he resumed the exchange.

"Did you say you *think* it's one vessel? Meaning, you've no way of knowing whether or not one vessel or many is…or are…nearing our town?"

Replacing his generally friendly demeanor with a hostile scowl, Duarte responded with nary a shred of patience in his voice.

"Afonso, it's one vessel, but you could mistake it for two, maybe three. It's big, and it's on its way here. Get *Capitão* Marius, now!"

As confused as he was frantic, Afonso darted toward the garrison quarters while Duarte turned his eyes back to the sea and to whatever was riding its waves toward Sesimbra.

Capitão Marius

Marius lived rather well by small-town standards. Being a harbor town, Sesimbra was surely home to a few luxuries and creature comforts to which a comparably sized country village would have little or no access. Spices, teas, foreign foods, and the occasional exotic woman passed through the harbor with enough frequency as to stave off any boredom a worldly, clever, and notably intelligent man, such as Marius, might otherwise have experienced as the garrison commander of so small a military force. It was the last of these creature comforts, an exotic woman, whose ears first detected Afonso's light yet urgent knocking.

"*Capitão, Capitão...*" the woman whispered softly to a nearly comatose Marius, who was wrested from his slumbering state only after a third whispering of his rank and title.

"What it is, you wicked Delilah?" replied the still half-sleeping captain, his eyes closed.

"A knock at your chamber door. I think it's that funny man who walked us to your house last night."

"Afonso? What in God's name does that bastard want of me at so early an hour?"

Rising from his bed and robing himself in seemingly one swift motion, Marius was at the door in less than a half dozen steps, so modest were his chambers, so long his stride. He was a tall man and strongly built. Years of soldiering and the requisite training that had preceded them rendered the man's body lean, rigid, and rocklike. His facial features seemed to channel every bit of this stoniness, particularly the cheekbones, which were preternaturally angular and seemed to strike out at any whose eyes lingered overly long upon the man's unforgiving countenance. Naturally, Marius's eyes seemed to drill holes into all upon which they were trained for more than the duration of a single heartbeat.

It was those very eyes that Afonso dreaded falling within the sightline of. And it was those eyes that had by that point begun the drilling act that was their nature.

"Afonso, I can think of only one good reason for your disturbing me in this way."

Summoning an element of composure suitable for the message whose delivery he was tasked with carrying out, the usually slumping sentry spoke truthfully and economically.

"*Capitão*, this *is* that reason."

With his blue eyes widening to an inhuman extent, Marius rose to a physical stature still greater than the respectable one he invariably inhabited, dwarfing an anxious Afonso in the process. Speaking to Afonso, though seemingly looking within himself while doing so, Marius then issued a set of simple orders as though putting words to a regrettable death sentence.

"Sargento, please see this—" he seized the sentence momentarily, as if to choose from a catalog of acceptable monikers, "—this 'lady of the night' from my bedchamber and report to the watchtower with every available soldier, save for those manning the northern road."

Allowing the rushed woman a brief moment in which to hastily clothe herself, Afonso then quickly made his exit, perplexed "lady" on his arm.

Soldier and woman having left the chamber, Marius delayed his own preparations with a brief glance at a large, locked wooden chest. With a look of some uncertainty, the aging veteran readied himself for God only knew what.

"Two years—so long a wait, so brief a time."

Marius made his way quickly through the sleeping streets of Sesimbra, the town whose safeguarding had been entrusted to him. Though not at all an ostentatious harbor town, Sesimbra was indeed handsome to the eye. Its homes and offices were well designed and properly maintained. The streets were devoid of waste and impoverished souls. It was a respected and known port city, sufficiently removed from the outside world to feel like a modest country unto itself, sufficiently trafficked by travelers and traders to enrich the daily happenings. Sesimbra was life as life should be, and Marius aimed to keep things exactly as such.

Afonso returned to the watchtower with just under fifty armed, armored, and mostly weary guardsmen a few moments after the *capitão* himself had arrived. With no clear instructions as to what should follow, Afonso placed the confused men at ease and ascended the tower's narrow staircase to join his leader and the perplexed Duarte.

"*Capitão?*" asked Afonso, who was slightly devoid of breath.

"Yes, *Sargento?*" replied Marius without so much as nodding his head in the inquiring soul's direction.

"Duarte wagered the ship would reach us within a couple of hours, *Capitão*. It's been half that time. What should I tell the men?"

"Are the men braced for whatever it is Satan himself might throw their way?"

"I suppose they like to think so, but who's to say?"

"Whatever the men aboard that looming monstrosity want of us they're likely to take regardless of our efforts to prevent their doing so. All I ask is that we not make it easy for them."

"But, *Capitão*, is there anything we can do *now*?"

"In fact, there is. Send one man to share with the town's elders what is upon us and another four to rouse the rest of the village."

"Yes, *Capitão*."

"And, Afonso," continued Marius, now looking with some sternness at the somewhat more resolved sergeant.

"*Capitão*?"

"Those guardsmen, they are *not* to spread panic. Is that understood?"

"It is, *Capitão*, yes."

"The elders concern me not; they will behave rationally and surely convene a council. But the townsfolk must be made to understand that they have options available to them."

"*Capitão*?" replied a now uncertain Afonso.

"Those who prefer it may flee to the countryside. What has brought that ship to our door is no more than a hundred or so paces inland; beyond that, our women and children, most importantly, will be safe."

"Yes, sir."

"However, those who choose to stay might consider arming themselves with whatever it is they have on hand. Such defensive measures may prove unnecessary…and ineffective…but the act itself will surely calm many a nerve."

"Anything more, *Capitão*?" Afonso asked this with a curious sense of hopefulness, as though Marius's words themselves might alleviate the morning's increasing tension.

"Only that you and the men move with some haste. We've perhaps an hour, no more, until the reckoning has reckoned with us."

As Afonso departed, Duarte looked to Marius with somberness in his gaze.

"Do you know why they're here, who that is?"

Marius, sighing heavily, looked down to the harbor itself, taking visual inventory of the activity surrounding both men-of-war. Then, as though he had not heard a word of Duarte's query, he asked a relevant question of his own.

"Did Modesto give any indication as to when the *Anjo* and the *Arcanjo* would put to sea?"

Duarte was clearly displeased with this evasive response but answered the counter-question nevertheless.

"Yes. He said soon, though likely not before our...visitor, such as it is, closes to within cannon range."

"No matter. Even combined in their firepower, our Davids are no match for this particular Goliath."

At this, Duarte resigned himself to a silence whose end he knew would come soon enough, within the hour, in fact.

The two men—tall and steely Marius, short and pensive Duarte— kept their eyes locked forcibly on the growing shape that had so suddenly disrupted their otherwise peaceful horizon. All about them more than a hundred sailors and a comparable number of dock laborers bustled about with clear and governing purpose. Marius's contingent of soldiers, having little to do, simply stared silently to the south, all while two of their comrades stared with far less intensity (and less curiosity) to the north.

Stranger

The view north of Sesimbra was one of lightly rolling hills and little else to occupy one's field of vision. A single road led from elsewhere in Portugal to the quiet harbor town, and a single road led out. This road was interrupted at the town's northernmost limit by a tower not all that dissimilar to the one in which Duarte had first eyed the approaching behemoth, though this one was a bit shorter and had at its base a passageway through which a medium-size wagon could just make its way. Lengths of prohibitive wall ran for hundreds of paces to the east and west of the tower—nothing over which a reasonably able man could not climb or jump, were he so inclined, but more than enough to hinder the entry of any animal-drawn carts and wagons. Commerce, after all, must be governed (and taxed).

Carts making their way through the northern gate required, of course, that the passageway's iron gate was not in its forbiddingly closed state, which it invariably was from just after dusk to shortly before dawn. Moments before the guardsmen Nuno and Horacio had dutifully cranked up those heavy iron bars, they had received word to refrain from doing so until further notice. The reason? A ship approaching the harbor.

"A ship approaching the harbor?" repeated Nuno in his predictably sardonic tone. "They are, I trust, aware that that's what ships do—they approach harbors."

Horacio, who rarely thought things through with any closeness, was, as usual, perfectly content in allowing Nuno to do so for the both of them.

"I guess they know what they're doing," Horacio replied with perfunctory engagement.

"We are keeping the *northern* gate closed because a ship is approaching our harbor from the *south*. Am I recalling those orders correctly?"

"As I said—they probably know what it is they're doing."

Horacio was often given to placating his friend's impatience and had inadvertently developed a system of doing exactly that. He was readying himself for just such a round of placation when a shape appeared on the northern horizon. Both he and Nuno strained their respective gazes in order to better assess what had populated the horizon line.

"Is that...?" began Nuno.

"A horse?" finished Horacio.

"A big one, if so. We'll know soon enough; it's moving down the road. And what the hell is on its back?"

"A rider? If so, why is he slumped over?"

"Suppose the rider died on the horse's back?" asked a confused Nuno.

"I can't tell. But I can just make out what looks like a knee...and a foot. And that's not a horse," replied a straining Horacio.

"Not a horse? What in Satan's hell?"

As the beast was moving at a rather slow pace, the cautiously intrigued sentries had another small passage of time in which to await their answers. What seemed like an eternity measured in small minutes elapsed, after which a clear picture of what approached was visible via proximity to the now genuinely confused Nuno and Horacio.

"Horacio, why don't you request a few men join us at the north gate? We may need the help or at least additional witnesses."

Irritated by the request, Horacio assumed a rare stance of recalcitrance.

"I've one or two questions of my own to run past this ox-mounted vagabond, Nuno. And I will satisfy my curiosity just as you aim to satisfy your own."

"Very well, but let me have the first word, assuming the rider's alive. If it's trouble he's after, we'd best have knowledge of it straightaway."

After another moment or so, during which the sentries had watched with unblinking eyes, the ox was within a dozen paces of the gate. The faint sound of patting, as in the patting of a hide, made its way to Nuno and Horacio's ears, at which point the ox stopped dead in its tracks. Resting along the beast's broad, powerful back was the darkly clad figure of a seemingly sleeping (dead?) man. From what could be made out in so odd a scene, he was fairly long and lean of build and had resting along the ox's flank a slightly-too-long rapier with a strong and intricate wired hilt. A wide-brimmed hat covered the man's head, face, and throat. If there was any drawing of breath under way, it was not evident in the rising or falling of his elegant chest.

Nuno and Horacio allowed their collective observation to endure for mere seconds before the former put voice to the most obvious of questions.

"In the name of our magistrate and the Crown to whom he is loyal, who are you and what business have you with Sesimbra?" demanded Nuno in a tone that to a nonmartial soul might actually have carried with it an element of menace.

Then a sudden rise of the chest, an exhaling of air, and a single motion, which saw the man dismount, retrieve his blade, right his wide-brimmed hat atop his head, and make eye contact with his questioner, Nuno, who now looked into a pair of the most haunting eyes he had ever encountered. The eyes sat handsomely spaced one from the other beneath a pair of sharp, dark eyebrows and above a nose and mouth of positively angelic shapeliness. The face, the gaze, the posture, the grace—all of this amounted to a man not to be taken lightly or in any way antagonized.

Recovering from an instant of apprehension and awe, doubtless shared by Horacio, Nuno returned to a version of the script he had improvised moments earlier as the ox had been making, slowly, its way to the northern gate.

"Sir, I ask you once again: who are you and what business have you with Sesimbra?"

Looking intensely first to Nuno then to Horacio, the long-, dark-haired man looked back to his ox while at last responding in accented Portuguese.

"The ox, he'll need water and rest." The man then turned to his questioners. "He's walked with a passenger since early yesterday evening."

"Yesterday evening? Where are you coming from, sir?" asked a somewhat calmed Horacio. This stranger meant to cause no trouble.

"From about half a day's ride north of here. And this beast endured my burden through and through. Water and rest, he'll appreciate both."

Nuno, less calmed than his comrade, now insisted upon an answer. "Sir! Your business with Sesimbra—what exactly is it?"

"My beast will have what I request for it?"

"I imagine we can spare a few drops of water and a bit of stable space, yes. Now then, what has brought you here this day?"

"Would I be right in saying this is a coincidental day on which a stranger should arrive in your humble town?" was the stranger's odd response.

Nuno and Horacio looked perplexedly at each other and then back to the apparently prescient stranger.

"Why would you presume as much?" asked Nuno, his tone accusatory.

"I'm guessing an unanticipated vessel makes its way to your harbor as we exchange pleasantries. Is that so, or is it instead that I am a sunrise early?"

"We are, good sir, a harbor town. Ships make their way to our shores on a nearly daily basis."

The man narrowed his eyes just slightly. "To be sure. However, this is no ordinary ship. Whatever is heading north has yielded a degree of concern throughout Sesimbra, thus the northern gate being closed at an hour during which it might otherwise be open for daily comings and goings."

"What do you know of this approaching vessel, sir?" asked Horacio, almost childlike wonder in his voice.

"Horacio!" exclaimed Nuno. "He doesn't know with any certainty that there *is* a vessel."

"Yes, I do. And had I not a heartbeat earlier, it's now a certainty."

"In that case, to Horacio's question," replied Nuno, "what do you know of this mysterious ship?"

"I know that danger looms. I know I may be able to help. And I know my ox will need to pass through the gate, which you've yet to open."

"You've no intention of betraying us, now do you?"

The man looked to both sentries, to his ox, to the rising sun, then back to the sentries.

"No, I do not. My journey is fated to cross with that ship; I've no interest in Sesimbra, save for the water and shelter it might offer this weary beast."

"May we have your name, sir?" requested Nuno, his tone polite.

"I am Xavier."

Looking to each other, Nuno and Horacio silently reached an agreement about which neither felt particularly certain. There was, after all, something compelling about this stranger. He was poised, keen, nimble, and rare. He was shapely of limb with forearms like edges and long legs, which even when fully straightened seemed eager to leap. His dark, black hair hung long at front, at back, and along the sides, though here his mane retreated from the angles of that sharp visage, framing the face—which bore a thin scar across one cheek—without crowding it. He looked as much *through* as *upon* those with whom he spoke, and this he did in strictly level tones. His voice seemed incapable of being coned into a shout, as though it would simply slip from under the effort, leaving only soundless air in its wake. His gracile motion was at once hypnotic and threatening, a fact of which he was doubtless aware. His dark leather clothing, well worn, was not ill-fitted nor did it appear to grip his skin with any closeness. It simply fell into place where needed and hung airily where not. His sword, a rapier of some length, dangled from a thick leather lanyard and swung slyly to and fro with every graceful step he took; it was as much a part of him as was his sharp jaw, which held the crystalline features above it in place. He was a breathing blade; of that, any soldier could be certain. And so, having made essentially identical assessments of the stranger, Nuno and Horacio did as he had requested.

Upon lifting the gate, Horacio joined the man and his ox within the now open passageway. Taking the makeshift reins (a mere length of cleverly tied rope), Horacio began leading Xavier and his beast into town. He then turned to address his cryptic guest.

"The *capitão* will surely want to see..."

Before finishing the thought, Horacio turned his head and quickly realized Xavier was nowhere in sight. Looking to the ox as though to demand of it an answer, Horacio then called out loudly to his fellow sentry.

"Nuno! Nuno! Sound the bell—Xavier is fled within the town!"

As Nuno raced to do as Horacio instructed, he realized doing so would create a redundancy of sorts. For the bell opposite his own, situated atop the harbor's watchtower, was itself being sounded, and Nuno could surely imagine why that might have been.

Envoy Vessels

As *Comandante* Modesto had known, the *Anjo* and *Arcanjo* had not been ready to depart the harbor prior to the enormous ship's reaching cannon range, which it had done moments before Sesimbra's two caravels were departing the harbor and moving more or less directly south.

Modesto had not heard *Capitão* Marius's voicing of a David and Goliath metaphor, but he would surely have found it apt. Both caravels in the harbor were fairly sturdy of build and armed with over two dozen cannon, more than enough to discourage attack from opportunistic privateers ever seeking the unguarded harbor town for a quick ransacking. No, between the *Anjo* and the *Arcanjo*, any ordinary raiding ship would absorb more damage than was worthwhile in attempting to sack Sesimbra. But the monstrosity upon which Modesto now gazed from the *Anjo*'s ship wheel was certainly not an ordinary raiding ship nor ordinary in any way at all.

The massive ship's alien features had come into clearer relief as Modesto, his sail masters, and a score or so of reliable crewmen and gunners had worked frantically to launch the town's only armed caravels. It was colossal, perhaps more than three times the length of a royal galleon. Modesto wagered it would take a hundred paces to walk from stern to bow, perhaps half that from larboard to starboard. And it was tall, essentially a floating fortress.

"It must be displacing seven hundred tons—maybe more." Modesto had said aloud, perhaps hoping a seasoned sail master would object to such absurdity.

No such objections were voiced.

Its construction was of a sort no sailor in Sesimbra had ever before seen. None could identify the wood type used for either hull or mast, and the sails were themselves of a peculiar appearance, as if the cloth had been merged with some sort of sturdy paper. There appeared to be a quarterdeck, as befitted sailing vessels of all extractions, a main deck large enough to house Sesimbra's town square, and a forecastle deck of one sort or another. But two additional decks sat atop this seaborne city, each of which was home to a number of house-like buildings around which dozens of people were clearly moving about.

It was vast in dimension, brilliant in design, beautiful to behold, and terrifying in its mystery. It seemed far too still for a ship at sea, as though it had commanded the ocean waters to halt their motions wherever it deigned to drop anchor. Its sails, spread across eight masts, were bright and tall, corralling enormous gusts of wind into knots the likes of which few Portuguese vessels could match. The wood of which it was composed was not European in its extraction while the masts themselves seemed to flex slightly and recover like a particularly well-made *epée*. Apertures lined the vessels endless flanks, though cannons were not visible to the naked eye from any great distance. Even from a distance of a half mile, a large number of long boats were visible across the top decks, as were a series of palace-like structures, two of which crowned the main deck.

"Or was that the quarter deck?" asked Modesto of nobody in particular. This ship did not comport with any boatwright blueprints he had ever before seen.

The ship was alien, enormous, foreboding, and arrived...in Sesimbra. And there was little to be done about that at the moment.

"It could be home to a thousand souls," the *Anjo*'s sail master Jhorge had posited while directing his immediate subordinates to and fro.

"Perhaps many more than that, my friend," had been Modesto's reply, though how many more was anyone's guess.

The vessel had a curious curvature to it. Up and down, left to right, there was a fluidity to its design, which, while perhaps not much greater than what one might observe of a beautifully designed galleon, seemed somewhat incongruous when characterizing so large a ship. It was as though the ship's designers had been dissatisfied with the prospect of merely creating a vessel of unholy size and had therefore taken it upon themselves to enhance the undertaking with an element of artistic ingenuity.

A *tenente* assigned to the *Arcanjo* had observed what appeared to be a large opening, nearly the size of a castle drawbridge beneath where the ship's bowsprit might have been placed had the vessel a bowsprit.

"Why do you suppose that ship doesn't have a bowsprit, Modesto?"

Modesto's brother Guaspar had joined him in readying the ship. A trader and occasional mercenary, Guaspar was eager to be involved with whatever promised to unfold that fateful day.

"Is the absence of a bowsprit the *only* concern you have at the moment?" Modesto had asked, his tone remarkably light given the circumstances.

"I suppose not, no. Just don't see any vessels larger than a canoe without one. That monstrosity must be guided by Beelzebub himself."

"Or simply very well designed. Are you planning on being aboard when we set sail?"

"Yes, brother, though I've been asked to round out the *Arcanjo*'s crew. They're light a few men, unsurprisingly; we're really only able to fully man one of these caravels at a time."

"Well, one and a half, anyway," replied Modesto with a rakish wink.

"Just don't tell *them* that," Guaspar insisted while nodding toward the towering ship. "They might see it as a vulnerability."

"Brother, another six ships just like the *Anjo*, fully manned or not, would be of little consequence at this point."

"Maybe. Although…" Guaspar's voice trailed off, an element of curiosity hanging in the air.

"Now's not the time for half-finished thoughts, Guaspar. What is it?"

"Of course. Tell me, do you see any cannons on that behemoth?"

Modesto turned to look more closely at the vessel, which was now perfectly visible to the naked eye. There did not appear to be any weapons protruding from its flanks, nor any cannons atop its decks.

"I suppose not."

Now quite enlivened, Guaspar continued, "And *I* suppose we could take aim at that easy target until sundown without so much as a single shot being fired in response. Hate to sink her, but we might damage her into submission."

"Guaspar, we could exhaust our every cannonball and still find ourselves looking upon a more or less intact ship. Besides, whoever we're dealing with has not made it this far without some sort of armament. We'd best presume they've enough firepower at their disposal to sink the Isle of Rhodes into the sea."

By this point, the twin caravels with their less-than-full crews were prepared to launch. The brothers embraced briefly and made their way to their respective ships.

As the *Anjo* and the *Arcanjo* cut their way through the calm sea, Marius and Duarte observed the improvised two-ship embassy from their watchtower perch. Both gripped the tower's upper railing with white-knuckled pensiveness. At that moment, a breathless Horacio interrupted their somber quiet. He was clearly in a state of panic, though whatever had the man panicked, the magnificent ship, which was well within sight, was of no immediate concern to him.

"*Capitão*, please, a word." Horacio had not so much spoken the words as hurled them like a misshapen stone.

"What is it, Horacio? We are, by this point, quite aware of our unexpected visitor."

"Yes, *Capitão*, of course. But it is another visitor about whom I bring you word."

"Another visitor? Should I trust the one upon which I am presently laying eyes is simply eclipsing the second of which you speak?"

"No, sir. A stranger made his way to our gate a quarter-hour past... he was on an ox. He vanished after we..."

"After you *what*, Horacio?"

After having paused for half a heartbeat, he said, "After we let him in. His ox, too."

Though at least a dozen questions materialized within Marius's mind at this point, he merely looked back to the towering ship, which had now dropped anchor and situated itself as Sesimbra's nearest neighboring city.

"Seems our harmless little seaside village is of great interest to strangers hailing from land and from sea, both. I'll politely await the dropping in of a windborne wanderer, as it would seem only fitting at the moment."

"*Capitão?*" Horacio quizzically inquired.

But the *capitão*, the man who perhaps knew exactly who was here and why, merely kept his eyes on the seafaring titan at his ocean doorstep and waited...

2

Council

"Silence. Silence, gentlemen, I implore of you."

On a high barracks rooftop not far from Sesimbra's harbor, a middle-aged man, small in stature, absent any hair, and loud of speech was attempting to be heard by Sesimbra's half dozen elder citizens, a group that had years earlier taken to regarding itself as a council. The elders were not in any way panicked at the moment, though each had plenty to say in regards to the foreign ship, which was now in plain sight of every Sesimbran resident.

The middle-aged man (not quite an elder himself) was the town constable, Rodrigo, who had some months past taken it upon himself to act as the council's spokesman, enforcer, and occasional mediator. Under the circumstances, the latter role was very much necessary.

"Gentlemen, please, I've spoken with *Capitão* Marius and can assure you he has things under control," said Rodrigo, apparently believing every word he had spoken.

"Come now, Rodrigo, you surely don't take us for fools, not after nearly a year as the town's constable," replied Llopo, a man who at not yet fifty was a younger elder, so to speak.

"Not at all, good sir. Not at all. However, we have all witnessed our fleet send wolfish privateers and their pirate brethren scurrying to the nearest tailwinds on more than one occasion, have we not?" A smile now brightened Rodrigo's face as though he were recalling a particularly brilliant instance of naval triumph.

"First of all, Constable," said Amdre, a powerful former soldier who, even at sixty years, was a man of considerable strength and vigor, "the *Anjo* and *Arcanjo* scarcely constitute a 'fleet,' as you've termed it. And second, the ship now sitting a half mile from our harbor is no mere privateer. It could suck the marrow from a rogue caravel with one pass through its jaws and find room for a dozen more meals like it before nightfall!"

A nervous round of laughter circulated through the council, though Rodrigo found nothing funny in the matter.

"The ship has no cannon visible to the naked eye, gentlemen. They may have no offensive capabilities of which to speak," was Rodrigo's seemingly rational response.

Amdre continued, though less joviality was apparent in his voice: "Constable, that ship is of no design any of us have ever seen. It is not of Christendom, nor of the North Sea. If it's Ottoman, I would be curious to know how it passed undetected through Spanish and papal waters en route to our shores. Wherever its monstrous design was realized, it has traveled far, and it has not endured such a journey without weaponry of some sort."

No laughter from the council followed this assessment. What instead followed was an interminable silence, thoughtful, even. A moment passed, then Llopo spoke.

"What orders did Marius issue the envoy vessels?"

"You do, of course, mean our 'fleet' of Olympian power?" jested Amdre.

"Yes, *that* fleet of ours. What orders?"

Rodrigo had not thought to ask this of Marius, which ended up being of no consequence; Marius had simply volunteered the information.

"He ordered Modesto to simply block the ship's route to our harbor as best as are they able."

"They are to *block* a vessel the size of Gibraltar?" asked an incredulous Amdre.

"Yes. They are to maintain an intercepting presence until..." Rodrigo realized he didn't know what followed the word *until*, as Marius had not elaborated on as much.

"Until *what*, exactly?" a now irate Amdre pressed.

"Well, until we know what the ship's intentions might be," Rodrigo submitted with some hesitation evident in his voice.

"It isn't the ship's intentions that should worry us," said Llopo, "but the intentions of those aboard it."

"Ahh, yes—a fair point, sir." Rodrigo mistook Llopo's tone for one of levity.

"He's right." Amdre was now more placid in his delivery. "Something has brought that remarkable horror to our ordinary haven. And while *most* of us may survive the day, I very much doubt the same can be said for *all* of us."

Amdre's final words had the effect of turning all council and constabulary heads toward the positively dwarfed *Anjo* and *Arcanjo*, both of which had the look of bees approaching a hive, though not a hive either bee would regard as home.

"They will leave," a strange voice volunteered, "when they have what they've come for—not a moment sooner."

All eyes quickly turned toward the unfamiliar voice, which had come from directly behind the council members. There stood Xavier, still as stone, eyes like knives, voice cool, almost soothing in its placidity.

Rodrigo, the group's only armed member, drew his heavy blade with practiced skill and some haste, lunging its lethal point toward Xavier's bare throat. A hand of great strength guided by healthy reflexes seized Rodrigo's wrist in midthrust, halting the sword's tip a mere finger's width from its target, who was himself curiously still.

Amdre, more than a decade Rodrigo's senior, had effortlessly caught the paranoid constable's sword arm as it was on path to administer a possibly undeserved death. To the eyes of every council member, and to those of Rodrigo himself, it seemed Amdre's rescue might itself have been unnecessary. Something in the stranger's visage suggested that Rodrigo's blade would not have found its target, with or without Amdre's interference.

"Constable, you would enact a unilateral execution as such? Perhaps our having named you to your present post amounts to an error on part of this august body." Amdre's tone was severe.

"Sir, forgive me. Under the circumstances I thought this…man… might be in league with our seaborne visitors."

"If so, we'll hear it from him."

Turning to Xavier, Amdre spoke with equal parts authority and courtesy.

"Sir, your name and business with our town, please."

"I am Xavier. My business has everything to do with that ship, nothing to do with Sesimbra."

"Yet here you are, in Sesimbra, which means your business now has at least *something* to do with the town."

"The sooner that ship leaves your waters the better for you…the better for me."

"And how might we hasten that end?" asked Llopo, who looked upon Xavier with utter curiosity.

"Demands will be made. Comply with them."

"Simply *comply* with demands about which we know nothing?" blurted Rodrigo, his pride bruised, his arm sore.

"You will either do so of your own accord, or you will do so unwillingly. It is of little consequence to those whose interests have brought that juggernaut to your harbor."

The councilmen looked one to the other, to the *Anjo* and *Arcanjo*, to the city-size vessel, and back to Xavier. Amdre then spoke.

"And if we resist?"

"You would do well to understand that your visitor is here upon invitation. As am I, by way of inheritance."

"You speak in riddles, sir, and tax our patience in so doing." Llopo's curiosity had given way to a seething anger.

"I speak as I see fit to speak. A former member of this council was in league with at least one man aboard that ship."

"A former member, you say?" asked Amdre. "But we are all here, save for..."

As Amdre put voice to these words, Xavier produced a bundled cloth and unfurled it before the council. The contents, a recently amputated hand, dropped to the councilmen's feet, a ring clearly visible on the hand's small center finger. The ring, exact equivalents of which are worn by every council member, bore a crest...the Crest of Aviz.

"Balltesar?" asked Llopo, in horror.

"Constable, I regret my interrupting of your earlier efforts," intoned Amdre. "Seize this man at once."

As Rodrigo attempted to close with Xavier, a series of swift motions disarmed and rendered the hapless constable unconscious. Then, having incapacitated the only armed member present atop that roof, Xavier turned deliberately to the council.

"Do not behave rashly. Balltesar lives, though minus the hand you see before you. Be assured, the hand you see before you carried in its grasp a blade all its own prior to my rendering it thus."

"You severed the man's hand? Why in God's name...?" began Llopo.

"With good reason. And Balltesar, as the more intelligent among you might be starting to understand, had his own interests in mind, not those of Sesimbra. Do you recall an agreement between your merchant marine and a German gunsmith?"

Amdre answered for the group, perhaps as only he was privy to the deal's particulars. "Yes, I recall. The deal was encouraged and brokered by...oh, dear God—"

"By Balltesar." Xavier completed the thought.

"But what does that have to do with the ship...with you?"

"With me, nothing. Save for the fact that I have unrelated business with a man aboard that vessel."

"So then…?"

"So then, have any large crates made their way to your town in recent days? Perhaps delivered by men of German tongue and extraction?"

"Dear God. The new muskets. They were to be sold to the English and at a decent profit."

"They'll not be sold at all; they'll be aboard the juggernaut by dusk."

Llopo then turned accusingly to Amdre. "What has Balltesar done? What do you know, Amdre?"

"I know what I've said I know—Balltesar was allegedly brokering an arms deal with the English, though this I knew only by way of rumor; the deal, it would have profited the town nicely.

"And doubtless profited that greedy bastard still more!"

Xavier interjected, "It'll profit him not at all now."

"So then"—Llopo stepped toward Xavier—"we simply deliver those damned crates to whoever it is wants them on that ship…?"

"It won't be made easy. First a message will be delivered, and it will be lethal. You still have time, so use it well. Ensure your largest building is empty of human life and of anything else you would like to see spared."

"What are you saying?" asked Amdre.

"I'm saying you have time to ensure that happens. Use it wisely."

"Are they…"

But before Llopo could continue with his line of questioning, the unmistakable sounds of chaos were visited upon his ears and those of every other Sesimbran. The chaos was unfolding in the harbor, as those there had witnessed dreadful activity aboard the exotic ship.

The vessel had systematically and very slowly circled in such a way as to direct its stern, which featured a drawbridge-like aperture, toward the town. And in precisely the same manner as a castle drawbridge, the aperture was lowered, revealing behind it only darkness, at least as was visible from Sesimbra's harbor. Mere seconds later, a large protrusion did as protrusions (large or small) do—it protruded. This particular protrusion had the look of a massive cannon, which, of course, is what it was.

"God help us," said Marius, still standing alongside Duarte, who noted the *capitão*'s tone was one of resignation; perhaps he was resigned to an event he had long suspected would materialize on his watch.

On the nearby rooftop where the council still stood gathered, a now conscious Rodrigo was being dragged to his feet by the powerful Amdre.

"What in the name of Saint Matthew is happening now?" Rodrigo asked, truly confused as to just what was happening around him.

"The visiting doom…it is soon to visit doom upon our town," replied Amdre in a mild tone of voice.

"And the stranger?"

"Ah, you mean Xavier. He vanished while our eyes were directed to the sea."

"Vanished?"

"Indeed so."

At this, the dazed constable looked with squinted eyes to the sea, to the harbor, and back to Amdre.

"God help us."

Sink and Destroy

"Ready starboard cannon! Prepare to fire on my command!"

Modesto had kept his sight locked on the massive ship's wheeling and now fully wheeled stern since prior to the *Anjo* having left anchorage. When it showed signs of opening, he had ordered his gunners to stand ready. Marius, Guaspar, and the others might have been curious as to what was concealed within the terrible vessel's wicked bowels, but Modesto knew *exactly* what to anticipate.

"That ship is armed," he had said to a young fellow *tenente*. "Be ready to answer hellfire with hellfire."

Opening the stern's hatch had required a lowering process of well over a minute, as unlike a drawbridge to which every soldier and sailor observing had made comparison, this hatch did not stop its descent once perpendicular to the ship. Instead it was lowered entirely until the outer planks rested against the lower stern. Modesto had then noticed a series of clamp-like hooks emerging from within the ship's lower decks. These clasped the hatch into place, doubtless to prevent it from slamming into the vessel when subjected to recoiling force.

"What do you suppose they've got in there, sir?" The young *tenente* had asked this of Modesto, perhaps in hopes of hearing a comforting lie of one sort or another.

Modesto did not afford that question the courtesy of a response. "Make certain your aim is true, your resolve steady. We are all that stand between Sesimbra and that monster."

At that moment, a number of crew members began pointing frantically to the juggernaut's open bow, as the protruding cannon was now visible to all.

"Your fire to that cannon, each and every shot!" shouted Modesto, knowing orders to that effect were doubtless being voiced aboard the *Arcanjo*. "Let fly our furies!"

And fly the furies did, fly in the form of fast-moving cannonballs. Would that they had been more effective, or effective at all. Neither caravel was of sufficient height or of the proper design to deliver sustained firepower against a target any higher than their own fairly low gundecks. Skilled gunnery could, of course, achieve accurate shots above and below the gundeck level, but this required the timing of one's shots with the rise and fall of one's ship as it rocked with the sea. And such precision marksmanship varied widely from gunner to gunner, as was to be expected.

The result: the *Anjo* and *Arcanjo* hurled an impressive barrage of cannon fire at a virtually unmissable target with fervor and intensity and accomplished nothing in so doing. Round shot after round shot struck the floating castle with considerable force, chipping bits of plank into the ocean below before themselves joining those insignificant woodchips in a vast watery grave. It was everything Sesimbra's defending vessels could produce in the way of offensive power; dozens of cannon, hundreds of round shots, most every cannonball impacting the ship's huge planks, if not the cannon itself—and it was not enough. For the waterborne juggernaut remained not merely unscathed (save for a bit of superficial scarring) but firmly fixed in its anchored state. If any sailor, soldier, or passenger aboard the recipient of the *Anjo* and *Arcanjo*'s combined firepower had detected the force of a single round shot's impact, they would surely have had their ear pressed to the hull at the precise place and moment of said impact. Otherwise, a somber prayer service within its confines could very well have been under way throughout the attack with nary a praying soul having been cognizant of a battle raging outside.

"Continue firing until we've sunk the beast or exhausted our round shot, *Tenente!*" Modesto shouted to be heard over the now sporadic sound of the *Anjo*'s cannon fire.

"Sir, I fear the latter will precede the former. We've round shot to last another six volleys, maybe seven, and the first dozen have had no effect whatsoever," was the *tenente*'s perfectly accurate response to Modesto's orders.

"*Tenente,* we will…"

Whatever words Modesto had intended to speak were fated never to be heard, for as he was reaching midsentence, the juggernaut began to turn slowly, deliberately, and by some nightmarish and unimaginable force of manpower and leverage. All aboard Sesimbra's twin caravels had suspended their activity to watch closely whatever it was that was about to befall them.

SSWW—BOOM!

What the caravels' crews heard was, in essence, a terrible blast preceded by the sound of air being quickly sucked into a passageway, as though some fire-spewing leviathan had inhaled deeply a full gust of air only to force that very same air out behind a murderous ball of fire.

Modesto and one or two others aboard the *Anjo* had remained standing as the shot had flown over their vessel. As the remaining crew members regained their composure, they looked to the *Arcanjo* with desperation, fearing their sister ship might have been sunk by that unholy weapon.

But the *Arcanjo* was unscathed, its crew likewise looking to the *Anjo* for fear that it had been met with a first fiery, then watery end. Both ships, however, were afloat; their crews stunned, but their hulls and sails intact.

"Sir, the cathedral!" the young *tenente* was pointing north to Sesimbra, pointing to where once had stood the town's beautiful house of worship. There was now fractured and flaming wood, shattered glass, crumbled stone—an instant ruin, blazing from the explosive ordnance by which it had been horrifically struck.

Enacting the *signum crucis*, Modesto spoke in response the only words he seemed capable of speaking in that moment after registering such horrific demolition to so holy a structure: "God in heaven."

"God in heaven." Guaspar had spoken those same words, a favorite saying of his (and Modesto's) father. "We haven't anywhere near enough shot or powder to answer that."

Guaspar had spoken these words to no one in particular, though they had been heard by Fernão, Modesto's counterpart aboard the *Arcanjo*.

"We've no choice but to answer, Guaspar. Your brother will surely do exactly that aboard the *Anjo*."

"Regardless of what we do, sir, we've no way of stopping this on our own terms. Perhaps we provide covering fire for my brother while he sails the *Anjo* out to the open sea. He could return with a whole fleet."

"Marius has already sent a messenger by horseback to achieve the same end. No, we hold here until we are sunk or captured."

"Sir, we cannot continue firing upon an impenetrable target. We accomplish nothing."

As Guaspar finished his impassioned plea, firing once again picked up aboard the *Anjo*, Modesto apparently intent upon letting loose his every round shot in retaliation for Sesimbra's cathedral having been destroyed.

"Signal him to stop, Fernão. This is madness."

"I will do no such thing. Modesto is...what on earth?"

Fernão had been distracted by the sight of the juggernaut's cannon being withdrawn from sight and of the juggernaut itself turning once again. This time, however, its bow was being brought into line with a smaller and more proximate target—namely, the *Anjo*, which had continued its barrage upon the impervious vessel.

"Modesto!" Guaspar screamed toward his brother, his voice drowned out by wind, by cannon fire, by distance. "Modestooo!"

Aboard the *Anjo*, Modesto was hurrying his crewmen below deck.

"Crank those damned cannon upward! Cut into the floor planks if necessary; we need to concentrate fire on the stern, on that gun port. Keep their gun withdrawn!"

A number of burly sailors began the hard work of repositioning several heavy cannon, hoping to situate them in such a way as to align their firing trajectories with the enemy ship's upper bow.

"Haste, men, haste! We've not a heartbeat to lose."

As Modesto spoke these words, he was looking through a gun port. He would personally oversee the aiming of a cannon and would create for his adversaries a good deal of trouble in so doing.

"Concentrate *every* shot on the upper stern. That beast has for its rear end a rather wide mouth—let's feed it accordingly!"

Seven repositioned cannons soon having been loaded, Modesto was heartbeats away from issuing the order to fire. He had attuned his equilibrium to that of the sea and was awaiting the perfect upsurge to bring his cannon into alignment with the murderous vessel in his sights. One swell, two swells, and three swells...

"On my command!" Modesto pushed these words out with enough force to have launched a round shot from his own lungs.

"Modesto, sir!"

"I see it, *Tenente*. Stand clear of me; this gun will likely dislodge after I fire."

The "it" in question was the juggernaut's enormous cannon emerging once more from its murder hole, this time being angled downward...angled toward the hapless *Anjo*.

"All fire on their gun, men; ALL FIRE!"

One swell, two swells, three swells...

"Now! Fire!"

SSWW—BOOM!

Heavy silence, ominous.

If a single round shot fired from the *Anjo* had struck its target, not one aboard was ever to realize as much. Their collective firing had been wholly drowned out by that of yet another terrific blast from the floating fortress—their own vessel's destruction had been almost immediate.

What Guaspar had seen from the *Arcanjo*, not least of which was the almost certain death of his good, and dear, and brave brother, was simply nightmarish. The *Anjo* had been punched straight through, its masts cut down like so many twigs snapping before a relentless boulder, its top deck obliterated, its crew hurled dozens of yards, save for those who found themselves in the path of the vicious projectile— they had been met with instant death...they had included Modesto.

"MODESTO!" Guaspar screamed his dead brother's name with the fiery rage of a thousand burning hells, all sense of humanity departing his mind in the process. Whatever mourning might darken his soul in the days to come would need to await its rightful turn; he became a living vengeance in that instant, looking with pure hatred upon the evil sea colossus, which had laid waste first to his town's cathedral, then to the ship of which his beloved brother had been captain.

"Guaspar, now is not the time for grief." Fernão had spoken these words, though was doubtful they had been heard. "We must return to harbor—there's nothing more to be done from where we now find ourselves."

"Sir, look. Just larboard the vessel."

The *Arcanjo*'s sail master, Diogo, had spotted a vessel perhaps equal the caravel's size. It was beautiful in design, dark in its coloring, lightly armed, propelled by a combination of oar and wind power, and it was moving directly toward the *Arcanjo*.

The peculiar presence of yet another alien ship had an oddly calming effect upon Guaspar, who voiced what surely all had been thinking: "What in the Devil's name does this mean?"

His question was answered in a fashion neither he nor any aboard the *Arcanjo* could have predicted.

"Is that…? Fernão began to ask.

"An olive branch, yes, in the mouth of a dove." Guaspar observed.

Indeed, an oversize flag, nearly the size of a mainsail, was flying high above the newly appeared vessel. Stitched expertly (and beautifully, all were forced to admit) into the wide canvas was a clear image of a branch held in the mouth of a flying dove.

"Now, *that* is a curiosity," said Fernão to nobody in particular, a mixture of dread and wonder giving his voice a certain hollowness.

"If it's peace they're asking," said Guaspar through teeth tightly gritted, "they'll not have it from me."

"No, I expect not," Fernão dutifully replied. "I expect not."

Terms

Terror had understandably taken hold of Sesimbra. The cathedral had been instantaneously reduced to mere rubble, which by itself had been enough to generate rampant fear and chaos. But it was seeing the *Anjo* destroyed, its sailors and gunners killed, their bodies hurled from the decks, that had resulted in a terrifyingly oppressive pall laying itself across the minds of Sesimbra's citizenry. Their sons had been aboard the *Anjo*, clergy and parishioners had been going about their duties and their worship within the cathedral, and there seemed to be no answer to the horror by which the survivors were now besieged.

"Marius, what recourse have we? Any at all?" Llopo and the other council members stood near the cathedral rubble with Marius and a half dozen of his guardsmen. The remaining guardsmen were assisting survivors and working to keep calm a population brimming with panic.

"I've signaled to the *Arcanjo*. They are to await our sending of an ambassador prior to parleying with whoever comes bearing that olive branch."

"Surely *Comandante* Fernão will represent our interests fairly. Why not allow him to begin the parley immediately?" asked Llopo, with Amdre nodding in agreement at his side.

"A parley? Is that what you imagine will be taking place?" Marius was amused. "No, councilmen, this will not be a parley—they will be delivering us terms, and I've a suspicion as to why it is they are in our waters in the first place."

"Perhaps we should tell him of the stranger." This was suggested to the council members by Rodrigo, who had joined the group after assessing neighboring damage around the obliterated cathedral.

"The stranger? You are the second to make mention of this mysterious figure, Rodrigo," replied Marius, more curious than he had been when first Horacio had informed him of as much.

"Indeed, a foreigner named Xavier inserted himself into our makeshift gathering atop the barracks." Amdre was explaining slowly, as though to ensure Marius absorbed every detail. "He spoke cryptically, until he spoke of Balltesar; then he spoke with some clarity."

"And what did the foreign Xavier have to say about the absent Balltesar?"

"First, it seems likely he will—with the exception of his right hand—remain absent in perpetuity."

At this, Marius's visage was mutilated by a pained grimace.

"And second?" he asked with pensiveness slithering just beneath the surface of his every syllable.

"And second," Amdre continued, "that Balltesar had been brokering a sidebar arms deal, one that may in some way have brought on the regrettable events of this day."

Marius sighed, turned his back on the council, looked to the ground.

"Snap locks. Modern design. Rifled barrels."

Each sentence spoken seemed to take a heavy toll upon Marius.

The council exchanged looks of concern before training their collective gaze upon the noble figure, his back to them still. It was Llopo who at last spoke.

"*Capitão* Marius, will you please reveal to this council just what it is you know? What were Balltesar's aims?"

"They were *our* aims, Llopo. Though it is of little consequence now."

Marius sighed, then turned to face the council members.

"We purchased from the Germans several thousand rifled snap locks over the past three years. At first we did so seemingly under royal authority, with the help of an official seal and a forged letter, which even the most trained of eyes would have believed was acknowledged and blessed by our king himself."

Amdre was at a loss. "But to what end, Marius? Angels above us, man! To *what* end?"

"We have been reselling these particular muskets to English and Dutch privateers, gentlemen, and at a handsome profit. Balltesar was the natural intermediary, considering his Habsburg ancestry. And he was untrustworthy—which meant, in a sense, that I could trust him."

"While we attempt to sort for ourselves just what the devil a statement like that means, perhaps you will explain just what it was that compelled you to arm Protestant criminals with first-rate weaponry." Llopo seethed.

"We armed criminals, yes. Criminals who happen also to be enemies of the Spanish, goddammit! We are increasingly powerless to contest their supremacy over our shared peninsula, but the English, well…the English have proven rather effective where plaguing Spain's seafaring career is concerned. If I could support that end while lining Sesimbra's—Portugal's—coffers, I was honor bound to do exactly that. The less you knew the better—and I knew I could trust Balltesar to keep quiet on the affair."

It was Amdre's turn to crank the interrogative wheel. "*Capitão*, tell me—what was it that troubled you so deeply following the raid of two summers past?"

"The royal seal, it was taken from my chambers. Along with the forged letter. And a sword of great importance to me, though that proved the least of my losses."

"And yet your elusive arms dealings, these would continue another two years thereafter?"

"Indeed. We had established financial credibility with our supplier by that point; the seal and letter had always been a formality—a formality that helped to inaugurate our transactions, but a formality all the same."

"Yet you were troubled deeply by the loss of this 'formality,' were you not?" Llopo was cross but genuinely intrigued at this point.

Marius betrayed not a scintilla of emotion in his terse response.

"I feared a blackmailing might ensue, or worse…"

"And you doubtless wondered," interjected a now familiar voice, "who held the seal in their possession."

All turned to face the source of this last statement. And there, in all his grace and guile, stood Xavier.

"You are, I take it, the stranger about whom so much has been said this day." Marius seemed entirely at peace with Xavier having inserted himself into the conversation.

"I'm becoming more familiar to your town, which is generally counter to my wont."

"Which suggests there must be sound, or at least *compelling*, reasoning behind your allowing as much."

"That vessel"—Xavier nodded lightly toward the sea—"it will be leaving here on a southern course before a new day dawns. I aim to be aboard it."

"Seems our interests are aligned to some degree," replied Marius. "We'd very much like for the ship to be on its way, and so would you... if for different reasons."

"Nonsense!" Llopo would hold his tongue no further. "We will sink that monstrosity and kill every last person aboard."

"No. You will try, valiantly even, to sink that ship. But you will fail, and in the end those aboard will have what it is they came to retrieve." Xavier was placid, which was seemingly the only manner available to him.

"And what is it they aim to retrieve?" Amdre was collected, reasonable.

"There are two thousand rifled snap locks—and a scroll containing their design and construction specifics—stored beneath the armory, all of which will be transported to that juggernaut by day's end."

"Jesus!" Rodrigo was as stunned by this information as he had been by Xavier's concussive blow earlier that morning.

"*Capitão* Marius, just how was it you managed to carry all this out under our very noses these three years past?" This had been asked by the heretofore silent Joham, eldest of the council members.

"With the help of Balltesar and his excellent capacity for discretion, particularly when his own potential for profit was at stake." Marius seemed to smile at some related memory. "A bit of clever crate labeling and the assigning of loading/unloading duties to a few of Sesimbra's more dimwitted of laborers. With the sheer volume of goods to come and go through this harbor of ours...the addition of a few crates every third month was no matter."

"Well, it is very much a *matter* now, Marius. Look what you've done." Llopo was on the verge of tears.

"And done it is"—Xavier's was the voice of a calculating man—"for which reason you must ready those crates to be transported."

"It isn't enough we've been arming English privateers with the finest snap locks; we'll now be doing the same for a ship of unknown allegiance?" Llopo was at his wit's end.

"The ship is allegiant only to itself. View it as a sovereign kingdom, and rest assured those muskets will not be brought to bear against your countrymen, nor anyone in Christendom." Xavier spoke only factually, not consolingly.

"And if they were intended for such a purpose?" Marius was suddenly returned to the present.

"And if they were, their fate this day would be the same—conveyed from Sesimbran storage to the lower decks of a powerful ship against which you are virtually defenseless."

"Can you at minimum assure us no further harm will come to our town or its people if we do as you insist we do?" This was asked by Amdre in a spirit of compassion, which was, for him, rare.

"I will do all of which I am capable to ensure as much prior to realizing my own purpose."

"Very well, but answer us just one more query: how was it Balltesar came to possess the knowledge for which you were yourself looking?"

Xavier looked coolly toward the massive ship, its cannon gate still lowered, its hull perfectly still in the lightly rocking waters below.

"Because he was in league with the man I am after—a man who has at least twice traveled the seas upon that juggernaut."

Aboard

"Move quickly, men, and be light of touch in handling those crates."

Marius had been directing activity in the harbor since an hour after the council had disbanded. Rodrigo, who had little else to do and always looked to be of use, stood at his side throughout.

"That's nearly all of them, Marius. Suppose we'll soon receive word back from Fernão?"

Marius had sent a small oar-powered boat to the *Arcanjo* with instructions to maintain his position until such time as forty large crates could be safely transported to his ship. Nothing about the eventual transaction was communicated, which meant curiosity would gnaw at the caravel's already shaken crew.

"It seems we'll have word fairly soon. There were seven men aboard our messenger boat—six oarsmen and Amdre—there are now eight?"

"Who is the eighth?" Rodrigo squinted sharply in hopes of answering his own question, which ultimately proved unnecessary.

"It's Guaspar. His brother was surely killed aboard the *Anjo*. We'd best be braced for the anger of a rightly angry man."

And angry Guaspar was. Upon reaching shore, he had jumped aggressively out of the boat and made his rage known to the stone-faced Marius and anxious Rodrigo.

"Something about forty crates, Marius? That has the sound of some goddamned trading deal. Modesto was killed this morning, along with dozens of others aboard the *Anjo*, goddammit!"

"There is no such trade deal under way, Guaspar, we are simply offering a concession in order that more of our townsfolk do not meet with your brother's fate—may he rest in peace."

"A concession? So it's a trade after all. We trade our dignity and right to revenge for the saving of your cowardly hide!"

Before the word *cowardly* had fully departed the lips of its speaker, Marius had closed the distance between himself and Guaspar so as to speak his next words within an inch of the grieving firebrand's face.

"You will hold your tongue, Guaspar, or lose it." Marius was murder incarnate in moments such as this, and all but the most foolish knew him to be sincere in the issuing of such threats.

"I will say as I damned well please, Marius." Guaspar was gripped by Marius's lethal intoning, but his grief and the rage born of it superseded any feelings of fear, which might otherwise have overcome him. "My brother, Sesimbra's best man by a wide margin, is dead this day."

"And we will grieve for him accordingly, Guaspar, of that much you may be certain. But first we must rid ourselves of that"—Marius paused as though to chew on the words before spitting them out—"foul menace. And the measures explained in my missive to Fernão will see to that end."

"What exactly is contained within those crates, Marius?"

"Our only recourse, Guaspar. If you'd like, you are welcome to oversee their being transported to the *Arcanjo*."

Guaspar turned to the sea at his back, then back to Marius. "By all means." This last he had said while gripping tightly the sword hilt at his side. "By all means, indeed."

Fernão had been waiting in war-torn waters for two hours, a panicked harbor to his stern, a curious envoy vessel at his bow.

"Any signal from the envoy craft?" He had asked aloud variations of this question since first the smaller ship had halted before the *Arcanjo* at a distance no more than twice its own breadth.

The responses had come from whichever crew member happened to be nearest him at the time of inquiry and had all taken some form of an answer in the negative.

"They seem to know far more than do we as to what will next occur in our waters." Fernão had spoken these words to Guaspar as the latter was preparing to make his way back to the shore—anger in his eyes, his fists, his heart.

A small two-oared boat had returned perhaps an hour after Guaspar had left the *Arcanjo*. Constable Rodrigo was the sole passenger, and he had come bearing truly unanticipated instructions.

"You are to signal to that envoy vessel informing them that they are welcome to position themselves alongside the *Arcanjo*."

"Alongside us? Have you taken leave of what little sense you once possessed, Rodrigo?" Fernão was nearing the end of his patience.

"There is to be a transfer of crates from our vessel to theirs within the coming hours. I am not certain how, but whoever is helming that vessel is prepared for this order of events."

Rodrigo's face betrayed his own confusion, though he had accurately conveyed the instructions with which he was charged.

"And what assurance have we, Constable, that no harm will come to my crewmen?"

"We have none, though it becomes clearer by the moment that theirs"—Rodrigo pointed to the juggernaut—"is not solely a mission of destruction; they've a material end in mind." The constable worked to soothe Fernão's pensive mind.

"And we will simply channel these crates—whose contents remain unknown to us—with nary a word exchanged between ourselves and these heathens?"

"Would you prefer a round of polite conversation, Fernão?" Rodrigo spoke in a manner pithy and unsuitable for the gravity of all that was afoot.

"I would prefer we not reduce ourselves to conveyors of mysterious goods to men who have wrought death upon our town, upon our countrymen!"

"Then we are of one mind, Fernão, but not carrying out the orders as I have described them would ensure further destruction, more death. Let us comply and, in the process, perhaps achieve a peace the likes of which our guns and swords cannot purchase."

Fernão relented, as he was not a foolish man, merely proud. A quarter-hour later a large white section of sailcloth was raised aboard the *Arcanjo*; on it had been hastily painted a dove, and in the dove's beak…an olive branch.

The envoy vessel immediately exited its suspended state, closing the small distance between itself and the *Arcanjo* before expertly maneuvering itself into position alongside the caravel. So much of this process was seemingly undertaken by an invisible hand, as very little of the top deck was clearly visible from a caravel's height. Even as the alien craft was at last sufficiently proximate to allow for the securing of a gangplank between the two vessels, only seven, perhaps eight men could be seen…

…for the most part. Each man was shrouded in dark and intentionally concealing clothing, their faces entirely obscured save for the eyes, which were themselves difficult to make out from any distance greater than an arm's length.

With the vessels securely adjoined one to the other via a sturdy and wide gangplank, Fernão kept his crew members at the ready.

Three men were assigned to keep the sails, rigging, and anchoring in order while the rest positioned themselves alertly on the top deck, eyes on the mysterious envoy craft with which they had now formed a tiny wooden island—an island beneath the looming shadow of a floating mountain, which appeared to see all. On the adjoined vessel, opposite the *Arcanjo*'s crewmen, stood only two men, their eyes looking straight ahead, their right hands resting on sheathed swords.

"Here we wait, men. Here we wait." Fernão had spoken the obvious; his men appreciated it all the same.

3

SHIP

The Crates

"The ships are joined. Fernão has done as instructed." Marius spoke nominally to the council members who had joined him in the watchtower, though the words were spoken as much for their own sake.

Below, several guardsmen and a score of dock laborers worked to load and secure forty large crates into a sizable barge, which had traditionally been used to convey men of prestige (royal, holy, martial) from their large oceanfarers to the Sesimbran shore. Within and upon the barge's two decks, which had been emptied of anything not affixed, and in the sole cabin, every crate had been made to fit. Even with such ample cargo, a crew of four sailors, ten dock laborers, and six guardsmen had room to move about, room to see that their task was carried out.

"We are prepared to leave this very moment, Marius." Guaspar had overseen the loading from beginning to end, had handpicked the laborers and crewmen who would accompany him back to the *Arcanjo*, and was eager to be on his way.

"You've the schematics on your person?" Marius asked, knowing the answer. "They'll not leave us in peace without the muskets *and* the knowledge of their design."

Guaspar patted his right breast with a powerful left hand. "It is on my person. Let us away."

"And do remember, Guaspar"—Amdre looked sternly upon the young man whose build and bearing so resembled his own—"yours is not a mission of revenge. Any actions along those lines will surely see further hellfire spewed onto our frightened townsfolk."

Guaspar nodded. "Still no sign of your stranger? Of Xavier, was it?"

"I'm afraid not," replied Marius. "He voiced so clearly his desire to board that terrible ship but does not seem interested in our transporting him to it."

"I've a suspicion he will realize his ends, regardless of our knowledge as to his means." Amdre was confident in this pronouncement.

Llopo was unmoved by his colleague's fascination. "We are, of course, speaking of the man who maimed and inadvertently exiled Balltesar, are we not?"

"Yes, we are. The same Balltesar who had been engaged in questionable dealings of a nature unknown to his fellow elders."

"For which reason he deserved a violent punishment?"

"For which reason his maiming should come as no surprise to you, to any of us. He assumed a risk in pursuing his greed and was rewarded with crippling and self-imposed banishment for his trouble." Amdre had never much cared for Balltesar, which made his seeming indifference as predictable to Llopo as it was enraging.

"Gentlemen, I was the author of Balltesar's actions in this matter." Marius was authoritative even when embracing culpability. "And when the present menace is behind us, I submit myself and my actions to further scrutiny."

"Yes, you will, Marius." Llopo continued to stoke the fires of his outrage.

"But for the time being, let us afford the present task our every attention."

With that, Marius trained his sight upon the departing barge. Sunlight would soon be fading, and all were praying this awful business would reach a conclusion before nightfall.

"Steady, men. Row quickly, but keep steady—those crates aren't particularly stable in their arrangement." Guaspar stood like an upright bowsprit at the barge's fore, looking behind him every other moment or so to ensure the top-deck cargo had not toppled.

The barge's two masts supported considerable sailcloth, but the day's winds were light, and Guaspar meant to make good time in reaching the *Arcanjo*. And so his crew rowed quickly and steadily. From what Guaspar could reason out, the *Arcanjo* would essentially serve as a passageway through which the forty crates would be carried en route to the envoy vessel. Once the ships were connected one to the next, and once the transporting of crates was under way, Guaspar would stand aboard the *Arcanjo*'s top deck and eye closely, vengefully, the enemy who had been foolish enough to come within striking distance. And strike Guaspar would...

An eye for an eye, a life for a life. Guaspar had been repeating those words to himself throughout the loading of those damned crates and would continue doing so until he had thrust his sword hilt-deep into the belly of whichever heathen had the misfortune of stepping to within a blade's length of him. *I will avenge you, Modesto. One among them will meet a terrible fate this day, a death more painful than that which you wrongly suffered.* Whether or not Guaspar had spoken these words aloud would have been a mystery to him. They had simply populated his inner monologue and would continue doing so until such a time as his bloodlust had been assuaged.

"We've nearly reached the *Arcanjo*, Guaspar!"

A burly dock laborer named Lluis had readied himself to join the barge with the *Arcanjo* once they were near enough.

"Help Lluis with that gangplank, men. We'll need to nail it down on our side once it's hooked onto their deck."

Guaspar had been gripping his sword hilt with sufficient might to have crushed an iron goblet. Relaxing his grip, he then set himself to the task at hand.

"Are we secure, Lluis?"

"It's locked in place and stable enough for the weight of a man and a crate at a time."

Guaspar nodded and looked to the top-deck cargo. A voice then arrested his thought process.

"Guaspar, you are returned?"

Fernão looked down at the barge from a man's height above, as the *Arcanjo* was a full deck taller than Guaspar's vessel.

"Of course I am returned. I aim to see that demon ship gone from our waters before the next sunrise."

"Yes, to be sure. But with your brother having…"

"Let's see to these crates, Fernão. Haste be our ally at the moment."

"Indeed, my good man."

The loading progressed somewhat more slowly than Guaspar would have liked. Though the gangplank was well made, it was narrow and the angle at which it was positioned was high. Simply lifting the crates overhead to the *Arcanjo* proved impractical. The height difference was too great, the crates too heavy.

"Haste, men, haste! Let us be done with this foul errand," Guaspar pleaded with the laborers.

He now stood aboard the *Arcanjo* for the second time that day and had taken note of those two heathens on the opposite end of the caravel's gangplank.

"I don't suppose they'll be offering us their assistance in completing the second loading effort?" he had asked Fernão as the twentieth crate had been brought aboard the *Arcanjo*.

"They've given no indication one way or the other, though I suspect we'll not be granted access to their vessel, even if it is a mere intermediary."

"When the time comes, I will do the speaking, Fernão. Is that understood?"

"Guaspar, I…"

"*Is it understood?*" Guaspar had snapped these words toward Fernão like the rapid blow of a skilled pugilist, though at closer range.

"It is, yes. But I ask that you keep front of mind our purpose here, son."

"Purpose is what brought me back to the *Arcanjo.*"

At this, Fernão merely sighed and returned to his largely unnecessary overseeing of the crate transfer. Guaspar's crew had found their rhythm, and the crates would all be in place aboard the *Arcanjo* just before dusk, after which, Fernão could scarcely fathom what would follow.

"And forty. That's the last of them, Guaspar." Lluis had spoken with neither pride nor relief.

"Bring yourself and our five strongest aboard the *Arcanjo.* Detach that gangplank and send the others back to harbor."

"Guaspar?" Fernão now looked quizzically at the grim man who wore the loss of his brother like a cowl of hatred.

"Calm yourself, Fernão. We may need the extra labor. Besides, do you have any objections to ferrying these men back to shore?"

"No, of course not. I just…"

"Good. Now let us see to the final step in this regrettable transaction."

Guaspar, with Fernão a half step to his rear, approached the *Arcanjo's* gangplank and the masked sailors who stood opposite it.

"Your godforsaken crates are here now. They are ready for your taking—so take them."

Guaspar hoped his white-knuckled left hand was not visible to either man. He needed only a heartbeat's time in which to bury the blade in his victim's skull. Would that the unlucky soul be definitely the man who fired the giant cannonball, the one who had taken his brother's good and noble life. But as it surely was not the man himself, he had perhaps been aboard the sea monster when the killing began…and so he was complicit, as even the elder Amdre himself might have reasoned.

"Or would you like that we deliver them ourselves?"

Upon speaking those words, Guaspar stepped a foot onto the gangplank and heard the distinctive sound of steel escaping a sheath—or partially escaping, in this case, as the masked sailors had drawn their weapons to reveal but a sliver of polished blade.

"Seems you were right, Fernão; we are not invited aboard their hellish ship."

What happened next had the dual effect of being both peculiar and informative. One of the sailors produced a small piece of parchment and, from its contents, read aloud in the most accented Portuguese to which Guaspar and Fernão had ever been exposed.

"One crate here," the man read while pointing to the section of gangplank immediately at his feet. "We will look. Once confirmed, one more, and one more, and one more."

"Saint Matthew in heaven," exclaimed Fernão, "we'll be here until the Rapture."

"Let us then to it, my friend." Guaspar betrayed no irritation, merely acceptance.

Both men were forced to acknowledge the efficiency with which their counterparts worked. Eight more men had materialized from their vessel's lower decks and were quick to open each crate, inventory its contents, then move it aside to allow for the next to take its place. Though the inspection ran perhaps a mere hour or so in its near entirety, by the fortieth crate, nightfall had begun to show its dark face.

"Stop right there, Lluis. I'll manage that one." Guaspar had taken the final crate from Lluis and positioned it in its designated space upon the gangplank. He now turned to face the men who had stolidly maintained their positions aboard the envoy vessel for several hours' time.

"Here you are, you heathen rats. Your fortieth crate." He then whispered to himself, "*Just step an inch closer my way...one of you, or both. It makes no difference.*"

All but one of the additional laborers had left the envoy vessel's top deck, and that man's task was under way that very moment. Upon finishing his counting of that crate's beautifully made snap locks, he began to hurriedly move it into place alongside the others. He, too, then left the top deck, leaving Guaspar to wonder just *who*, aside from the originally stationed two, sailed the bloody ship. It was now those same two who commanded Guaspar's firm attention.

Stepping closer, Guaspar assumed the most disarming posture of which he was capable. "OK, then, we'll just detach that finicky gangplank and be on our way." His hand tightened still more upon the sword hilt, for he knew he was within mere heartbeats of drawing it in haste and fury.

"AHHHHHHH!"

A scream, but from where? From which ship? Guaspar turned to his rear, then looked back to his quarry, only to realize he was himself the quarry. For had he turned an instant later, a mere instant, his life would have brought to a painful and violent end. One of the two men with whom he had been exchanging tense eye contact for hours had closed to within inches of Guaspar and was on course to thrust a medium-size sword into his broad, flat gut.

"Damn you! What have you done?" he exclaimed and demanded while catching his attacker's sword arm in midstab. "*What have you done?*"

SNAP

Always an unusually strong man, Guaspar's power benefited now from the slow-boiled rage, which had been stewing inside of him since that morning and had now flowed over as he realized the day's slaughter was not yet at an end. Guaspar had, to his own surprise, broken his assailant's wrist.

AHHHHHHHHHHHHHH! AHHH! ARGGG!

The screams below deck continued, and those men of his who had been on the *Arcanjo*'s top deck a moment earlier had gone below to aid their town brethren. Guaspar aimed to join them but had men to kill here before doing so.

CRACK!

He drove the fore of his head into the already wounded man's face and watched his body lose all animating energy; it was as limp as wet cloth. Discarding that assailant into the water below, he then faced the other in a similarly unprepared state. For the second man was delivering a flurry of sword strikes against the larger Guaspar, who had drawn his blade in only just enough time to block the first round of attacks.

But there were more rounds to follow.

Clang. CLANG. CLANG!

The blades struck one another in a storm of steel and fury. Feeling himself overwhelmed by the swordsman's speed, and realizing he was needed below, Guaspar resorted to creativity of a masochistic variety.

SLICE

Nearing his wit's end, Guaspar had allowed his opponent's sword to stab directly into his own shoulder, which had effects both desired (stopping the blade) and undesired (intense pain). With only an instant in which to put down his foe, Guaspar struck swiftly, mercilessly—and when he allowed himself to assess the conclusion he had brought about, the sight was one of butchery. In his frenzied state, bloodlust upon him, Guaspar had driven his heavy sword through his enemy's left collarbone, through the ribs below, and nearly into his abdominal cavity.

As the dying man slid back and away from the sword by which his body had been cleaved, Guaspar allowed himself only a split second in which to comprehend his kill. But another scream had the effect of moving him below decks, where God knew what awaited his already bloodied blade.

"Fernão? Fernão?" He was screaming at this point, though his doing so served little purpose.

For the gun deck was an abattoir in which all but two of the *Arcanjo*'s crew members were lying dead. Fernão himself had been sliced deeply across the waist, his entrails spilt out before his still body. Lluis had been nearly beheaded, though he still held in his dead hand a bloodied club.

"Goddamn you!" This Guaspar screamed toward the six shrouded men who surrounded the *Arcanjo*'s remaining crew members, bloody sword gripped with ferocity in his bright red hand. "GODDAMN YOU!"

Four of the six broke away from their murderous semicircle and moved strategically toward a man they clearly regarded as a greater threat than the cornered crew members, both of whom were run through before Guaspar could engage with the four now closing in on him.

"I'll take you bastards with me; I swear it. I fucking swear it." Guaspar drew a dagger from his boot and hoped against all hope that the second blade would allow him to fulfill his questionable promise.

CRASH

A lantern to the rear of Guaspar's now six attackers was destroyed, its flame extinguished.

CRASH

Then another. Then a scream. One of the six, the man who had been nearest the second lantern, had been opened up across the chest with a deep cut.

CRASH

Another lantern. Another scream. The man nearest that third lantern now lay dead, his own chest cut deeply.

While two of the remaining four ambushers turned to face this hidden threat, the other two charged the similarly confused Guaspar. Fortunately, his confusion quickly gave way to resolve as he ducked a swinging blow from his nearest attacker and plunged the dagger into that man's exposed groin.

He then turned to the other and readied himself for a more skillful attack.

CRASH

Yet another lantern. Yet another scream.

Guaspar could only fathom what force of nature had come to his aid, though he'd not share too generously of what little honor might be salvaged from this hideous combat.

A series of sword blows not unlike those he had fended off on the top deck had him backing up toward the *Arcanjo*'s bow, only a few steps remaining until he would be cornered and likely killed.

CRASH

The destruction of that lantern plunged the lower deck into almost total darkness, save for a bit of moonlight making its way through the hatch through which Guaspar and the others had entered.

Guaspar knew only one other remained, the one with whom he now fought for his life...well, aside from the unseen dealer of death, but...

One thing at a time, Guaspar thought.

Another stroke of combat genius: dropping his sword to the floor after feigning a heavy-handed parry, Guaspar then caught his opponent's arm in midswing, clearly surprising him greatly, and delivered a brutal succession of hard fists to the man's wide-eyed face.

CRACK. CRACK. CRACK. CRACK. CRACK!

The last of these five punches almost certainly had the effect of collapsing the man's cheekbones, to say nothing for liberating his every tooth from his now destroyed jaw.

CRACK!

This last one killed him.

As the body dropped to the floor, a limp pile of flesh, bone, and blood, Guaspar himself fell to his knees in exhaustion, in anguish, in resignation.

"Who are you?"

Silence.

"I asked who you are! You killed my enemies. Why?"

K'TCH

A lit lantern. A face illuminated. A diamond-like voice.

"I did not wish to see two sons of one womb die this day."

The voice was that of Xavier.

"You? You're that stranger of whom Marius and Amdre were speaking." Guaspar spoke with the voice of the dead. "How did you get aboard?"

"In a way not unlike the manner these men employed. Are you wounded?"

"Not badly."

"You'll not steer this vessel back to harbor on your own. I will signal the barge; they've not yet docked."

"And what will you do after?"

"What I came here to do—I'll be boarding that juggernaut."

"How do you—?"

"I've left alive a number of that smaller vessel's crew—bound but alive."

"Who are you? Truly—who *are* you?"

"Tonight? A man fated for a journey." Xavier stopped as if to consider something he had forgotten to remember. He then looked to the dazed Guaspar with discerning eyes and procured a rolled cloth from within his black cloak. "Make certain this finds its way to Marius. I understand it took its leave of him some years past."

Xavier gently placed the cloth at the wounded and now grinning Guaspar's side.

"Stolen during our piracy episode that summer night?" Guaspar asked this while unfurling the cloth, revealing its sole content—the royal seal, about which Marius had fretted for countless nights. "I'd wager that envoy ship is the infamous *Djinn*, is it not?"

Xavier merely sheathed his sword and knelt to help the wounded sailor stand. "Be well, Guaspar, and live."

The Captain

Xavier moved quickly. He had helped Guaspar to the *Arcanjo*'s top deck (with strength Guaspar couldn't fathom existed in so gracile a frame) then made his way to the envoy vessel, which was casting off well before the barge made its way back for the *Arcanjo*'s sole survivor.

And he was gone, leaving behind the corpses he had created, the Sesimbrans he had perplexed, and the ox upon whose back he had lightly slumbered the night prior.

As the ships separated one from the other, Guaspar attempted to visually register what was happening aboard the envoy vessel. He could vaguely make out a tall, lean shape that must have been Xavier. He appeared to have his hand on the wheel while closely watching two other figures, both shorter and stockier in outline, as they manipulated the vessel's rigging and readied it to join the floating city a quarter-mile to the south.

"What I wouldn't trade to have seen that wicked leviathan from within, even if only for a few moments." Guaspar was cradling his wounded shoulder and wincing from the pain of bruised knuckles, the very knuckles that had ruined an assailant's skull. His killer punches had done their business at a price. The voice within continued in a largely ordered manner. *Goodbye, Xavier. I owe you my life and hope one day to settle that debt.*

Aboard the crate-laden envoy vessel, Xavier kept a guiding hand on what proved to be an ornate ship wheel. The two sailors whose throats he had left intact were managing between them to catch sufficient wind for a swift return to the large vessel from which they hailed. They had observed this leopard-like swordsman quickly and effortlessly kill three of their shipmates below decks before themselves being rendered unconscious. They had also deduced, upon being awakened from their painful slumber, that the same man had almost certainly murdered those comrades who had snuck aboard the Portuguese vessel earlier that evening. He had awoken them and spoken words in their own tongue (accented though it was) to the effect of "Sail. Now."

Fearing for their lives and realizing their brethren were dead, they had done as they were told.

The distance was short; the sailing brief. Within a quarter-hour of having detached from the Portuguese ship, they were steering themselves alongside the *Ocean Castle*, as Xavier himself understood the translation of those intricate exotic etchings, themselves carved deeply into the vessel's broad stern. The *Ocean Castle* had lowered a rigging contraption into which the envoy vessel was to be guided. This would allow, Xavier also knew, for a stable transferring of the crates. Once that transfer was complete, the vessels would again separate, the smaller of the two maintaining a miles-wide satellite orbit around the *Ocean Castle* scouting for foreign vessels that might be curious as to what business a ship the size of a small fiefdom had in their waters.

But for the time being, Xavier had focused his energies upon a proper aligning of the envoy vessel with the ingenious rigging setup.

"They will be docking shortly, men," came a voice from aboard the *Castle*. "Be ready to swiftly secure that cargo. We are to be hundreds of miles south by morning."

The voice, which Xavier could faintly hear even from hundreds of feet away and far below the deck from which they were spoken, belonged to Nam, the *Ocean Castle*'s quartermaster, who was wholly unprepared for what he was soon to discover.

Nam watched closely as the small scouting ship, which had traditionally been purposed for missions identical to the one it had just undertaken, was tightly affixed to the rigging platform he had lowered an hour earlier.

"Shin? Move your men to the top deck to assist with the unloading. *Tokoh* ordered our sails to be set within the hour. We've not a moment to spare. Hurry!"

Silence.

"Shin?" Nam, a man accustomed to feelings of uncertainty and paranoia, was now doubly so on both fronts. Pointing to a group of equally perplexed crewmen, Nam directed that they lower themselves down to the scout vessel via rigging ropes and investigate, which they expertly executed within a few dozen heartbeats.

Observing the men from his perch, Nam demanded answers: "What is it? Where are Shin and the others?"

"All are dead, save two, and they were unconscious until we brought them to," was the response shouted from a terrified crewman.

"Nonsense! All dead? How? What are you saying?"

"Master, there is more…"

"Go on! What is it?"

"There was another with them, a Christian from his look."

"And where is he now?" Nam had been shouting more than was necessary given the evening quiet and his proximity to the men below.

"He is nowhere to be seen. He must be…"

Sun and moon! Nam said to himself, *He is aboard the* Castle.

"Nam, what would you have us do?" his crewmen stared in angst at the equally anxious Nam, who knew what needed doing.

"Keep eyes on those crates; I will send more men to assist with their unloading. Have you affixed the ship?"

"It is secure, sir."

"See that it stays that way, and stay vigilant; I'll not have you meet your end this night."

And Nam was away, moving with haste to the *Castle*'s central top deck on which the ship's primary guardhouse stood. Storming with purpose into the large room, he turned to those six men who nightly manned this post. Their eyes went to Nam with some surprise, though nothing in the way of alarm, certainly not panic.

"We've an enemy aboard." Nam was frank.

"One enemy? How?" The senior *jungsa* had responded coolly, as Nam anticipated he would.

"He returned with the *Bocho* moments ago, killing many before reaching us. Two survived; they were unconscious when we found them." Nam labored to maintain a calmness equal to that of the *jungsa*, who had drawn his short blade while absorbing the information.

"Three of my men will remain with you on the top deck. Have the crates been loaded?"

"The *Bocho*'s crew is dead, or most of them. I've more men coming to assist with that."

"You will be safe with these three." The *jungsa* then looked to the two others: "You, come with me. We've a hunt to undertake."

The search party departed with a shared look of purpose about them. Nam then addressed the three who had stayed behind: "Let us see to those crates, lest the deaths they brought about be in vain."

The *Tokoh*

Tokoh Jaidev, a lean and gaunt man of almost exactly fifty-five years, sat comfortably behind his large desk. He was refined in appearance, with intelligent eyes set deeply in sockets that seemed cavernous yet open, not unlike the cabin in which Jaidev saw to his work. It was approximately twelve paces from doorway to the rear wall and just under that from side to side. Adjoined were the sleeping quarters in which the busy *tokoh* rarely spent more than four hours in a given daily cycle. The ship's responsibilities, after all, were not wont to subside on account of an aging man's desire for sleep.

The evening's tasks were not so much different from what they might have been on any other evening. Course charting, ship logs, promotion and demotion filings, and, of course, the entering of thoughts into what was now a decades old journal, one that preceded his own captaincy by many circumnavigations of the world. Of course, this night was unusual in at least a couple of respects, though neither was yet in any way worrying to the oblivious *tokoh*, who was now in his twelfth year at the *Ocean Castle*'s nigh mythical helm.

There had been a show of force, as scheduled, which Jaidev had not deigned to oversee; destruction of that sort, though necessary, had never proven delightful by the sensitive Jaidev's measure. If such things could be avoided, he would avoid them, but they could not invariably be avoided, and so he did not invariably avoid them.

A pity, that, he had said to himself upon hearing the *Castle*'s thundering cannon deal its death upon the harbor town, which, had he simply troubled himself with turning around and standing from his seat, Jaidev could have seen through one of his cabin's two large windows. *Would that we might someday keep from exhibiting power thusly during ventures of this sort.*

THUMP! THUMP! CRASH!

Two figures crashed through Jaidev's heavy cabin door, iron-braced though it had been. One figure now stood atop the other, a figure graceful in bearing, acrobatic in build, dark in cladding, and grim in visage. He had rendered unconscious Jaidev's eunuch corridor guard, a warrior of considerable height and girth, when jump-kicking the man into the *tokoh*'s outer cabin door. The door had given way, as, presumably, had a number of the poor eunuch's ribs.

A number of Sesimbrans would have known the man as Xavier, the ox-mounted stranger who had, as a parting gift, saved Guaspar from certain death and avenged a number of the *Arcanjo*'s crewmen by visiting brutal killings upon those aboard the *Bocho* (or *Djinn*, as it had been known in Sesimbra years earlier).

But to Jaidev the man was merely a stranger, as Xavier so often was to so many people.

"This may come as a surprise to you, sir," the *tokoh* said in broken and violently accented French, suspecting it to be the stranger's native tongue, "but I have been expecting you."

"Takeru." Xavier spoke with crisp, icy French, as the tongue was to him, indeed, native.

"Ah, yes—Takeru. You *are* the very man I have been expecting. And Takeru, I should say, sends you his regards. Something about a hope that you have made your peace with, well, whatever it was." Jaidev was fairly confident tonight would not see his life thread severed, his mortality exposed at its frayed ends. "I expect you've not come for my life; after all, we've only just made each other's acquaintanceship."

"That gun of yours"—Xavier nodded curtly below decks—"it's rather deadly." Xavier had taken a step closer though was still several paces from the *tokoh*'s desk.

"It is, yes, and a bit older than it appears. My predecessor insisted it was present at the siege when Constantinople met its end." Jaidev looked down for a moment, as if attempting to witness that historic siege replayed on the parchment before him. "But who can say with any certainty?"

"Their cathedral, their sailors—you brought death with you this day."

"And with those two thousand snap-lock muskets—rifled, each—aboard, I will be departing with it as well."

"Takeru had kind words to say about the man whose chair you now occupy."

"Ah, yes, my predecessor was beloved. A gifted sailor, a good leader. But we struggled in those years, I spent most of my early manhood under his leadership."

"Learning little in the process."

"Learning much in the process. We lived lean for far too long. I turned to the trafficking of modern weapons to ancient cultures, and we struggle no longer."

"These muskets, they are for Takeru?"

"These muskets are for a *Nihon* bidder with some distant relation to Takeru, yes. I suppose you will request passage?"

"Not requesting, no."

"I might insist you do so. Your being here tells me a number of my sailors, men who have entrusted their lives to me, will not see another sunrise, to say nothing for my eunuch whose body is surely broken."

"Consider as retribution the lives I've taken—recompense for the Sesimbran sons whose wives and mothers weep this night and will continue weeping for days to come." Xavier's words implied compassion even if his voice conveyed nothing approaching it.

"*Tokoh!*" came a frantic cry from just within the ruined doorway.

The *jungsa* and his two men had successfully tracked the stranger to their captain's quarters and, paying the conversation no mind, were moving in for a swift kill. The kill was indeed swift, as one of the *jungsa's* men found himself disarmed and hurled headfirst to the floor with herculean strength, his neck succumbing and snapping crunchily upon impact. That man's short blade now in hand, Xavier had sidestepped a skillful slash from the *jungsa* himself, positioning his borrowed blade in such a way as to cut deeply into the fierce warrior's wrist, then across his abdomen with calculated force sufficient to yield only a superficial wound.

Wasting no time, the third warrior had charged recklessly toward Xavier with a heavy slashing blow. Xavier easily avoided the attack and drove the short blade still in his hand directly into the man's lower jaw, through the mouth cavity, and ultimately punctured his assailant's lower skull. Allowing man and borrowed blade to fall, Xavier then drew his elegant rapier and walked slowly toward the bleeding and enraged *jungsa*.

"This is but a beginning, Jaidev," Xavier said to the still calm *tokoh*, who looked upon the bloodshed with the curiosity of a man who had seen little if any such brutality in his day. "I will kill relentlessly, leaving your ship in the hands of a mere skeleton crew." At this he pressed his rapier with not inconsiderable pressure to the *jungsa's* exposed throat.

"Or?" *Tokoh* Jaidev was more concerned with Xavier's lingering alternative than in saving the life of a man who had endured severe injury to save his. Xavier took note of Jaidev's indifference.

"Or, *Tokoh*, you deliver my person to the very same destination you've in mind for the murderous cargo your men are this moment bringing aboard."

"Interesting proposition. You do understand it's no short journey, do you not? Even with our expert knowledge of the routes, of the winds, you will be aboard for no fewer than three lunar cycles." Jaidev sensed he was sharing with the lethal Christian familiar information.

"Can you spare the space?"

"Naturally. I expect you've reduced my crew by many a soul this day. Two dead in here, not including my poor eunuch. Still unconscious, is he?" about this man Jaidev seemed somewhat concerned. "How many did you murder aboard the *Bocho*?"

"Fewer than I killed aboard the Portuguese vessel. So many had made their way over to carry out the massacre. Was that by your order?"

"Not directly, no. My *panglima* operate with an element of autonomy. If their judgment suggests the leaving behind of no direct witnesses is sensible"—Jaidev paused as though to consider leaving unsaid that which might go unsaid—"well, then, they leave behind no direct witnesses."

"They left one in this case."

"Ah. You managed to save a life in taking so many from us. You know, Portugal is a bit more populated than is our floating state."

Xavier's eyes narrowed in a rather feline manner, then looked to the *jungsa*, nudging him toward the shattered doorway. The bleeding man looked to his captain, who spoke a number of words in a tongue that was surely unknown to Xavier. Rising with some difficulty to his feet, the man made his way to the now semiconscious eunuch. Once he, too, had fought his way to a standing state, the two exited their captain's quarters, each leaning against the other.

"They will receive excellent care in our infirmary. I've instructed them to say nothing of how they acquired their rather cruel injuries; that much will be made known soon enough. Takeru had said you were well trained, though I confess he seems to have understated things."

"He also mentioned your 'floating state' took very seriously its imagined sovereignty." Xavier's sardonic narrowed eyes widened slightly.

"Imagined? Not in the least. You are the first uninvited passenger to have boarded the *Ocean Castle* in more than a century's time and the first to survive more than a moment after having done so."

"Truly. But, nevertheless, sovereignty seems a rather lofty presumption for a people whose 'country' is best measured in hair widths, lest the true dimensions betray a minuscule domain."

Jaidev laughed a sincere laugh. "Indeed, sir, indeed. Despite our vessel's enormous size, it would not register as even the smallest of inkblots on most ocean maps. But ours is an exchange of our own choosing: the liberty born of moving about every sea, sound, and ocean on earth, unmatched in might by any ten ships, in exchange for never declaring allegiance to a landed kingdom, empire, or city-state. We live well, we travel freely, and we are ghosts. But, then, being acquainted with Takeru, much of this is known to you."

"Will you grant me my requested passage? Or would you like that I cut so deeply into your crew—or, rather, your countrymen—as to render this sovereign state a mere floating husk...a fallen empire?"

Jaidev exhaled audibly, looked to his dead men, then back to Xavier. "You do perhaps overstate your killing capacity, Xavier, but I'd prefer to not lose so much as one more man this night. Enough blood for one day"—then looking to his land-facing window—"both ashore and at sea."

"And the crates...?"

"Yes, theirs is a destination near to Takeru's province."

"As is mine." Xavier sheathed his rapier.

"Tell me, Xavier, this journey of yours—"

"Yes?"

"Is it driven *solely* by vengeance?"

"Did Takeru truly share with you so little over so long a voyage?"

"Assume he did."

"I assume nothing where Takeru is concerned." Xavier's voice was flatly conversational in delivering that pronouncement, nothing more.

"I see. Well, let us see you to your quarters. Under less, shall we say, mortal circumstances, I might have asked my eunuch to manage this task."

"Had he granted me my requested access, he'd have suffered no injury at all."

"He is among my more skilled of warriors, Xavier, and certainly my strongest."

"Thus his duty."

Jaidev, who had stood and was now readying to lead Xavier into the *Ocean Castle*'s depths, then looked ominously to this living blade of a passenger. "But he is not my *most* skilled of warriors, Xavier. You might bear that in mind."

Xavier seemed to consider this for a moment, though only as a courtesy.

"Your French is stronger than I might have expected, Jaidev, though I'd wager you speak at least ten other languages with greater frequency."

"We are men of tongues aboard the *Castle*, and we have recruited French sailors from time to time. None walk among us these days, the last having died nearly five years past."

"And you and Takeru?"

"We spoke many languages in conversation, your native French included, if rarely."

Xavier narrowed his eyes perceptively. "Indeed."

As the men exited Jaidev's chambers, a number of crewmen entered with litters, bundles of cloth, and a bucket of boiling water. The *jungsa* had apparently ordered men to clear the *tokoh*'s chambers of those corpses Xavier had left in his wake.

The Ship

The *Ocean Castle* was vast, seemingly larger within its mighty hull than what an outside look might have suggested was in any way possible. *Tokoh* Jaidev led Xavier not through the lower decks of a mere ship but through the halls, rooms, passageways, and staircases of a massive palace. People of widely varying facial features, physical frames, and languages moved about in a manner that seemed to them nothing other than mere routine, simply the productive rhythms by which their days and nights were governed.

"We number over a thousand, minus those we leave behind this night." Jaidev looked disapprovingly to Xavier, who chose not to acknowledge as much. "The *Castle* is crewed by one hundred and twenty men at any given moment, with an additional fifty standing by should the sea determine our need for additional sail, or less."

Xavier took these words in while allowing his eyes to absorb a story of their own. "Even assuming four shifts each day, your crew represents less than half of your"—he paused to arm and curtly deliver his term of choice—"population."

"Well under, in fact." Given that he presumably provided vessel tours rather infrequently, Jaidev was clearly reveling in the role. "The *Ocean Castle* is supremely well designed and requires far less manpower per sail or displaced ton than do its European counterparts, at least under ideal sailing circumstances. Our sailors number under five hundred, soldiers and gunners a mere one hundred fifty. Those nearly six hundred not responsible for the sailing and safeguarding of our vessel-state are everything else one would expect to find in a civilized community: physicians, carpenters, metalworkers, scholars, performers, and so on."

Xavier had observed clear evidence of this "community" while Jaidev was speaking. A blacksmith was giving shape to a tool of one sort or another in a sizable forge whose fumes were cleverly directed outside via a network of ducts and an ingenious, air-powered fanning system. In a neighboring room, a potter wheeled away mere feet from the smith, while, another dozen paces on, Xavier laid eyes on a particularly clever bakery or something not unlike a bakery. A skilled and highly focused baker was massaging vast quantities of—dough, was it?—while three assistants did their part in either feeding additional flour and water into the accumulated mass or shaping the prepared portions into large rolls.

"The daily bread," Jaidev said with some pride. "Those men are as responsible for keeping this ship afloat as are our deckhands, sailmakers, and even the masters of wind themselves."

"Crews tend to sail well when fed." Xavier was terse.

Jaidev looked to the man as though feeling slighted. "Come now, Xavier, our people subsist off of far more than flour and water. We eat quite well, in fact. The bread is simply a unifying measure; we break it as one, essentially, and take heart in knowing that its taste and nourishment are shared by all."

"I see."

"Let us hope you do, Xavier." Jaidev had donned a conspicuously focused countenance when speaking those words. "I suppose a man whose stock and trade consists of administering mortality with the cut of blade has little interest in those daily functions that sustain life for the living."

"Takeru told you nothing of our own bread and water regimen?" Xavier asked while continuing to observe the bread-making process.

"As it happens, Xavier, we spoke of topics beyond that which concerned your training under Takeru."

"Yes, I imagine you would have. Nevertheless, he did share with you a great deal; otherwise, you'd not have granted me passage."

"The passage was demanded at sword point, Xavier."

"So it was. But you must have a sense of my purpose."

As they walked, Jaidev noted the enormous cannon whose murderous belching had only hours earlier abated.

"That gun predates my time aboard this vessel by nearly as many years as those I have lived. Your father's father was not yet conceived when this cauldron of death was purchased thousands of miles from where we now float."

"It's really rather terrible, is it not?" Xavier studied the cannon with a cold eye.

"It is unequaled in all the waters of *sasāra*—of our *world*, as you might say."

"In Sesimbra, a cathedral stood this day."

"And another will rise in its place. Christians build well and quickly in service to their God."

"Need it have been destroyed? Truly?" Xavier's words suggested compassion, his tone coldness.

Jaidev then turned to face Xavier with greater speed and force than a man of his age and stature should have possessed.

"Yes, its destruction was necessary, Xavier. Were the deaths of my sailors necessary? If you could have achieved your ends more peaceably, might you have done so?"

"No. I meant to kill, and I killed. Witnessing what I witnessed in town, though, I knew to expect it, and again at sea, I sought to balance the affairs as best as was I able. My sword dealing death more intimately than this"—he then harshly acknowledged the simply gargantuan cannon—"monstrous thing. And perhaps more painfully."

"Those men, Xavier, had comrades and, some of them, families aboard this vessel. Seeing to your safe"—he then remembered the scene in his own cabin—"or at least uneventful passage these next three months will be no easy task. I acknowledge the debts between my country and the Portuguese as having reached parity—"

Xavier interrupted crisply, "As well you should, though I am not Portuguese."

"But I must insist," Jaidev went on, "you not call attention to the misery your blade hath wrought for many aboard our home this night."

The men looked one to the other for a tense moment, before Jaidev ultimately returned his gaze to the brutal engine of mayhem of which he had spoken so reverently moments earlier.

"And I recognize ours is an expensive business. Fear is our only currency, particularly as Christian vessels populate our waters in greater numbers with each passing year. This weapon"—he patted the cannon's cold iron—"is the source of that fear and a guarantor of our continued sovereignty."

"I'll make you this promise, *Tokoh*: upon realizing my purpose in Takeru's homeland, I'll not request of you return passage."

"A curious vow. How, then, will you return?"

"That much is my concern."

Jaidev studied this curious, lethal, beautiful force of human will… this archangel…and wondered. Wondered on a number of thoughts.

"Well, then, being as we've scarcely departed Portuguese waters, let alone the larger ocean to which they belong, let us see you to your promised quarters."

The two proceeded through a positively wondrous, to Xavier's eye, and labyrinthine series of decks, corridors, and shared rooms en route to the promised quarters. Along the way, Jaidev continued to provide his—guest?—with ship history, guidance, and information of variable relevance to a man who was, by his own reckoning, merely a passenger. Citizenship aboard the floating kingdom interested Xavier not in the least, even if the *Ocean Castle*'s dimensions, ingenious use of what was still rather limited space, and sheer population were duly impressive.

Stopping before a doorway that, as both men quickly observed, would require Xavier to duck somewhat more than slightly upon each entrance and departure, *Tokoh* Jaidev, captain of what was surely the world's largest and most powerfully armed vessel, looked with some pleading to Xavier. His eyes betrayed an angst he had heretofore kept tightly contained.

"There will be delicate days ahead, Xavier. You've ended many a life, a tragic fact that has yet to be made known throughout the populace. Your presence aboard cannot be kept hidden, nor will it be overly long before the more intelligent of my citizens identify you as the murderer of their countrymen. The *jungsa* himself might be ordered into confidence, but knowledge does have a way of making itself known, thus, for instance, your having learned of and subsequently boarded the *Castle*."

"Indeed." Xavier was wholly unmoved by Jaidev's plaintive soliloquy.

"I will exercise my considerable authority in assuring your safe passage is honorably fulfilled, but do understand the limitations inherent in any such exercise."

"The risk I assume, I knowingly assume."

Jaidev smiled softly. "Do watch your head."

And with that, Xavier entered a quarters far larger than what the short doorway might have foretold. A ceiling several hands above the uppermost reach of his floppy hat, a long sleep rack, and a window through which Xavier would see the very same waters upon which Takeru himself had lain eyes during his own passage.

"I do hope you've some sense of my impending arrival, Takeru." Xavier's inner monologue was charged with a sense of adventure, and of impending perils.

The Mysterious Man

"Make ready for anchorage!" a sailor called out from his perch well over fifty feet above the *Ocean Castle*'s spacious top deck.

This was the translation Xavier was able to mostly assemble from his knowledge of Punjabi, the language spoken by this particular sailor and also *Tokoh* Jaidev's preferred tongue as Xavier had quickly realized in his first exchange with the man.

"Make ready for anchorage!" the sailor bellowed once more.

The *Ocean Castle* had been at sea for twelve days' time since having left Portuguese waters. A large wooden map of the world and its waters was kept in the pilot's cabin. It was dotted with holes in which a handsomely crafted miniature of the *Castle* was routinely pegged and repegged to represent each leg of a given seafaring odyssey. Early on the twelfth day of his journey, Xavier was invited into the pilot's cabin by Jaidev himself, who proudly noted his ship's—er, kingdom's— progress thus far. The map was as well detailed in its rendering of the New World as it was of the Old, and of the Orient. "They have been traveling thus for some time." Xavier concluded, noting that the wooden map was clearly very worn with time, with saltwater air, with use.

We will be cresting the lower extremity of mighty *Fēizhōu* in a week's time, Xavier! The winds have been with us since our second day on the high seas!" Jaidev referred, of course, to the vast continent Xavier knew as *Afrique*.

Xavier had kept his eyes largely to the east as the *Ocean Castle* made its way south. The shores of Africa had previously been known to him only by way of maps, all of which were attributable to the foremost cartographers Italy, Spain, and Portugal had produced throughout the former half of the century. Accurate though they surely were for charting purposes, the maps did little justice to a coastline that Xavier found endlessly fascinating, beautiful, and alluring. He wondered at life upon that big continent, large enough to swallow France ten times over, a Jesuit had once calculated for Xavier's benefit and that of his brothers. Being that over a week had passed since Jaidev's crew had set sail from Sesimbra, and given that *Afrique* lands had populated the eastern horizon all but one of those days, the first, Xavier began to question the Jesuit's calculation. "Surely this enormous landmass could cover France one hundred times over."

Occasionally, when the *Castle* would sail near enough to shore, Xavier would lay eyes upon fauna he had been taught to recognize; more often, however, he saw only creatures that even the imaginations of Ireland's skilled story weavers could not have summoned into existence: birds of preposterously bright hues; ungulates with heads so strangely horned; and swine of angry, cruel features.

Of course, Xavier's introduction to exotic beasts and creatures was by no means limited to what he saw on dry land. The *Ocean Castle* itself kept caged, penned, and, in some cases, neither, a panoply of animals and birds, many of which seemed to Xavier as though they had been plucked into being from the fibers of a particularly inventive tapestry: feisty canids, a number of cats larger than those found in a Parisian alley but smaller than the leopards to which they might have been compared given their colorings, and a brilliant aviary replete with winged specimens too numerous (and active) to be reliably counted. Many of these, Xavier later learned, were used in an intricate messaging system that helped ensure, among other things, the *Ocean Castle*'s open sea lanes.

As for the latter, Xavier had not been wholly uninformed as to just how a ship so conspicuous as the *Ocean Castle* had made its way to and from Christian waters largely unseen by vessels navigating the very same winds. The answer, Xavier had learned from a knowledgeable source, is that the *Ocean Castle* did not go unseen. It was simply seen when (and by whom) it chose to be seen. Over the course of several decades' time, Jaidev and his *tokoh* predecessors had cultivated a series of mutually beneficial alliances and understandings with tightly controlled networks of privateers, merchants, and coastal fishing communities. For its part, the *Bocho* was ever vigilant in its perimeter watch around the *Castle* and was often first to signal allied vessels in known waters, determining the degree of openness within an impending passage. Routes deemed overly active were circumvented entirely.

On rare occasion, the *Bocho* would go to great lengths in drawing away vessels whose routes might otherwise have intersected with the *Ocean Castle*. Agreed-upon rendezvous points ensured a reconvening of the two ships should such distracting measures require extraordinary dedication on the *Bocho*'s part. Otherwise, the *Castle* would simply pace itself for a day or so, thereby allowing the dark Valkyrie (as Xavier thought of it) to reenter orbit.

Many of the birds upon which Xavier now looked were, in fact, used in a courier capacity. Some hailed from the African coast and were dispatched with highly cryptic messages to inform deeply trusted souls in unassuming coastal hovels of the *Ocean Castle*'s impending passageway. Potential dangers were reported via land signals or a dispatching of vessels in the *Ocean Castle*'s nominal employ. Those that did not first reach the *Bocho* would simply enter a patch of shared ocean with the *Castle* itself, a circumstance in which Jaidev reveled. He was sincere in his gratitude to those who entered alliances with his wandering kingdom, a point that he invariably articulated as ardently with gifts as with his words (almost always in the ally's native tongue; Jaidev was truly a polyglot).

"Will the anchorage impinge upon your schedule?" Xavier studied closely the wall-size representation of earth and ocean in the pilot's cabin.

"You understood our lookout? What do you know of our *Pajāba* tongue?"

"Had I not known a word, the man's meaning was still perfectly clear."

Not fully convinced, Jaidev conceded the point. "Perhaps so. In any event, we dock on account of several countrymen who are nearing a full month on foreign lands. We, or rather the *Bocho*, will retrieve them. Once they've boarded the *Castle*, we will recover the anchors and welcome this charitable wind back into our sails."

"For what purpose were your men sent ashore?"

"We see rather well to our many needs aboard the *Castle*, Xavier, but there is always need for trade and occasionally for new manpower."

Those aboard the *Ocean Castle* certainly did see very well to their own needs, as Xavier had observed while aboard. Perhaps most remarkable was the cultivating and harvesting of certain crops throughout the second deck. Various herbs and beans were grown in an elaborate series of hanging pots, while a small fruit both sweet and tart in flavor grew in trees that ran adjacent to a long row of tall windows, their soil tightly packed into deep boxes in which each tree enjoyed secure rooting.

But it was the field itself that most stunned Xavier. It was exactly thirty paces in length, half that in width, and was nearly deep enough to allow for the burying of one's arm up to the elbow. Produce was cultivated across two-thirds of the field's surface area at any given time, with the other third being rotated out for soil replenishment. Light was cleverly showered upon the half dozen vegetables grown therein by way of a circular opening in the top deck whose perimeter opened sharply outward, thereby maximizing the exposure sufficiently to ensure no square foot of dirt went untouched by the life-bringing rays.

Such wonders had not ended there. The *Ocean Castle*'s multitiered top deck was replete with smaller vessels, the long boats, most of which were used for fishing, whaling, and the transporting of small land parties. And the *Bocho* itself engaged in the occasional harvesting of the sea's vast bounty, even seeing to its own provisioning so as not to tax the *Castle*'s food stores. But the *Ocean Castle* employed a fishing method the likes of which Xavier had never seen aboard a Christian vessel nor even heard described as a possibility.

On the lower deck, nearly thirty feet beneath Xavier's own quarters, a brilliant concept had been expertly realized. A square approximately a man's height across had been carefully cut into the *Ocean Castle*'s ballast and keel. The opening's perimeter was surrounded by a knee-high enclosure that prevented water from spilling into the lower deck. And should stormy seas imperil the ship, the opening could itself be tightly sealed with a two-layer hatch, effectively rendering whole the hull.

This passageway to the deep sea below served a number of purposes and was quite essential to the *Ocean Castle*'s adequate provisioning. Several fishing lines ran at varying lengths beneath the ship and were affixed firmly to the opening's perimeter. A large cage-trap was also lowered during periods of anchorage, which promised to endure for at least the better part of a day. It had even been lowered into Portuguese waters while the chaos and carnage unfolded above. Such measures yielded remarkable bounty for those aboard, and nothing was wasted. Those charged with food preparation were also charged with food preservation. Some of what the cage and lines yielded was kept alive in large tanks designed strictly for that purpose while others were partially readied for the diner's plate before being submerged in *vinaigre* or packed in heavy salt pouches. Bread was indeed a cornerstone of the *Castle*'s meal design, but not for lack of alternatives.

During longer anchorage episodes, both cage and lines found themselves withdrawn into the vessel to keep them from becoming intertangled with the most peculiar of contraptions aboard the *Ocean Castle* and its equally peculiar pilots: the *bada piteu*, or "sea walkers," as Jaidev would loosely translate for the intrigued Xavier. These men were tethered to the *Ocean Castle* in a threefold manner. The massive iron bell in which they descended, sturdily constructed and cumbersome, was home to heavy steel rings adorning each shoulder. Running through the shoulder rings was a thick, durable, sturdy chain, the other end of which was fastened to a crank-powered wheel mechanism allowing for the swift retrieval of these "sea walkers," provided a pair of stout men were on hand to crank quickly enough the enormous wheel. The third point of tethering was that of a thick (also watertight) air tube that kept nourished the *bada piteu*'s lungs as they scavenged the sea floor for shellfish, seaweed, and the occasional pearl.

Provided they were uninterrupted by disruptive goings on in the ship above, the *Ocean Castle*'s "sea walkers" were capable of spending hours scouring the maritime bed below, their tethering system allowing for a descent of well over one hundred feet. They also employed intricate communication with those who stood alertly by the cranking wheel above. A single tug of the left lanyard, for example, indicated a need for a loosening of the chain. Two tugs indicated a need for chain tightening, while four rapid tugs of either lanyard was a plea for swift retrieval.

The *bada piteu*, of which a mere six were actively employed (though others aboard had simply retired from the duty), were cherished for that bounty their labors brought to *Ocean Castle*'s banquet tables and treasure reserves. Theirs was difficult duty, but it was by no means thankless.

Xavier had marveled at the *Ocean Castle*'s nearly self-sufficient agricultural system and might have found himself soundly charmed by the bustling, creative, and harmonious life aboard. Had he not witnessed the expense such life carried with it—the *Anjo* was, after all, resting eternally at the bottom of Sesimbran waters—Xavier might even have deemed the *Ocean Castle* a worthy civilizing project, a harmless testament to human ingenuity. It traversed the world's vast waters with impunity, this floating city-state, and maintained for its people a way of life cosmopolitan, stimulating, and dynamic in the extreme.

No two sunrises were alike for Jaidev and his seafaring citizenry, nor did the stars repeat themselves in quite the same way. Even return trips to familiar ports and coastlines would doubtless occur at different times of year, rendering the night sky slightly distinctive from previous visits.

"We know no borders, Xavier," Jaidev had explained (unasked), "nor do we conduct business with crowns and imperial robes. We answer only to the winds, to the waves, to ourselves."

"For how many generations has the *Ocean Castle* been at sea?"

"You surely know of *Kalamabasa*—your Columbus—do you not?"

"I do."

"This vessel was old when *Kalamabasa* was only a boy. It has undergone one major overhaul, as you might call it, and countless planks, masts, and sails have been replaced over the past one hundred and fifty years. I very much doubt more than a fraction of this original ship still sails, but it *is* the *Ocean Castle* all the same. The blood of generations is soaked into those decks, which have endured the footsteps of ancestors and descendants for thrice my time in years."

Jaidev looked thoughtfully to the sea, though *Fēizhōu* itself was practically within swimming distance and breathtaking in its beauty. Something about the surrounding waters had struck a melancholy chord with the *tokoh*.

"My assuming the captaincy was as unlikely a happening as has ever come to pass aboard this storied ship. I was born in the lower decks to a sail weaver and her sailor husband, my father, in the *Ocean Castle*'s hundredth year at sea. Both of them had come aboard from *Bhāratī* shores, along with a score of others not unlike them. The ship's population had declined for over a decade, with mortality and a number of ill-advised battles on land and at sea claiming more lives than could be quickly replaced by newborns alone. A recruitment effort was undertaken in the homeland of my parents, whose waters we will deal a glancing blow during this voyage, and the population soon burgeoned to near its current numbers, far exceeding the original need."

Jaidev then looked with sad eyes to the politely listening Xavier.

"Many of those whose lives your sword cut down were direct descendants of those brought aboard that year. Tell me, do you suppose their ancestors would ever have come aboard had they known what fate awaited their unborn grandchildren?"

"Would they have done so had they any sense of the destruction you so often leave in your wake?"

"They were made aware of how it is this ship achieves its enduring survival."

"It might then be argued that the fate of their descendants was of their own choosing."

Jaidev turned quickly away from Xavier, looking back to the sea.

"The *Bocho* will join us soon, delivering its cargo—human and otherwise."

An hour thereafter, the *tokoh*'s words were borne out, as the *Bocho* affixed itself in precisely the same way it had done two weeks prior in order that the musket-laden crates could be transferred to the *Ocean Castle*'s vast holding bay. Twenty passengers had boarded the *Bocho* from the southern coast of *Fēizhōu*, around half of whom were clearly unaccustomed to the sea and were new to the *Ocean Castle*.

"New blood," Jaidev said with some happiness in his voice, "new blood for the arteries of our vessel."

"Recruiting?" Xavier imagined Jaidev's mother and father having boarded the *Ocean Castle* some sixty years earlier in much the same way as these nervous souls were now doing.

"Indeed. Our ship can, if necessary, house eleven hundred. We were under that even prior to your bloodletting two weeks past. And there will be work to undertake in keeping afloat our beloved vessel."

All but one of those now boarding, crew member and recruit alike, carried with them cargo of one sort or another. Some brought aboard small wooden chests, perhaps containing coinage, while others had on their backs large sacks that seemed to be filled with seeds and bulbs. The man who boarded with only his body and two medium-length swords (whose design Xavier vaguely recognized) was darkly swathed, precise in movement, and seemed to observe at once all that transpired about him.

Xavier kept his eyes trained closely on this man, a killer no doubt, and wondered not at all as to his purpose on the soil *Fēizhōu*—he was a protector, an extension of Jaidev's intermittently murderous will, not unlike the cannon, which had several weeks' sailing to the north been brought to bear on the people of Sesimbra. Has this man also been brought to bear? How many lay dead in his wake?

While Xavier considered the *Ocean Castle*'s influence upon seafaring lanes and coastal settlements the world over, a violent happening did then occur. One of those whom Xavier had correctly identified as new to the sea quickly seized a large club-like section of wood from near his feet and brought its mass down hard on the shoulder of a nearby crewman, breaking it in the process. He then drove the makeshift weapon into the ribs of a sailor who had run to his comrade's aid.

All of this had unfolded in the space of an instant, which rendered it all rather overwhelming to those in the situation's midst. Making sense of the attack's neutralization would prove even less achievable still. The killer, who Xavier had also correctly identified for what he was, had closed quickly with the clobbering man, whose skin was twofold darkened—once from birth and once from a life spent unshielded from sunlight; the man was nearly onyx black, was beautiful in build, and now lay dead. For the dual-bladed killer had, while closing with his quarry, been seemingly in middraw of one sword. He had then ducked a brutal swing of the club while fully drawing the narrow, perfectly straight blade and finally coming to a stop fully behind the powerful bull of a man.

A strange stillness had followed this exchange. Those watching had seen the darkly swathed swordsman close with and avoid a blow from the dangerous attacker. They had also seen him draw his blade while dodging what would have been a fatal club blow to his skull before ultimately ending up at the clubber's back. What had not been anticipated was what they then witnessed: the tall, powerful, purely black, club-armed man turned very slowly to face this swift opponent, then fell suddenly to his knees. Motionless, the man then cried out in abject pain, as several of his fingers and two sections of the wooden club themselves fell just as suddenly to the deck below. His cries would surely have carried on long thereafter had the swift blade of his killer not been plunged artfully into the very throat from which they emanated. Whatever knowledge of his exotic lands behind those wide eyes, whatever love for others once beat in his breast, whatever skills and trading or hunting wisdom he had possessed, all of this drained from his heavy corpse into the planks, which now bore his dead weight.

The mutilated corpse had collapsed in tandem with the sword, which had ended its life being sheathed. And silence befell the normally vibrant main deck. Xavier noted a look of satisfaction on Jaidev's face. "There are often reluctant recruits," he said as though some macabre plan had been artfully realized.

"No," Xavier observed as the once vibrant body was thoughtlessly cast overboard. "That man was intended to be example." Xavier did not meet Jaidev's eyes; there was no need. His suspicion was correct. While the others had perhaps boarded of their free will, one had been brought against his own in order that such a display might unfold exactly as it had.

"You see much with those icy eyes, Xavier." Jaidev was in mid-stride while responding, on his way to the pilot's cabin.

He was death, this shrouded man, and few warriors would have survived an encounter with him. Half a hand shorter than Jaidev, himself of average height, Chau Hai Fan (as Jaidev would later identify him) was tightly muscled and seemed to walk a finger's width above the ground. Every aspect of Chau suggested threat. His every movement was economical, his every breath imperceptible, his every glance a challenge...or an assessment. The swords he wore on his back were approximately equal in length to his own arms, which is to say not overly long. They were straight, simple, single-handed swords that flexed considerably when subject to impact or rapid striking, the very sort of striking Xavier had observed when visually acquainting himself with the nightmarish killer.

At one point in his life, Xavier had known the finest sword masters from Christendom, from the Near East, and from lands still much farther east. But from what he had observed of Chau Hai Fan atop the *Ocean Castle*'s main deck, Xavier was not certain any one of them would have been equal to the diminutive man had their blades crossed. Not one would have proven an effortless kill for Chau Hai Fan, but a kill they might ultimately have been. He was death.

4

NIHON, MIKAWA PROVINCE, EIROKU 11 (GREGORIAN YEAR 1568)

Lord Sakurai Takeru

Mikawa Province was experiencing a beautiful summer season, and Sakurai Takeru of the Matsudaira clan was savoring it all, each and every breath drawn, every glimpse of plant and wildlife, every sight of impossibly white clouds soaring in overhead from the sea beyond. It was the third summer Takeru was now enjoying since having returned from endless days in the distant west and only his second full summer, having returned somewhat late that season in what his Christian brothers knew as 1566.

The Matsudaira clan had accumulated for itself much prestige across the preceding generations. Its very name had become a metonym for Mikawa Province itself and was thus used routinely in precisely that manner, with "Matsudaira" and "Mikawa" spoken almost interchangeably. And the Sakurai branch of Matsudaira, to which Takeru belonged, had entered a period of eminence just prior to Takeru's birth, an eminence his brother, Daimyo Lord Sakurai Kiyoshi sought to preserve (if not expand) with his every waking breath.

"Takeru! *Oji* Takeru!" intruded an earnest voice upon Takeru's peaceful morn.

His *oi*, Hiroshi, son of Sakurai Kiyoshi, Takeru's venerable and respected brother, was running toward him, two *bokken* held firmly in hand.

"I expect you'll be demanding the daily sparring round with your *oji* Takeru." Takeru was a living smile while speaking those words. How he loved his *oi* Hiroshi.

"Of course, *Oji* Takeru. I wanted to practice before Osamu finishes speaking with our father."

Osamu was, of course, Lord Sakurai Kiyoshi's other son. Having two *oi* (or "nephews," as the Christians knew them) in Mikawa was perhaps the sole reason for Takeru's having returned after more than ten years spent in Christendom and another two at sea or elsewhere on land.

"Why are your hands bound in cloth, Hiroshi?" Takeru knew the answer to this.

"Because I know you will strike them during our sparring. I'm not a fool, *Oji*."

"Indeed not. But remove those rags. You will strengthen either your hands or your reflexes. After all, the hands are—"

Hiroshi quickly interrupted. "The ambassadors of your strength, *Oji*, I know. You tell us every time."

"And it is true every time, Hiroshi. Your hands keep hold of your weapon, of your enemy himself if necessary, and are the vessels through which your might is best channeled."

"Didn't you tell Osamu that you learned that from a *hakujin* months and months west of here?"

"That much is true."

"Was he better than you?"

Takeru considered the question for a moment. "Perhaps. He was remarkable with a sword. Among the best I've ever seen."

"Did you ever best him at anything?"

"Only at *shōgi*." Takeru smiled.

"Ugh! I hate *shōgi*."

"So did he."

"Were there any others better than you with a sword?"

This Takeru did not consider. "Yes. One. And he was...he *is* far better than I and any other I've known. Better than any I will ever know."

Hiroshi quickly lunged at his uncle with a crisp, skillful blow, which Takeru effortlessly deflected. "He's not better than me!"

Thrust, Thrust, Slash, Slash

These, too, were deflected or dodged altogether.

"I'm afraid he is. You may be my beloved *oi*, but I'll not deceive you on matters of such import."

"He was a fellow teacher at the holy place?"

Takeru smiled softly. "Come now, let us work on your stance. You're all energy and might, but your feet tend to be a step behind your torso."

The sparring continued for some time thereafter, with Hiroshi's limitless energy and eagerness to improve eventually wearing down the middle-aged Takeru.

"You show great promise, *Oi*. As much as any I trained in Christendom. If stamina alone were the mark of a good swordsman, you'd be among the world's greatest."

"But it isn't, is it? Stamina isn't enough." Hiroshi appeared dejected.

"No, Hiroshi, it isn't. A master of lesser energy, diminished strength, and no swiftness of which to speak might very well disarm you before your considerable energies, your youthful strength, your inherent speed could be in any way brought to bear."

"And what of those masters who are strong and fast? How am I to defeat such men?" Hiroshi drew his *bokken* into his shoulder, perfectly situated for yet another forceful attack.

"You are to hope your blade never crosses with that of such a man, not until your own expertise has"—Takeru deftly parried Hiroshi's forceful thrust—"matured." He spoke this last word while bringing his *bokken* to his nephew's vulnerable neck. "After all, not all opponents will be of your blood, and any number of men would as soon open your veins as not. In almost any duel, a man will know whether or not he is overmatched within the first few heartbeats. Be mindful of your instincts, Hiroshi."

"I hope one day to be the best swordsman you know, *Oji* Takeru." Hiroshi looked with a degree of solemnity to his smiling uncle.

"One day you may well be exactly that. Though your brother is rather formidable himself. He knows his weaknesses and trains intensely to overcome them. Not unlike myself at his age."

"And still there are better than you walking among us?"

"At least one, yes. And I'd wager a few I've had the good fortune not to encounter." Takeru was laughing warmly at this point.

"Well, you're the best I know, and that's what matters."

The two then readied themselves for another series of strikes and counterstrikes. Takeru appeared as calm as Hiroshi was intense.

The Daimyo

From within the *moya* of his elevated palace, Lord Sakurai Kiyoshi, Matsudaira daimyo and loyal vassal to the recently installed Shogun Yoshinaga, observed with some happiness and considerable pride his long absent brother Takeru engaged in sparring with his beloved younger son, Hiroshi. It was Osamu, Kiyoshi's eldest son, who stood to inherit the Sakurai legacy in title and duty, but Hiroshi was daily proving himself every bit the man his father had hoped—had known—he would become.

Lord Sakurai Kiyoshi knew much of Takeru's travels, the two having found many an evening in which to speak during those initial months following the latter's return, but he did not know all. A merchant ship had ferried Takeru from *Nihon* shores fourteen years past, after which he had boarded a far larger ship in a port town of southern *Ajia,* and from there had traveled to lands so far west Lord Sakurai wondered how the gods themselves could possibly have kept their protective eyes on his wandering brother.

Takeru spoke of political dealings, of working in the employ of a *Kirisutokyō no* holy man, a *saishi* whose rank was "archbishop" as Takeru had explained it. This archbishop, named Romero (after one of their great holy cities), had encountered Takeru in a great Ottoman city, *Isutanbūru*, many, many years after that city had fallen to the *Toruko-go* Empire with which Kiyoshi was even himself vaguely familiar.

While in this great city, Takeru had been witness to negotiations between *Kirisutokyō no* from their own western lands and the Ottoman conquerors. Certain texts and relics were of some concern to Archbishop Romero, who had traveled far to see them returned unharmed. To his great credit, Takeru had assisted in the bringing about of terms acceptable to both sides and had then agreed to escort Romero back to *Rōma*, the greatest of the *Kirisutokyō no* cities, from which the holy man took his name.

Takeru bonded with Romero during their days and weeks spent on land and at sea, finally returning to *Rōma* nearly a month after their having met. And from there, at this point in the tale, Takeru was invariably cryptic. There was talk of betrayal, of treaties, of power, and of regret. The details, Kiyoshi lamented, were always lacking. One thing was certain: something had sent Takeru racing back to his homelands, and whatever it was, he hoped never to encounter it in this life or any that might follow.

"Hiroshi's swordsmanship is developing well."

Lord Sakurai Kiyoshi turned around to see his eldest son Osamu, who was then bowing, in the eastern doorway, the Mikawa Bay waters just visible over his back.

"Yes, your *oji* Takeru's influence has been favorable in that regard. Why do you not spend more time in lesson with him?" Lord Sakurai indicated his son should rise.

Standing at his full height, perhaps a sword's width taller than his father, Osamu smiled. "You suppose I need still more training?"

"Ah, mastery of the sword is lifelong in the making. Even the best in *Nihon* will acknowledge as much."

"Yes, *Otōsan*, but I have spent thousands of days in close study of my swordsmanship and under several teachers. My skills are sharper than my blade." Osamu spoke with some hubris, but he did not speak untruthfully; he had worked diligently to prove himself a warrior capable of leading the Sakurai family in their stewardship of Mikawa Province and more specifically of *Hazu* District.

Seated directly upon the Mikawa Bay waters, *Hazu* was important to Mikawa Province for reasons of commerce and fishing. The district had also produced respected and decent *daimyō* in its time, men answerable only to the shogun. Osamu very much expected to equal his father's greatness and believed the skilled wielding of weaponry to be instrumental in that regard.

"Did Takeru not disarm you fairly quickly when first you sparred upon his return to Mikawa?" Lord Kiyoshi grinned impishly and took in his son's presence with careful attention. Osamu was sturdy in his build, not unlike his father, and cutting in his movements, also not unlike his father. He was well muscled and had an intensity to him that spoke of both ambition and earnestness. Throughout Mikawa and its (more powerful) neighboring provinces, Osamu was known, and some said feared, for his swordsmanship. Notoriously relentless on the attack and rarely willing to yield ground, Osamu had bested warriors many years his senior in many a contest. But he had not seen warfare and had never taken a life. And he had, indeed, been disarmed by his much older and somewhat smaller *oji* Takeru, reluctant though he may have been to acknowledge that fact.

"Takeru brought back some demonic swordplay from his *Kirisutoky no* lands. That trick, whatever it was, won't work twice." Osamu was indignant.

"It doesn't have to, not when the stakes are life and death!" A glistening Takeru had entered from the western doorway, the courtyard and Hiroshi visible at his back. "Had I wanted your life that day, I'd have had it. And, as I just told your brother, there are many as good as me, some better." Takeru had a way of putting voice to warnings as though he were sharing celebratory news.

"They are welcome to try their steel against my own, *Oji*. I'll not be so polite in my strikes as I was with you. Besides, I've gotten the better of you several times since then."

"Yes, it was *my* turn to be polite." Takeru was always able to invoke laughter from his otherwise stern brother, and this day was no exception. The daimyo laughed heartily and patted his irritated son on the shoulder.

"Come now, my son, let us be grateful you have as an ally the great Takeru. And he is blood, which means you'll needn't ever risk losing your life to his *Kirisutokyō no* tricks!"

"Considering my age, Osamu, you'll inherit the mantle of *Nihon*'s best blade soon enough; I'll be in the heavens with our ancestors long before you and Hiroshi. Speaking of whom, it is your brother's skill you'll need to mind in the months and years ahead. He lacks your strength, but there is a cunning in his way. And the strength will reach parity within a year or so."

"Ha! The day Hiroshi brings me to the point of yielding, I will sell my sword for a few coins and gamble them away that same eve!"

"May as well find a buyer now!" Takeru was quick in wit and in all else.

Lord Sakurai turned with smiling eyes to his dear brother. "Come, Takeru, we've matters to occupy our hours."

Middle age sat well with Sakurai Takeru of *Nihon*'s venerable Mikawa Province. Years spent at sea and elsewhere had left their lines upon his otherwise handsome face, and a lean life had kept his musculature very much intact. While his brother, Lord Kiyoshi, had softened in the middle and wore a bit of weight just under the chin, Takeru had always lived a meal behind—never quite slowing himself enough to fill out as so many men his age ultimately would. He was sturdy, formidable, limber, and composed of fearsome sinews. Prior to leaving behind his beloved *Nihon* for what would end up amounting to a more than ten-year odyssey, Takeru's reputation throughout Mikawa, Owari, and a handful of neighboring provinces was that of an especially gifted swordsman and combatant.

Trained alongside his brother from a very young age (from birth, it was often said), Takeru responded well to his lessons and created for himself an exercise regimen that had shaped his limbs into muscled extensions of his ingenious swordplay. In his fourteenth year, Takeru had bested a *masutā* under whose guidance he had studied *koryū* for a decade's time, disarming the seasoned swordsman with such ease as to stun all who had witnessed the remarkable feat. The *masutā* is said to have retired from his discipline that very day and pursued as a way of life austere holiness. Though probably apocryphal, the story tacitly conveyed one truth: the *masutā* never again matched *bokken* with the prodigious Takeru. Many others would do so across the years, with very few proving more than child's play for Takeru, whose skill had reached a hypertrophic level the likes of which few men in *Nihon* could equal.

Of course, these were stories from another time. Nearly twenty years had passed since last Takeru had engaged in a contest of swords on the soil of *Nihon*, the training of his brother's sons notwithstanding. He had laughed when, upon returning from his years' long travels, Osamu had put to him a rather unexpected question: "Is it true?" he asked, his tone insistent.

"Is what true, Osamu?" Takeru genuinely had no sense of where that line of questioning was heading.

"That you left in search of a swordsman who might be your equal?"

At this, Takeru laughed the charismatic laugh that his stern brother had always envied. "Were it so, I should say I was not disappointed in that regard."

"Go on, *Oji* Takeru. What do you mean?" Osamu pressed with force similar to that he exhibited in his own swordsmanship.

"Within months of reaching *Yōroppa*, I was asked by a holy man—in whose employ I then found myself—to demonstrate the *kendō* I had worked my many days to master. After a simple exhibition of our forms, I was presented with a *Furansugo* sword master, meaning he was from *Furansu*, a great kingdom. The man used a light, thin, flexible blade unlike any I had ever seen, though that I would come to know very well in the years ahead. We were each advised not to kill the other, both of us being needed for the holy man's purposes, and were then politely asked to fight to the best of our respective abilities."

"And you surely beat him, *Oji* Takeru, this *Kirisutokyō no* from *Furansu*." Osamu was known to demand the answers he wanted to hear.

"Yes, I did, eventually—but not that day." Takeru was pleased to disappoint Osamu, even at the expense of confessing a loss.

"He beat you, *Oji*, with a small sword?" Osamu was incredulous.

"Not small, Osamu, thin. It was actually rather long, and in any event it was enough to place me at the man's mercy within a moment's time. I was no fool and moved cautiously, even caught him off-guard with a more brilliant series of strikes, I might add. But his blade was quick, his corrections quicker, his form mechanical, and his every step deliberate."

"That is how you were often described in your absence, *Oji*."

"I imagine so. Mind you, disarming me was no easy feat, and the sword master, Reynier, credited me as the best he had ever bested. Praise I warmly accepted before resolving myself to learn the technique that had separated my sword from my grip."

"You traveled hundreds of days to lose a contest in *Yōroppa*?"

"I traveled thousands of days to learn things I might otherwise never have learned, Osamu."

Of this memory Osamu was reminded once alone in the *moya*. He looked about him, at the palace's great room, and wondered at the future.

The Matters

"Owari Province." Lord Kiyoshi spoke gravely and leadingly, hoping Takeru may have insights to offer based on the voicing of those telling words.

"Our old allies, our old enemies: what is it they want of us now?"

"There has been talk, Takeru. Our spies and theirs, an ongoing conversation in which neither acknowledges the other."

"You walked a fine line with Yoshimoto, and, it could be argued, the present shogun is as much in your debt as not."

"Mikawa is bordered everywhere but the sea by powers greater and more numerous than itself. We broker peace where we are able, we take sides where we should, and we support the present shogun because it is right that we do so."

"But despite the prudent course you have charted for our people, Owari beckons."

"We fought against them eight years past, on the side of Yoshimoto, who merely used Mikawa as a conduit for his army. Perhaps better we had not joined him at all. Tensions with Owari...and with Daimyo Oda...they do persist."

"And likely always will, Kiyoshi, until such a time as the hunger for power is absent human experience or one of our two provinces slips wholly into the waters they neighbor."

"I would wager on the latter coming to pass well before the former." Lord Sakurai Kiyoshi had grown still more pensive in the time it had taken to speak those words. "Lord Oda requests our support in his effort to unite all of *Nihon* under one rule."

"Under *his* rule, you surely mean." Takeru had a sense of what was afoot.

"Under *his* rule, naturally. We've only just installed a suitable shogun with the aim of securing peace for some time. Lord Oda, with the considerable resources of his Owari Province, threatens that peace."

"And needs the support of Mikawa Province to achieve that end?" Takeru's questions tended in such instances to be of the rhetorical sort, whether speaking with student or daimyo.

"He does not need us, no, but our support at present will ensure no harm comes to Mikawa Province should his attempted overthrowing of the shogun prove effective."

"But you object on principle?"

"I object on grounds both practical and principled."

"You spoke of spies and of conversations."

"Yes, Takeru, and it is here your knowledge of the world beyond might be of some help in the addressing of our problems."

"Had I my own way, the world beyond would never step foot upon the soil of my beloved *Nihon*, certainly not that of my cherished Mikawa."

"Agreed, brother, but it now seems poised to do exactly that. There is talk of weapons…of weapons that even now are on course to reach our shores."

Takeru's mood degraded rapidly from one of thoughtful conversation to one of sincere alarm.

"What has been said of these weapons, Kiyoshi, aside from their being destined for *Nihon*?

"They will reach Owari Province within the summer, they could conceivably hand Lord Oda the victory for which he yearns, and they could very well tear apart these lands far beyond the shores they first reach."

"And was any indication given as to where these weapons originated?"

"Of course, Takeru, thus my mention of your great knowledge. They are from the *Kirisutokyō no* lands in which you spent so many a sun and moon."

Takeru turned away from his brother, Lord Sakurai Kiyoshi, daimyo of Mikawa Province and respected figure throughout the land. After a moment spent looking intently upon the neighboring bay, Takeru looked back to the still pensive Kiyoshi.

"My brother…"

"Yes, brother?"

"I am being followed, and across a distance much farther than most minds can rightly fathom."

The Rival

Daimyo Lord Oda Nabunaga sat perfectly still within the *moya* of his great palace, *Kiyosu-jō*. Accompanied in the *moya* by vassals and advisers, Oda looked to the east, to Mikawa Province which had been for Owari a source of pain and of occasional reprieve.

"What of Mikawa? What of Lord Sakurai?" Oda asked this of no-body in particular, a habit he had developed in recent years.

"No word as of yet, Lord Oda. Though our ears in the province suggest official neutrality is possible, perhaps even likely," replied Hayato, a more revered one of Oda's vassals. A tried and tested warrior, said to be the equal of three men on the field of battle, he was also trusted with the overseeing of Oda's vast network of spies and assassins, a duty in which the killer quite clearly reveled.

"They will either join in my worthy cause or Kiyoshi's dynasty will be relegated to the soil once I have disposed of this weak, puppet shogun." Oda's words were laced with venom and seemed to seethe forth from his otherwise calm countenance.

"Yes, my lord, but bringing these threats to light may result in a problem of our own making. Mikawa has no stated interest in impeding our known plans." Hayato sensed that these seemingly innocuous words would serve to fan the flames of his lord's rage. He certainly hoped for as much.

"They also had no such *stated* interest eight years past, and still their army entered into a foul league against my own. I'll not afford them any benefit of any doubt, not this day, not any that follow!" Oda was indeed cross and suspected he had been manipulated into this emotional state. "Nevertheless, we'll not stoke the fires of animus just yet. Let us extend a formal offer of alliance to Daimyo Lord Sakurai Kiyoshi and his rambunctious heir to render official that which now exists only as unspoken possibility."

"And should they reject the offer entirely?" this was asked by Shinichi, an elder vassal to whom Oda often turned for philosophical insight.

Oda seemingly ignored the question, turning instead to Hayato: "When is it, exactly, we might expect the shipment whose arrival we have so anticipated?"

Hayato grinned as though having been invited to join an inside joke. "Two moons hence, or perhaps as the one that follows is upon us."

And the training of your selected conscripts in battlefield *masukettojū*? The shipment will be useless if our men have no idea as to the weapons' function."

"We have made good use of the improved *tanegashima*"—this word was often spoken in carefully administered syllables—"as our agent calls them, which he left us last winter. The conscripts will be ready. Even minimal training will render them more than lethal."

Oda then turned back to Shinichi. "If they reject the offer, Shinichi, Mikawa Province will become a proving ground for our newly minted *ashigaru* army. And theirs will be a fate well deserved."

After another few moments of administrative discourse, all but Hayato stood, bowed, and departed Oda's great *moya*. The brutal vassal looked to his ambitious lord and nodded knowingly. The nod was almost imperceptibly returned.

5

LIFE AT SEA

The *Ocean* Rhythms

The *Ocean Castle* sailed swiftly, keeping in sustained contact with the ever scouting and circling *Bocho*. Though far heavier than any galleon the Spanish were capable of producing, the *Castle* moved at a respectable speed, covering one hundred fifteen miles in a day, sometimes closer to one hundred twenty five. At this pace, the enormous mass of wood, sail, and humanity would indeed reach *Nihon* in under four months' time.

"Over a century spent mapping these routes and learning these winds has contributed greatly in that regard, Xavier," Jaidev explained to his passenger. "What takes your people five and six lunar cycles we achieve in just under four." There was detectable not a trace of arrogance in Jaidev's words; he spoke truthfully. "And our sail masters," he continued while observing one of the towerlike center masts, "they are heirs to a system of wind-harnessing, which predates even the eldest among them by fifty years. Each is capable of pulling into our sails enormous power. We forfeit little time to the whims of nature."

As Jaidev expounded upon the *Ocean Castle*'s impressive properties and the marvelous seamanship by which it was propelled, Xavier was marveling at the vast desert that had monopolized every waking hour of the previous four days' sailing. Jaidev consciously kept the vessel within sight of land for reasons yet unknown to Xavier.

"An early predecessor of mine, *Tokoh* Li Mu, whose captaincy ended almost a hundred years past, deemed this desert the *Yŏnghéng*—the *Éternel,* as your French would have it."

"Is it inhabited?" Xavier had seen no signs of life, though the ship was far enough removed that seeing more than a quarter-mile inland was quite impossible.

Jaidev nodded knowingly. "It is, yes. We have traded with the peoples there, the Bantu, for hides, stones, and dyes."

"Not at the barrel of a cannon, I'd wager."

Jaidev's smile vanished. "No, Xavier, not at the point of a cannon. The politics in these parts are more, shall we say, conducive to peaceable transaction."

In the days prior to this conversation and in those following, Xavier came to appreciate much of what Jaidev held dear aboard his seaborne polity. Life carried on below and above decks with a certain harmony, a creativity, a cooperation that spoke rather well of the human condition. Pedagogues carried on classes with the vessel's sixty or so children and adolescents while astronomers and cartographers busied themselves with the revising and perfecting of maps and charts quite literally decades in the creating. Artisans worked with wood, copper, and in some cases marble to produce wares, crafts, and tools for both use aboard the *Castle* and trade ashore. The sail masters were always tending to something above or below decks, with maintenance of cloth and masts taking precedence above all else.

Just as eminently occupied as any of the craftsmen or sail masters were the ship's forty skilled carpenters. Work orders within the master woodworker's cabin rested in two stacks that quite truly never diminished in height. They were organized very sensibly by orders pertaining first to the ship's hull, decks, and all other integral structural components; second were orders pertaining to individual requests placed by citizens. Warped doors, broken shelves, unhinged sleep racks, and so on. If any aboard earned their keep, it was these carpenters, men and women whose efforts kept the *Ocean Castle* from springing leaks, its masts from succumbing to strong winds, its planks from collapsing under the pressure of ten thousand footsteps each day.

Yes, the *Castle* was a testament to cooperation and to shared purpose. It was a marvel to behold. Xavier wondered what the nonmartial aboard thought of Jaidev's brutish methods in acquiring weapons and whatever else he deemed to take by force. It was a question he would never ask, too precarious was his position. Jaidev had been correct—all eventually came to know Xavier as the man who had taken the lives of their seafaring countrymen. Had they been women, children, or even those of the scholarly/artisan class, Xavier's passage would have been an impossibility. But he had killed warriors, men who were themselves responsible for much death, and as recently as their time in Portuguese waters.

Thus, Jaidev's decree had found itself honored, reluctantly, which allowed for Xavier's ongoing inquiry to continue unabated. "Did these people—a broadly fluent and hyperliterate citizenry if ever there was one—imagine themselves carrying on as such in perpetuity? That the ship had endured and even thrived for well over a century was itself miraculous and doubtless a testament to the godly craftsmanship that had brought it into existence."

Some several evenings later, Xavier stood upon the top deck while a score of astronomers looked to the heavens above. Employing remarkable instruments and referring to charts, many of which appeared to be rather ancient, the men (and seven women) busied themselves with a thorough charting of all they saw overhead. A number of cartographers participated in the project, applying annotations to their maps that seemed to take into account the stars themselves.

"We round the horn of this mighty continent." Jaidev had appeared at Xavier's side. Torchlight had been almost entirely extinguished above decks in order that it would not interfere with the astronomers' view of the night sky. The men therefore spoke in something approaching total darkness. "This is a stretch of land that our cartographers seek to chart with perfect precision and to understand in direct relation to the stars that crown it. Not a detail goes unmentioned. Wind behavior, wave patterns, all of it—the transition from south to north is of endless fascination to their ordered minds."

"How the sailors of Christendom would surely benefit from time spent with your learned folk."

"Perhaps so, Xavier, though they will learn themselves, and sooner than I care to acknowledge."

Tokoh Jaidev and Xavier then retired to their respective chambers, each reflecting upon the significance of the former's words.

The Lands and Waters Unknown

The *Ocean Castle* was two days into its northward journey, when Xavier was summoned by a crewman to join *Tokoh* Jaidev in the pilot's cabin.

"Xavier"—Jaidev was in high spirits—"ready yourself, heart and mind, for a sight to behold."

"I've beheld many a sight in recent weeks, with scarcely a readied heart or mind."

Jaidev gave a curt shake of his head. "To be sure, you have. You will recall my having spoken to you of the *Castle*'s overhaul some many years past?"

"I recall."

"In a few hours' time, you shall lay eyes upon the evidence of that remarkable episode in our ship's history. Until then, place your eyes upon what the Portuguese know as *São Lourenço*, a massive island to the east of *Fēizhōu*.

And massive the island was, as though France itself had been plucked from Christendom and dropped with a huge splash into these waters a thousand miles, more, to the southeast. Xavier knew the name *São Lourenço* and recognized the island from his own cartographical studies years earlier. "This titanic vessel truly had made breathtaking time in its southward journey," he acknowledged, marveling at the sail masters' capacity for extracting propulsion from even the faintest of winds.

Xavier and Jaidev watched as the *Ocean Castle*'s progress was carefully adjusted on the cabin's wooden, peg-holed map. Centered somewhere between the continent and the island in a sea passage through which the ship now journeyed, a small red representation was evident. It was apparently indicative of an island too minuscule to be properly represented, in terms of scale, upon the map.

This supposition was borne out in, as predicted, a few hours' time. Jaidev simply pointed knowingly over the vessel's bow, wherein a small patch of land jutted out of the water like the finger tip of some ocean deity reaching toward the air above. Xavier watched in quiet anticipation as the island came to consume more and more of the horizon, which, in response to its doing so, the *Ocean Castle* began to slow rather than to adjust course. Jaidev meant to suspend the voyage for a time, and the sail masters, knowing this, were surrendering their command of the winds.

When at last the small patch of sand and stone had come into full relief, Xavier realized what it was that had Jaidev feeling sentimental about this island and its place in the ship's history. A fairly deep cove cut into the island's southwestern corner; therein was an enormous structure that had at one point in time served as a dry dock for the world's largest sea vessel.

"The dock has for long years been out of serviceable repair, I'm afraid," Jaidev said with some regret in his voice, "but shortly after my own birth, the *Ocean Castle* saw its hull restored anew, and with the help of those blessed souls who inhabit this unassuming island."

"They helped with the overhauling of your ship?" Xavier had not taken his eyes off the largely rotted but nevertheless discernible dock since first it came into full view.

"And with the construction of the very dock we see before us. A predecessor of the *Bocho*, long since scuttled, sent a crew aboard to make contact, to offer gifts, and to conscript manual labor for the ambitious project."

"With some success, apparently."

"Ah, with remarkable success. Under the supervision of our carpenters, the islanders had constructed the dock in under a month's time, after which the *Castle* entered its embrace and enjoyed eleven days of intensive overhauling. Hundreds of souls laboring day, night, day, and night to rebuild the ship's hull from bottom to top. It was an incredible rate of work, even by the standards of Admiral Zheng He's blessed day."

"You were but a boy?"

"Very much a boy. I helped where I was able but spent most of my time running 'round the island, playing with children my own age. I befriended a number of them in a lifelong capacity and know many of them still."

Though the foremost reasoning behind the *Castle*'s suspension of travel was for certain provisions to be brought aboard and to allow for the carpenters to conduct exterior work upon the hull (minus the aid of any full-scale dry dock), Xavier quickly realized that Xavier's tertiary motivation was the reunion he would soon enjoy with those boyhood friends of so many years past.

And reunite Jaidev did. While several laborers and sailors saw to the loading of foods and materials native to the island, Jaidev could be observed cavorting with middle-aged and elderly men and women who clearly cherished his presence. It was, Xavier later learned, a quadrennial visit to which the ship had adhered since the overhaul process had been completed nearly half a century past.

Xavier did not accompany Jaidev ashore but did bear witness to the festivities on land from his perch atop the *Ocean Castle*'s quarter deck. He would return to his chambers later that evening and awake the following morning to feel the ship very much under way, sailing for *Nihon* having been resumed in full.

The Chase

Three days' east-by-northeast sailing from the no longer visible *São Lourenço* island and the *Ocean Castle* was again covering miles by the hundreds.

"We'll soon enter the very seas wherein Admiral Zheng He himself once knew unrivaled dominion!" Jaidev spoke for the benefit of all on deck, and there were at least fifty crewmen, carpenters, cartographers, and civilians carrying about their business. "Those very same seas in which the Ming under *Yongle,* that visionary emperor, subjected man, tribe, and kingdom alike to knowledge of his own eminence."

Xavier had, in his day, known men to lean toward the sentimental. Jaidev dwarfed them all in this respect. Every mile of water to crash beneath the *Castle*'s indomitable hull, every flapping of a vast sail, every turning of the mighty rudder—all of this belonged to the pages of a saga that populated both the pages of history and the present moment at once. For Jaidev, his captaincy placed him in league with Zheng He and with the *Yongle* himself.

"*Tokoh!* We are seen!" a sentinel occupying one of the ship's three crow's nests pointed firmly to the south, to the *Ocean Castle*'s starboard flank.

Jaidev raced to what would have been, on a galleon, the *Ocean Castle*'s poop deck, a perch from which he was able to see clearly just what it was the sentinel now pointed toward. And so the inevitable proved itself so—a group of three privateers, English, now were moving on an interception course with the far larger *Ocean Castle*.

"Strength in numbers, they wager." Jaidev was visibly cross. "Let us show them that numbers count for *nothing* when men face dragons."

"Suppose them to have been in pursuit since Sesimbra?" Xavier asked in his calm, whispery voice.

"I expect not. Legends of our existence have populated this side of the world since long before your kind made their way 'round. Any number of privateers would risk life and ship to bring us to submission."

"They must not know of your firepower."

"Or believe rumors of it to be precisely that." Jaidev turned to a deck officer, who was quite distinctive in appearance, taller, broader, and darker than most others aboard. Xavier would later learn this man hailed from an archipelago in the center of the ocean known in Christendom as *el Pacífico*. "Ready the cannon. We will be firing while at sail."

Voice calm, Xavier addressed Jaidev coldly: "They'll not give chase overly long, and they can deliver serious fire only with the broadside. Can we not simply outsail our pursuers?"

"Of course we can, but in so doing we may well place ourselves in the paths of others who mean us harm. And I'll not afford any ship a clear look at my own when doing so can be avoided. We will sink one, cripple another, and hope the third has enough sense to abandon the fool's errand."

"More will surely come, Jaidev."

"To be sure, Xavier"—Jaidev turned and smiled wolfishly—"but not this day."

As they spoke, Jaidev's sailing crew had turned the ship to a straight northward course, allowing the gun at its stern to align with its targets, all of which had closed considerably while the *Ocean Castle* was laboriously turning (a vulnerability the ship's crew openly acknowledged).

Jaidev then spoke to his deck officer, the man of noteworthy appearance: "The gun crew may identify and sink a vessel of their choosing," he said, voice steely, "but their following shot must do nothing more than de-mast the second vessel."

The deck officer went below to relay Jaidev's orders. Some time passed, and the pursuit continued. *These men are fools to not know they are overmatched,* Xavier reflected, *but pride exists nowhere at all if it does not exist in the bones of a sailor...to say nothing for privateers.* After the pursued and the pursuers covered what must have been another three miles of turbulent sea, during which time the English had closed considerably (Jaidev had reduced sail), Xavier heard for the third time in his life that distinctive sound.

SSWW-BOOM!

Distance being long enough, velocity slow enough, and cannon-ball large enough allowed for any aboard the *Ocean Castle* so inclined to quite literally watch the projectile make its way toward the Portuguese warship, a warship that, when struck, seemed to collapse under its own weight immediately thereafter. The massive shot had struck that vessel's main deck, crashing through the two below and either severely cracking or breaking through the keel itself.

The medium-size vessel would be lost to the seafloor within moments.

While all aboard the *Ocean Castle*'s stern deck, perhaps more than one hundred, looked on in equal parts pity and righteousness, Xavier's fourth experience with the sound came to pass, some short while after the first.

SSWW-BOOM!

Again, all eyes on deck watched as the projectile covered just under a mile of ocean air, soaring rather majestically over the ocean's wavy surface, its shadow appearing as some submerged and rapidly swimming marine life. The gunners were skilled, they were fiercely accurate, and they were ones to follow orders. This round had struck the main mast of its target vessel, destroying the rigging and sail and bringing the mast itself crashing down upon the deckhands below. One seaworthy English vessel remained and did then, as Jaidev had wagered, abandon its pursuit.

"Between the two floating vessels, some of those men aboard their wrecked companion may survive." Jaidev spoke not with elation, nor with regret, simply as an experienced man of winds, and waves, and seafaring. He knew his craft.

"Join me in the pilot's cabin, Xavier. We've a matter to discuss."

Xavier had watched the devastated English warship slip beneath the waves and was now watching the survivors swim to the sister ships. Confident that many would, in fact, find salvation, he joined Jaidev in the cabin, as requested.

Guns of Nihon

None save Jaidev were present in the pilot's cabin when Xavier entered. There was work to be done in returning the *Ocean Castle* to its largely eastward course, which all hands on deck saw to carrying out.

Jaidev had his hands on the massive helm, his eyes on the horizon.

"Xavier, the *Nihongo* have known gunpowder and musketry for nearly two decades' time, or, if you will, since only a short time after your own birth."

"Yes, Takeru was familiar with muskets and their usage." Xavier had said nothing to invite this line of conversation.

"But their integration has been slow…a stubborn process. Traditions and customs, as I can certainly appreciate, are difficult to overcome. And in *Nihon*, tradition is like an emperor unto itself. It governs, unites, and wields awesome power…awesome control."

"And the cargo two decks below?"

"Will find itself in the possession of a man who ranks tradition at least one rung below ambition and custom well below martial efficacy."

"Your buyer?"

"My buyer, and an enemy of Takeru, yes."

"These are going to Owari Province." Xavier remembered well his conversations with the forthcoming Takeru. "To a Lord Oda, correct?"

"They are. And when they reach Owari, they will be employed with such effectiveness as to ensure a shift in power within that pristine realm of tradition and custom."

"And this catastrophic change is one you are willing to implement for gold alone?"

"That, my friend, is why we are now speaking."

"So there *is* more to this than a mere sales transaction."

"Look astern of this ship, Xavier, or starboard momentarily. There you will see not the first, nor the second, but the third Christian fleet we have crippled in as many years."

"I expect that rate will increase, perhaps sooner than you have anticipated."

"Then we are of one mind." Jaidev paused briefly. "What is it you want of Takeru? It's something to do with his having fled the holy place you shared, isn't it? Is it vengeance as I have presumed?"

"What has that question to do with the English warships? Or with the *Nihon*-bound muskets?"

"Perhaps everything, Xavier. Takeru's knowledge of Owari, of its ambitious daimyo, it was all instrumental in making this…well, let us revisit the topic in a few days' time. I understand your tendency toward discretion; that much you certainly do not share with Takeru."

"No, I do not."

"Very well. Another time then. Do enjoy what remains of the day."

And with that, Xavier was gone, leaving Jaidev to helm the vessel as he saw fit.

6

ITALY, 1558

The Monastery

The monastery was constructed politely within a woodland cradle set in the northernmost papal lands. Such lands were often regarded as a sort of intersection of kingdoms, of politics, of interests. Thus was erected an edifice and a place of rare importance and singular significance. It was known to some, acknowledged by few, and guarded by a protective recipe of secrecy and denial. Built on an ancient foundation, the monastery's most recent incarnation was no more than a decade in age, and it had been built to serve a unique, important, and likely unprecedented purpose.

Vincenzo and Alexandro—both Italian, both ordained Jesuits, and both sworn to the cause that animated their monastery's daily goings on—walked the garden grounds and talked of matters noble and petty. At thirty, Alexandro was the elder of the two priests and had been ordained for nearly ten years' time. Vincenzo, who had only just entered his twenty-fifth year, had been ordained five years prior. Both were plainly garbed, slender in build, serious in bearing, and thoughtful in visage. There was a mutual respect between the two Jesuits, each admiring the other's intellectual heft and mental discipline, each pleased for the other's involvement in the worthy task that was their charge.

"The *apprendisti* are doing well in nearly every aspect of their training, I am told." Alexandro looked not to Vincenzo but to the garden through which they meditatively strolled, as was his wont.

"That is as much a credit to the instruction as to any aptitude on their part." Vincenzo tended always to withhold (or at least prune) praise at every opportunity. He had devoted himself, blood, bone, spirit, and mind, to the Jesuit pathway and saw no reason to cheapen the efforts of others on similar paths with unwarranted adulation.

"I should think so"—Alexandro was often agreeable—"particularly given that we were not overly selective in selecting each *apprendista*."

"No, though the orphanages did oblige us in a number of regards—limbs and senses intact, no obvious mental impairment, sturdy. Anything less and your reports as to their training would surely be less favorable."

"Indeed. Good steel yields good tools."

"And good swords." Vincenzo channeled his usual pedantry.

"Make no mistake of it, Vincenzo"—Alexandro assumed the pedant role—"a sword is as much a tool as is any hammer."

"Were that the case, proverbs about beating swords into plowshares would carry less meaning." Vincenzo lived to argue such points.

"Perhaps they would. Nevertheless, weapons and tools, if you insist upon the distinction, serve no other purpose than to augment power of their wielder. If commanded to construct a house in the absence of hammers, nails, and saws, the most skilled carpenter whose life God has seen fit to author would stand helpless before the commanding party."

"And a sword is to the swordsman as the hammer is to the carpenter?" Vincenzo was leading.

"To be sure." Alexandro was led.

"So, then, do you suppose the swordsman stands, sword in hand, before his Creator with the same register of sin and foul deed as does the carpenter?"

"That much depends upon the man, not the profession."

"Yes, so we have taken to assuring ourselves since embracing this charge."

"As a blade is the tool of the swordsman, so shall our *apprendisti* be tools of Rome, augmenting her power, extending her reach, a weapon in her blessed hand."

"May their purpose be realized." Vincenzo crossed himself while voicing the Trinitarian Formula.

"And it shall." Alexandro likewise crossed himself but voiced silently the Trinitarian.

The priests' conversational walk had led them to a less than conspicuous doorway built into one end of the monastery's long northern wall. Dark stained glass covered the same wall from east to west, the lower edges of each just over a man's height from the ground below. Little expense had been spared in the monastery's design and construction as well as in fulfilling the training that was undertaken within.

Alexandro placed his hand on the heavy door latch and pulled it leftward with some effort. He and Vincenzo then entered the large hall to witness what was invariably a series of extraordinary sights.

The Training

The *apprendisti* numbered twelve, naturally, and were in the third year of an intensive physical, mental, and spiritual conditioning battery the likes of which had never before been equaled in Christendom or elsewhere. Selected from childhood, the boys now ranged in age from ten to fourteen and had been subjected to a near ceaseless state of martial discipline, intellectual rigor, and physiological strain since having been plucked from orphanages throughout France, Spain, and, of course, Italy itself.

With but a single exception, the orphans whose lives now intertwined quite profoundly with what was indeed a remarkable fate, had exhibited trepidation and reluctance in being spirited so clandestinely to the largely hidden monastery that would become the entirety of their adolescent existence. There had been weeping and clumsy prayers; there had been pleas for answers; there had been attempts at fleeing, many; and, ultimately, there had been acceptance of the path charted by God himself for these once wretched souls.

And on this day, three years hence, as Alexandro and Vincenzo stood observing within the cavernous hall, the *apprendisti* demonstrated skill and strength that the watching Jesuits might never have imagined achievable within a human organism.

A near score of thick ropes were suspended from the hall's ceiling, itself five times the height of a given man. Exactly one dozen of the ropes were in use by the *apprendisti*, who ascended them single-handedly, holding in their spare (all left) hands the blunted blades with which they daily practiced. Employing an acrobatic technique of encircling the rope with one's legs while using the right arm to ascend—*what extraordinary strength!* Alexandro thought—the *apprendisti* made quick work of reaching each rope's securing top-knot before quickly switching the practice blade from left hand to right and descending using the former. This process was to be repeated by all until such a time as only one climber remained. And Vincenzo suspected just who the remaining climber would be.

The boy went by his disciple name: Mathieu.

Each of the *apprendisti* had been blessed by Archbishop Romero with such a name as a sacred moniker, of sorts. The obvious exception of "Judas" having been replaced with "Judah" and assigned to the kindest of the dear orphans—"No need to plant the seeds of treachery in this particular garden," Archbishop Romero had mused. "The servants of our pope will encounter plenty of it beyond these walls."

"Mathieu is inordinately strong, even when compared to his brothers." Vincenzo spoke in clinical tones, though admiration was also in evidence.

"He is indeed a prodigy." Alexandro had been observing the rope climbs with a fascination that might otherwise have abated long ago but persisted as the *apprendisti* developed more spectacularly with each passing month.

"Not one among them will be anything less than a force with which to be reckoned," Vincenzo accurately predicted.

"I'd wager few swordsmen twice their age would best them at this point." This from Alexandro was also accurate. The *apprendisti* had, after all, been immersed in acrobatics, strength building, horsemanship, musketry, and, of course, swordsmanship for more than a thousand days' time while nearly double that duration remained ahead of them before their place as Papal Blades (the title had been suggested by Romero) would be wholly realized.

"They've years ahead of them, though for Mathieu many of those may prove unnecessary. He may soon surpass those under whose instruction his rebirth as a weapon has flourished," observed Vincenzo, presciently.

"Let us hope that day is many days in the coming," said a warm voice in smiling tones and violently broken *Français*. "And that those of us who have trained him are long dead and buried when he reaches his—what do you call it?—potential."

"Lord Takeru, a good morning to you!" Alexandro had forged a close bond with the enigmatic, intelligent, and appealingly exotic *Nihongo* sword master, traveler, and circumstantial emissary.

"And to you, Alexandro. Have you taken your morning walk?"

"Yes, we have. Vincenzo spent the hour talking of remembered futures and forgotten pasts."

"And of the exciting present"—Vincenzo joined in—"as it does so clearly exist all around us."

"It does," agreed Takeru, "what a truly special cause that unites us. Had I any idea of what adventure awaited me in your *Kirisutoky no* lands, the long journey would have been more than I could bear."

Alexandro smiled. He had always enjoyed Lord Takeru's curious translation of *Christian*, the syllables somehow seeming more poetic, more elaborate in his own tongue. For their part, the Jesuit priests, under whose scholarly and theological stewardship the monastery fell, had mined from Takeru's memory every item of knowledge he was willing to share about his native and immensely distant *Nihon*.

This was ostensibly a gesture of sincere curiosity and polite interest but also carried with it the implication of worthy missionary work in a supremely foreign land. And the implication was by no means lost on the intelligent and shrewd Takeru; for him, the benefits of stimulating conversation outweighed the risks of religious proselytizing in his native lands.

"A journey we are surely pleased for your having undertaken." Vincenzo found intoxicating Lord Takeru's effortless charisma.

"My presence before you now we owe to Archbishop Romero. I had intended to reach only the Ottoman lands when first I set out on this *tankyū* of mine."

Takeru's version of "quest" was also enjoyable to Alexandro. "Indeed, Lord Takeru. The good archbishop must surely have seen in you something good and worthy."

"As you surely saw something in each of these pupils. In my case, Romero was more intrigued by what he regarded as the oddly shaped *katana* at my side and imagined I might be of interest to his own warriors."

"Which you, of course, were. As for these pupils, we selected only for health and soundness of mind. Whatever it is they have become, whatever it is they *will* become is attributable to your efforts and to the efforts of your fellow cadre."

"And how very well they have indeed come along." Vincenzo contributed while observing that, since their conversation with Lord Takeru had commenced, all but one of the *apprendisti* had succumbed to fatigue and were no longer able to ascend single-handed the tall ropes. The sole exception was, as predicted, Mathieu.

The *Apprendisti*

They had been mere children, orphans all, when the robed clergy and uniformed warriors had taken them. Of course, the process had all seemed a far less sympathetic circumstance when viewed from the limited vantage point of childhood. Conversations had been overheard, with talk of health, of limbs, of minds, and of nature swirling about the rooms and halls of orphanages throughout Rome, Paris, Lisbon, and any other city in which the Church wielded some degree of influence.

Scores of such conversations yielded nothing for the clergymen, Jesuits each, who searched for wretches of a certain age, of solid constitution, of detectable intelligence. But as those chosen would so often be told in the months and years ahead, the choosing was not nearly so intensive as the mission's overseers would have preferred. Once a child well enough for long travel and healthy to the naked eye had been identified by a given vetting party, he was plucked from the orphanage and thrust into a future no more certain than any other, though far more unsettling initially.

But the chosen souls had by and large been chosen well, for all responded favorably to what was by any standard a brutal and relentless training regimen for body and for mind. They had entered the monastery as formless iron; they would one day emerge as brilliantly shaped and tempered steel, their first-rate instruction proving the necessary carbon to yield such a transition.

Archbishop Romero had insisted upon that very number of souls with which the Savior had seen fit to surround himself, and though each had lived with names (some Gallic, Germanic; others Christian) of their own for years prior to being recruited into papal service, it was Romero who had deigned to transpose these with the far worthier names of Christ's loyal apostles. As for the disloyal exception—well, Judas would go unnamed among the Papal Blades, and Romero had always liked the name Judah. The twelve *apprendisti* had, for their part, accepted their mandated pseudonyms with negligible reluctance, none possessing the energy in those initial days to protest any aspect of their circumstances. For the regimen had been inaugurated immediately, and all would soon embrace the destiny to which Romero's vision (a conduit for God's will, naturally) had given marvelous form.

There were the Italian recruits, six in all, who were the first taken into papal service when Romero began the realizing of his zealous vision. They were Thaddaeus, Simon, Peter, John, Andrew, and Thomas (their given names long forgotten or never known by Romero), and they fell within approximately a year of one another; the oldest, Simon, having been eleven upon entering the monastery; the youngest, Thomas, estimated to be nine. He, like two of the others, had no idea as to his actual age. Most of these were plucked from within twenty miles of Rome itself, though Peter hailed from a region just north of Naples, and John from Florence.

At the outset, these boys had maintained a cohesion born of shared language, similar appearance, and of having endured together that long and secretive journey from their native lands (which none could have identified on a map) to the monastery they would eventually come to know as home (and whose location all were taught to identify on a map). The tribal impulse would soon be overcome as bonds were forged among the *apprendisti* on grounds of mutually experienced suffering, achievement, and intellectual enlightenment. Furthermore, as each found their sole and native tongue joined by a plurality of languages, courtesy of sustained and well-conceived lessons from the monastery's resident man of tongues, Greve Christiern of Denmark, the common ground of familiar speech was quickly cross-fertilized with linguistic expertise spanning the whole of Europe and much of the world beyond.

There were also the Iberian *apprendisti*, Philip (Spain) and Judah (Portugal), who did not share a language and had arrived at the monastery nearly a week apart. Their initial association had existed only in the minds of the Jesuits and only for purposes of administrative organization. Philip and Judah were very quick to assimilate with their adoptive brothers.

There was a boy of Germanic extraction, Jakob (in order not to be confused for the Italian James), though his recruitment had come to pass in a Swiss convent that had assumed the housing of several orphans shortly before Archbishop Romero's Jesuits were passing through en route to France. The very image of resilient health and budding strength, Jakob had been plucked from the convent almost upon sight. He, more than any others, struggled to be understood by peer and instructor alike. It was the sensitive Greve who had assisted most charitably in this regard, helping the linguistically beleaguered Jakob to develop a working shorthand with which to be heard and understood, then ensuring his command of core tongues was achieved swiftly and with function aforethought.

And there were the French *apprendisti*: Bartholomew, Mathieu, and James, the final recruits to reach their monastic home, and the widest ranging in age with nearly three years separating eldest from youngest. Like their Italian brethren, the French orphans had kept to themselves, at least initially: language, a shared journey, and so on. But one among them, Mathieu, had donned the bearing of independence almost immediately and merged his every energy with the regimen that was his immediate calling. Inherently aloof and sufficiently intense in bearing to stir anxiety in nearly all, Mathieu was purpose incarnate. Whether it was he who had inherited Romero's purpose or the other way around was the source of much debate among the masters charged with his training. There was little doubt that a determination on the matter would one day be made.

Before the eyes of all to whom the training of these *apprendisti* fell, each boy was transmogrified from hopeless orphan, child of God though they all surely were, into vessels of papal agency. Even at this fairly early stage of the decadelong program authored by none other than Archbishop Romero himself, the boys had advanced in mind and in body to a degree few could have foreseen. The learnedness, the strength, the experience, the very will itself of Romero's carefully selected cadre was channeled daily into these living weapons and coursed through their veins, their sinews, their hearts.

Philip, who had from an early age shown himself preternaturally agile, had taken well to the acrobatics, which inaugurated nearly every morning's sword and body drill. Like a spritely circus performer, he seemed to defy all known laws of motional mechanics and effortlessly incorporated his aerial abilities into the sword training that followed.

Thomas, who had let loose a storm of tears upon first seeing the monastery, had proven himself a remarkable intellect, routinely proffering (uninvited) challenges to the often obliging Alexandro. For his part, Vincenzo entertained no such false promise of cerebral parity with a mere boy and responded to one such challenge with a firm rebuking and a warning to never again trespass upon the soil of authority. The haughty priest did eventually offer the precocious child, which is indeed what he was, sparing praise after observing a blindfolded sword display that had impressed even the venerable sword masters.

And Thaddaeus, the severely charismatic Thaddaeus, who was indeed beloved by all and who also excelled across the range of arts, disciplines, and studies whose mastery he (like all the *apprendisti*) was expected to achieve. He was graceful and composed in his swordsmanship, well versed in studies both ecclesiastical and secular, developed quick intimacy with foreign tongues, and was possessed of a calming manner that contributed to excellence in the saddle, in conversation, and in strategic games, the last of these being an arena in which he was virtually without equal among his peers.

If any of the *apprendisti* could be said to have struggled in any way, it would have been Jakob, to whom few new tasks or concepts came easily. His brute strength, however, was well in evidence even in childhood, and his supreme and abiding loyalty was never once in question, so committed was he to the cause into whose fold he had fallen quite accidentally. A number of the cadre, intuitive to a man, saw to it that Jakob's unique way of learning was accommodated and that his innate strengths—namely, muscle and resolve—were developed and emphasized accordingly. When Jakob would best an opponent in one of those nigh infinite duels fought within the *apprendisti*, the victory was invariably achieved via stubbornness, stamina, and sheer might, all of which he possessed in droves. The recipe was met with success as often as it was with failure, and by the regimen's third year, Jakob had disarmed or forced into submission nearly every one of his peers (including Thaddaeus), all save one. He had not enjoyed any such triumph, nor would he ever enjoy a triumph, over the preternatural Mathieu.

Mathieu. A wonder. Swift as he was strong, graceful as he was forceful, brilliant as he was measured, skilled as he was talented. Nothing came to him with any detectable difficulty, and it was not long before the youthful creature began to exhibit signs of surpassing those to whom he owed his growing abilities. It was Takeru who first voiced what many had considered.

"He will eclipse us all, each and every one. I've not seen his equal, here or in any land whose earth I have touched."

"Does this knowledge frighten you, Lord Takeru?" inquired Alexandro, sounding himself somewhat frightened.

Takeru, rarely serious, replied with a grin on his lips. "I've made certain to plant the seeds of friendship, my dear Alexandro."

"What nonsense! Hernan, the stern Andorran sword master, planted a hand squarely on the table around which he, his fellow cadre, and the Jesuits were standing. "He's not gotten the better of any blade in this room. And if he imagines himself capable, I will swiftly divorce the child's mind from so arrogant a thought."

"He has not bested one of us, no, and he may not for months to come." Takeru, though hardly harsh in tone, had arrested his earlier levity. "But that day will surely be upon us before we are prepared to accept the accompanying humiliation. I was among the best *Nihon* in my youth; my skill then would have been soundly outclassed by his now."

This had been followed with the sort of silence that always follows the voicing of irrefutable truth. The meeting had adjourned with all minds focused on the question of Mathieu's relentlessly mounting greatness. What design did heaven have in store for such a creature? Was he fated to serve the pope, Christ's vicar on earth, or was he fated to serve God himself? A veritable archangel—Mathieu.

Like all of the *apprendisti*, Mathieu's name was a pseudonym. Even so, Greve, the Danish man of tongues, would occasionally use the name "Achilles" when speaking about (never to) the boy. And

Takeru, importing from his own lands a similar sentiment, used the term *kami*, which he had loosely translated as *demi-dieu* or "demigod" in the English occasionally spoken by one of the masters. Forbidden by the Jesuit clergy to allow such talk to be overheard by Mathieu or his adoptive brothers—it was, after all, a sacrilegious notion—a peculiar theater was overlaid atop the monastery's austere environs. In it, cadre and clergy alike were compelled to behave as though Mathieu's prodigious qualities were of no particular relevance to any involved in this papal charter. Despite what all knew to be true about the force of nature into whose being they continued to pour their collective knowledge, he received neither praise nor discipline that differed in any significant way from that enjoyed and endured by his brothers… brothers who themselves recognized the supremacy Mathieu so singularly embodied.

Mathieu and Jakob on either ends of the *apprendisti* talent continuum, the remaining ten falling somewhere between those extremes, Cardinal Romero's cadre laboring with diligence and by design to yield men of paramount quality—the monastery's was truly a breathtaking testament to all that was achievable within human experience.

The Masters, 1554

Would that the masters in Romero's employ had so gleaned from collective expertise in the way their twelve pupils themselves now did. These men were each remarkable in their own right, representing disciplines spanning from horsemanship and language to acrobatics and the way of the sword; the monastery was a trove of marvelous skill, unimpeachable pedigree, and resolute devotion to the Church and its presiding pope. Whereas Romero's Jesuit disciples had carried out the task of scouring orphanages across Christendom for worthy pupils, the assembling of suitable cadre members was undertaken almost exclusively by the cardinal himself.

Accompanied solely by a pair of Swiss Guardsmen, a young priest pressed into clerical service, Lord Takeru, and Archbishop Romero (always in search of good cause for travel) had traversed much of the *Europa* landmass in a recruiting effort that spanned nearly four months' time. Benefiting greatly in his mission from a series of correspondences with military leaders, purveyors of circus theatrics, university overseers, and a lifelong friend whose wages were earned via translation and embassy interpreting, Archbishop Romero had identified by kingdom, name, and physical description his every cadre member before stepping so much as a single foot outside the limits of Rome. He had then charted a sensible west-east-to-west pathway that had his modest assembly passing through and, in many cases, lodging in more than a score of Christendom's capitals and leading cities.

Beginning in the Greek islands—the only portion of their journey to necessitate travel by sail—Romero aimed to intercept a wandering circus about which he had read a great deal and in which worked the archbishop's initial recruit.

Born in Athens to Turkish parentage, Ismail Öztürk's was a remarkable life of travel, of showmanship, of pedagogy, and (as understood by Romero) of spiritual resolve. Conditioned from an early age for the rigors of soaring acrobatics, vaulting, and a host of equally breathtaking physical feats, Ismail had spent decades robbing crowds of their collective breath while exhibiting his extraordinary acrobatic prowess. Eventually, thousands of performances having exacted of his limbs a heavy toll, Ismail devoted himself to the life of a teacher, passing along his knowledge of high-flying performance to pupils destined for the traveling circus and coupling this education with an evangelizing penchant he had cultivated within himself throughout his early life.

"One does not tempt the earth below with a promise of a brutal falling death and not forge a relationship with one's heavenly savior," Ismail was once heard proclaiming.

That the Turkish-born, Greek-raised traveling acrobat was of decidedly Catholic persuasion owed itself largely to chance.

"Or to divine overseeing," Romero argued.

For had the Turk's mother and father not spent a year's time on Italian soil, much of it in Rome, theirs might not have been loyalty to papal sanctity as it would ultimately become. Their journey had, blessedly enough, come at a time when both were experiencing a disillusionment with the Orthodox faith to which they belonged. For whatever reason, neither sensed any cause for such apathy to the Roman counterpart; thus did the pope win, absent any effort on his part, two converts and the faith of their infant son: Ismail Öztürk.

And thus did Archbishop Romero, nearly half a century hence, recruit to his cause a well-traveled Turkish acrobat of Greek upbringing, Roman Catholic faith, and a gift for instruction. Romero had first encountered Ismail many years prior to the cause that now re-united them. Passing through Thessaloniki en route to Istanbul, Archbishop Romero had enjoyed a performance of Ismail's acolytes as they soared on ropes in a decidedly avian exhibition of near-flight wonder. Striking up conversation with Ismail shortly thereafter, the holy man and the holy acrobat developed an immediate affinity for each other. Correspondence was established, maintained, and ultimately brought the men together under rather important circumstances some years subsequent.

"It will be a commitment of a decade's time, my friend." Romero spoke such words to each of his cadre. "And yours will be vows of secrecy, of devotion, of sacrifice."

Not a word of this was unknown to Ismail, who replied simply, "It is as God wills it."

Archbishop Romero had directed Ismail Öztürk to Rome with official documentation and papers ensuring safe passage throughout papal lands and allied lands thereof. He had also provided money, sealed orders, and a map. In six months' time, Ismail would trek to an obscured corner of the papal lands. There stood a specially constructed monastery that would be home to Ismail, numerous fellow cadre, a number of Jesuits, and the souls into whose minds and bodies would be invested the shared brilliance of Christendom's finest men.

And on and on did scenes of this sort take place across the weeks and months ahead. *To the north and west,* Romero thought upon departing from the Athenian hovel that had been, until that moment, Ismail's modest home.

The coming chapter of Romero's sweeping journey would have him pass through Bavaria and its ancient city of Ingolstadt. There stood a marvelous and venerable university that the Jesuit founder Ignatius had himself visited in an evangelizing capacity some years earlier. But this was incidental, at least for Romero's purposes, for the *Universität Ingolstadt* was also home to a strongman of considerable fame.

Long ago abandoning his given name, which was unknown to all, the extraordinarily powerful specimen had taken for himself the title and pseudonym of Herr Samson.

"A rightly conceived pseudonym, to be sure," noted Archbishop Romero upon reading of the man's godlike strength demonstrations. The bending of iron bars, the lifting overhead of large swine, the throwing of heavy logs over tall hurdles, and so on.

"If we are able to engender within our chosen twelve a mere fraction of Samson's power, his contributions will be well worth their while," Takeru had suggested. Romero was in agreement.

Securing the Bavarian titan's participation in Romero's project was a foregone conclusion. Mere mention of papal involvement and of *Il concilio di Trento*, which would eventually gave rise to this undertaking, was enough to have Samson kneeling obediently (unprompted) before the bemused archbishop. And while the giant—he was a full head taller than the himself tall Archbishop Romero—had cast a suspicious look toward the extremely foreign Takeru, the latter's accompaniment of Romero seemed to dispel any significant concerns.

"You will need to extend sincere overtures of camaraderie in winning Samson's trust, I would imagine," Romero foretold.

"I will share with him my famous wit and find myself with a *Kyojin* for a protector," Takeru countered while observing Samson demonstrate his power for an audience of enamored students.

Heartily laughing, Romero replied, "So you shall, my friend, so you shall!"

The archbishop's journey would next take his party many weeks to the west, where taught a swordsman of tremendous reputation, his name, Reynier Galante, having long ago become synonymous with the art of dueling upon which he had built his career.

Reynier now instructed would-be warriors in his art, often in the employ of royal figures minor and great alike. He lived in the very academy where he, along with several of his comparably skilled disciples, taught every day save the Sabbath. And even on that holy day, Reynier was known to move systematically through a series of prescribed sword movements derived (and often improved upon) from various weapons training manuals: Spanish, German, Italian, and even a rare Egyptian text he is said to have inherited from his own teacher upon the latter's death.

A maze of intersecting wires was set up at ankle height in precise fashion to ensure proper foot placement and movement throughout these exercises. Should a skilled practitioner prove himself capable of negotiating the wiry lattice while correctly exhibiting various strokes, thrusts, and parries, that practitioner would rightly be deemed a formidable swordsman. Should one do so while sightless, well, that person would indeed be a master of the highest order.

And Master Reynier strictly moved himself through these intricate exercises while his eyes were wholly covered by cloth, the training hall closed off from any inquisitive rays of sunlight, and the candles firmly devoid of illuminating flame. Such genius had been observed in no other swordsman throughout the whole of France.

"If any are his equal, they surely do not live within ten days' hard riding of the *Dauphiné Viennois*," one of Reynier's acolytes had assured Romero, who turned furtively to Takeru.

"How many days' ride might you suppose your *Nihon* to be from where we stand this very moment?"

Takeru seemed to seriously consider Romero's question, the answer to which was surely unknowable.

"Let us hope for the horse's sake that a determination is never made," was Takeru's evasive response.

"But we may presume your native soil sits somewhere outside of this man's ten-day ride threshold, may we not?" Romero politely persisted.

"My friend"—Takeru, to his great credit, was game—"if one day consisted of ten, my native soil would still sit beyond any such ten-day threshold."

Romero allowed himself a grinning moment in which to marvel at the fluency Takeru had cultivated in the speaking of both Italian and, to a lesser extent, the French they were presently using. He then turned back to Reynier's associate, Gaston.

"We have in our midst a swordsman of some skill, a man who calls home lands that sit scores of days—by horse and sail, mind you—to our east. Perhaps we'd enjoy an examination of your thesis, Gaston."

Gaston turned to Reynier, who had overheard much and was amused by this Italian archbishop with whom he had been in correspondence for some months.

"Master Reynier?" Gaston had no interest in serving as intermediary for so unanticipated a challenge.

"As you yourself said, Gaston"—Reynier stood to his decidedly average height, releasing from its scabbard a brilliant, polished rapier while doing so—"no man within ten days' ride. This is a rare occasion, indeed."

Gaston was handsome in his way, with sandy hair, fine proportions, and deep brown eyes that conveyed an inexplicable sadness, as though the world and all in it had failed to match his exacting standards. When he had sword in hand, however, the sadness gave way to a dignity and formality that crowded out all else.

"Gentlemen, I only implore you not harm each other in the realizing of this transaction." Romero's voice now lacked its prior levity. "I trust your combined skill will allow for a victor to be known without injury presenting itself as deciding factor."

Both men nodded to Romero, then to each other. Takeru drew his katana and handed the scabbard to the nearest Swiss guardsman. Stepping into an adjacent enclosure that was clearly used for precisely this purpose, Takeru stopped within two body lengths of his new acquaintance...of his unexpected opponent.

"Romero spoke well of you during our journey." The always courteous Takeru was, indeed, courteous.

"He does me great honor, seeing as we've only just this day met." Reynier stood perfectly still, eyes narrowed.

"Yes, but he met your reputation long ago, which says more about us than does anything else."

"Indeed. Speaking of which, the good archbishop saw fit in one missive or another to make mention of you. Seems yours is a style of remarkable property and potency."

"Ah, now it is *I* Romero does honor." Takeru spoke these words from a statuesque and entirely still stance.

The great swordsmen, Takeru some ten years younger than Reynier, afforded each other the kindness of a measured start. It was Reynier who initiated.

"*En garde!*"

In near perfect harmony, which all present found breathtaking, the masters each assumed a defensive posture that betrayed the vastly distinctive forms to whose respective mastery their martial lives had been devoted.

The swords, how quickly they moved. It would have been difficult to state with certainty whose blade was first thrown forth, as a profound symmetry characterized this terrific contest. Strike and counterstrike seemed to happen at once, with Takeru's movements materializing like so many gusts of wind and Reynier's parries being carried out with mechanical precision, fluid though they certainly were. Mere heartbeats after the men's swords had first crossed, Takeru's victory appeared rather likely, as he had forced a seeming misstep on Reynier's part, placing the French genius off balance. Takeru rounded to ostensibly bring his katana to his opponent's throat, thereby achieving a submission. But Reynier righted himself and redirected Takeru's blade harshly downward. What followed was a rapid succession of thrusts that kept Takeru in firm defensive posture. Seemingly relenting for a brief instant, Reynier lowered his sword and almost imperceptibly raised his free hand to chest level; Takeru moved quickly with an expertly rendered slash intended to decisively separate Reynier from his blade. A mere blink of an eye subsequent and the reverse had unfolded. Reynier, anticipating the counterstrike (or one like it), had placed his left hand into pursuit of the katana's hilt as it made its downward trajectory and swiftly withdrawn his rapier from said trajectory. Takeru's Katana was wrenched from his grip by the sheer force of Reynier's, as the Frenchman torqued his body and spun 'round to place his rapier flatly at the throat of Takeru.

"*L'émissaire de force*," Reynier then said while making a fist of his left hand, not a scintilla of hubris in his tone.

Takeru was intrigued. "Indeed, my friend. The hand is the emissary of one's strength. I applaud you!"

"Would that more could have witnessed this moment!" Romero exclaimed.

"In order that my *kutsujoku* might then be complete." Even this, Takeru spoke with humor on his breath.

"Nonsense, my friend. You acquitted yourself nicely and represented your *Nihon* honorably."

"Indeed"—Reynier had sheathed his blade and placed a hand of friendship on Takeru's shoulder—"yours was the swiftest swordsmanship I've yet encountered. A missed parry here or there, and the defeat would have been mine."

"That is true of *all* duels, *Masutā* Reynier," said Takeru the conciliator.

"I suppose it is, Takeru. But in this case, my erring was far more likely than ever before has it been. I'll not invite a second challenge with you if one can be avoided."

"Dignity and skill, both." Romero's eyes glowed warmly. "The monastery will surely benefit from your combined presence."

"And I eagerly await the cause's commencement. I am to understand my wife and daughter shall be invited to join us."

"And so they shall, Master Reynier."

Farther west now. Reynier having been left with papers and coins not unlike those bestowed upon Ismail, Archbishop Romero and his group set about to visit the three remaining recruits, neither more than three days' ride from the next, though the first was indeed some distance further from Dauphin.

Malcome Munro, a Scottish Lowlander if ever one can be said to have walked God's earth, had made himself known in cavalry service under two French kings, Francis I and his successor, Henri II. A horse warrior of legendary courage and prowess, Malcome had retired from service in his fortieth year and found himself in the employ of numerous stallion breeders. The profession ultimately opened itself to the training of cavalry officers in and around the ancient city of Troyes and proved itself work for which he was uniquely well suited. The fiery Scotsman had also made known his papist sentiments on many an occasion, sentiments that at times ran quite contrary to the mood of French royalty. "But, at least he isn't a Protestant," or so a courtier of Henri II's (himself an admirer of Malcome) is believed to have said at one point.

Archbishop Romero, who famously kept open lines of communication with many an influential figure throughout Christendom (including Scotland), had come to know Munro by name shortly before the brilliant cavalryman's career collided with a retirement brought on by age and injury.

"See to it that I am made aware of any threatened punishment directed toward this man Munro," Romero had written to a French Jesuit who invariably kept his ear to political whisperings, "he will enjoy my full support, legal or otherwise, should such a foul development come to pass."

He had then initiated direct communication with the surprisingly literate Lowlander and, perhaps a year hence, planted and nurtured the seeds that would blossom in the form of Munro committing to Romero's rather special undertaking. No dramatics or anything in the way of a lengthy visit had proved necessary in seeing Malcome

Munro off to Rome, a city upon which he had, since childhood, longed to lay eyes.

"And I am to meet Christ's vicar on earth?" he had asked plainly before setting off.

"Indeed, Munro. That much is a certainty." Romero was pleased to offer the man this deserved honor, though all cadre were to make the acquaintance of Pope Julius once assembled.

"Very well. I look forward to our meeting in one month's time."

And with that, the bravest (retired) horse soldier in France made his way south to Rome, documents bearing Papal authority held close to his body in a tightly secured satchel.

"Our numbers grow, Takeru. Let us now go and retrieve our man of tongues."

"Ah, yes—Greve. You know him well, do you not?"

And Romero was, in fact, quite well acquainted with Greve Christiern, a Dane who was thought to be intimate with over twenty living languages and half that number of dead.

"Indeed. It was Greve who accompanied me on my first trip through the Habsburg lands six years past. He had ensured my communication was unhindered, my precise meaning faithfully conveyed at every turn."

"They speak a difficult language, these Habsburgs?"

"They speak a great many, and many minor variations of those many. In Greve's absence, I'd have been reduced to illustrating my meaning in the dirt at my feet."

Takeru roared, "There would be a sight to behold, my friend."

"Well, a sight, anyway." Romero was less amused by the thought.

"So, Greve speaks these Habsburg tongues?"

"Many, yes, and he is uniquely gifted in the way of acquiring new language, seemingly within days. A better sense of human communication I've not encountered."

"In *Nihon*, we refer to such gifted souls as *tsūyaku*."

"I'd wager confidently that Greve could discern the meaning with little context."

"Let us place that wager." Takeru smiled.

Born in *København*, Greve Christiern's merchant father had sent him, when the boy was in his tenth year, to Paris for a worldly and rigorous education. Recognizing in his son a profound cerebral talent, he had imagined Greve might one day inherit the shipping house he had worked for years to build, crate by crate, shipping order by shipping order. Supreme intelligence enriched with knowledge and advanced ways of thinking; the boy would return a man and expand his inheritance tenfold.

But Greve was not a man of commerce. He loved only language and returned to his native *Danmark* only three times in the decades since having left. The third visit saw him bury his father; the second to wed his beloved wife; the first to bury his dear mother. Greve had little left in his native land, much language experience in the world beyond.

"I understand you hail from lands a hundred days' eastward sailing." Greve spoke to Takeru in beautiful French, having learned from Romero that the man of *Nihon* knew this Christian tongue fairly well. The three men sat in a large study replete with books, maps, and parchments. Paris suited Greve nicely; Romero knew his friend would miss the ancient city.

Responding in French far less beautiful, Takeru's wit nevertheless survived: "Would that a mere hundred days at sea were all this visit entailed, might have made my friendship with the archbishop moderately worthy of my while."

A wit himself, Greve smiled the smile of a kindred spirit. "So you come from farther still? In that case, you must have gleaned many a new word throughout your quest!"

"Or *tabi*, as we might roughly translate in my tongue."

"*Tabi!*" Greve beamed widely. "I cherish its sound."

"Well, then, it seems your sharp minds will enjoy intertwining throughout the years ahead." Romero had afforded himself the brief luxury of merely observing this exchange rather than participating as might normally have been his wont. "All will surely revel in that discourse."

"Indeed, Archbishop, and I should say just how good it is to behold you once more."

"Mine are identical sentiments, old friend. And your wife, your daughter—they pose no objection to a life on the Italian peninsula?"

Uproarious laughter by Greve was followed by a cheerful response: "My good man, this brilliant cause of yours may very well be the salvation of which my marriage was in need. Prior to your welcoming me into the cadre's ranks, I had begun preparations for a visit to the *Ny Verden*. I understand the Spanish have encountered tribes of red men in those lands."

"And considerable gold, I am told."

"Of no concern to me. Language is my gold; exotic vocabulary my coinage."

"You truly are a fortune unto yourself, Greve Christiern."

"So, you see, my wife had no interest in accompanying across the Atlantic to explore—under Spanish protection, I should hope—lands in search of new tongues and greater understanding of *menneskehed...* of mankind."

"No desire to explore distant lands populated by hostile peoples? It beggars belief." Romero, himself a traveler, was in no way interested in New World exploration. Too much to be done in Christian lands.

"It certainly does. In any event, would you like that I make my way to Rome at once?"

"You've some time to spare, though departing within the week might be sensible. As I recall, yours is not a particularly swift rate of travel."

"Agreed. Within the week it is." Greve then turned in coy manner to the exotic Takeru. "How might I say 'farewell' in your faraway *Nihon*, my new friend?"

Takeru's face illuminated. "You are the only man to ask since first my feet touched Christian dirt."

"It is my eternal wont, sir."

"In my land one would say to another when bidding farewell, *'sayonara.'*"

"Now *that* is a term I shall adopt immediately. My good men, I bid
you both *sayonara* and eagerly await your arrival to those lands below
the *Alperne*."

Takeru looked back to Paris on more than one occasion as he,
Romero, the Swiss Guardsmen, and Romero's secretary made their
way southwest from that storied city.

"It grew on you quickly, did it not?"

"I am reminded of a city I visited once in childhood and again on
my journey to *Yōroppa*. It is known in my homeland as *Pekin* but to its
people as"—Takeru paused as if to perfectly form the name—"*Běijīng*."

"You are reminded by our Paris of a distant eastern city? I find
that remarkable, even breathtaking." Romero was alight.

"There is, to be sure, as much distinctive as there is common between them, but the city's spirit is old and worthy and good. It is *Pekin*
of the West, I shall call it." Takeru looked to the horizon while sunnily
stating his proclamation.

"Perhaps you will inform those in *Pekin* of their having a distant
sister city when passing through."

"If ever again I do see that ancient city, I will do just that."

The five walked in silence for some time, making their way to a
highway stable in which passage by wagon had been arranged for
this, the final stretch of their long travels.

"I very much doubt the village our final *praeceptor* calls home
will bring to mind any such jewels of the Realm Oriental," Romero
predicted.

"You have said the country is both France and Spain and neither France nor Spain. I am reminded of riddles our province's *shijin*
would pose in order to drive mad my brother, the heir, and myself."

"Ah, yes—Andorra is not French, and it is not Spanish. It sits high
atop the uneasy border between both kingdoms and guards its identity closely."

"And the man we seek?"

"Also sits high atop the border. And he, too, guards closely his
Andorran identity."

"I shall look forward to meeting this elevated master."

"Those dual meanings of yours, Takeru, they will surely be a source of amusement to Greve."

"Should I expect to cross blades with the Andorran?"

"I should hope not. Certainly not by my design. He is by far the eldest of those I have sought to assemble; he no longer duels for sport."

"And in his day?"

"In his day, Hernan was the finest blade in Europe"—Romero glanced in prodding fashion to Takeru—"perhaps in the world."

"To have seen the man in his prime—a blessing would that surely have been."

Vexed at having had his bait go unseized, Romero abandoned the effort. "Make no mistake, my good man, even now there are few who would chance with him a test of skill. His knowledge of technique is ancient; it is practiced; it is proven." The archbishop then sighed. "But this flesh of ours, it does inevitably rot off the bone. Mortality levies all, genius and jester alike."

"For many in *Nihon*, the chance to die in battle carries with it the blessing of averting the infirmity—the indignity—of aging."

"So, too, in these Christian lands, though few in my profession are inclined to actively promote such a philosophy."

"To be alive is to wonder at such things; to be dead is to know the only answer that matters." Takeru spoke in a way Romero had never before heard; sadness gutted his voice of its characteristic warmth.

A day into their southwestward travel, Romero halted the large and mostly comfortable wagon. The passage from Paris had not seen them cross arduous terrain, certainly nothing of which to speak. But there was a not inconsiderable ascent ahead of them, and Hernan had advised, via written correspondence, that Romero begin the upward journey into Andorra with a new and rested team.

"Halt your travel in the village of Foix, our old neighbor," Hernan had written. "There you will find any number of stable masters willing to accept your papal coins in exchange for strong oxen. Most of these will have traveled to Encamp, where I instruct my foolish students. Tell the stable master, whichever you meet, that Hernan says hello and that if they owe me money, I will be down with sword in hand before the coming autumn."

And Romero had done exactly that, with the exception of issuing what he hoped was an idle threat.

"I've no objections to being an intermediary between men and greetings," he had explained to his secretary priest, "but I'll not lower myself to the role of debt *dominatore*."

The oxen team had come at a high price, but Romero's venture was well funded…the expense worthwhile. This particular team came with a guide who, while strictly walking alongside the beasts, ensured their progress en route to Encamp was steady and without incident. He did indeed know the roads, as did the oxen themselves, Romero expected.

Andorra was simply transcendent in its beauty, as the traveling party discovered upon their second day since having departed Foix. Even the Swiss Guardsmen betrayed upon their faces a hint of wonder at what Takeru, Romero, and the secretary priest had all conveyed openly—a serene landscape of pristine hillsides, palatial mountains, and an innate vibrancy that suggested a realm only lightly disturbed by time's passage. And the effect was lasting, just up until the moment…

"Archbishop Romero!"

…Hidalgo Hernan de la Vega called out from what was a heavily floral porch, itself attached to a pleasant cottage. All approaching were able to see an adjacent structure whose large windows made visible an elaborate studio dedicated to the art of swordsmanship.

The genius that must surely unfold therein, Romero thought before acknowledging Hernan's boisterous welcome.

"My good man, an honor to see you in the flesh." Romero leaped from the wagon and walked with some haste toward the venerable old blade, who appeared to be perhaps in his sixtieth year.

The greeting and countergreeting were spoken in a tongue that both Takeru and the secretary priest were unable to fully decode. It was, both knew from Romero's forewarning, Catalan, and the only language Hernan spoke with any degree of fluency.

"The stable master did not rob you blind, I trust." If Hernan was asking in jest, Romero could not know with any certainty.

"Actually, he did exactly that. But I consider the coinage a worthy loss, as its absence from my pouch assured my—*our*"—Romero turned and directed his arm toward his companions—"safe and timely arrival to your handsome doorstep."

"So it did." Hernan nodded as though some words of wisdom had been exchanged. "And this is the foreign master of whom you made some mention in your letter?"

"It is, Hidalgo Hernan. May I introduce Lord Sakurai Takeru of far-off *Nihon*?" Romero gestured reverently to the politely composed Takeru.

"Hello, Lord Takeru. Perhaps a demonstration of your skill would be in order."

Laughing with some nervousness, Romero quickly interjected, "Ah, firstly, I assured my companion he'd not cross blades with the great Hernan de la Vega on this day."

"And secondly?"

"And secondly, though Takeru has proven himself brilliantly adept at the acquiring of foreign tongues, Catalan is as yet alien to his ear."

"I see. Well, time spent in my company will correct *that* language shortcoming"—the Spanish-born Andorran was haughty—"as for the demonstration…"

"I'm afraid we'll not be—"

Hernan interrupted. "If not against me, then perhaps one of those Swiss fools at your back. I've long suspected theirs to be an undeserved reputation; let your foreign sword cut down that inherited pride."

Takeru had inferred quite clearly just what it was the old master now proposed. Impish grin gracing his visage, he spoke quickly to the secretary priest, who nodded along in hesitant agreement.

Stepping out into a patch of land well clear of wagon, beast, and man (save for his recruited assistant), Takeru placed a hand firmly upon his sheathed katana and, looking only to the now inquisitive Hernan, bowed deeply.

This having been the agreed upon moment in which to enact his essential part, the young priest procured from his flowing robe a bright red apple and, with some effort, threw the hapless fruit straight above the ground on which he and Takeru stood. Darting quickly from the samurai's side, the priest then turned to observe what lay in store for the apple.

Rising from the deep bow and drawing his katana in a single fluid motion, Takeru then spun with wind-like speed. The whipping blade, which moved horizontally across his bodily hemisphere, sliced neatly through the rapidly descending apple. His second revolution was compounded in complexity as Takeru dropped to one knee and intercepted one half of the split apple with his katana's point. Then, as one might expect from Takeru, the gifted samurai recovered to a standing position and took a generous bite of the spitted fruit.

All were duly impressed by that which they had just borne witness, but only the observant Hernan noticed the final element of Takeru's splendid display.

Pointing somewhat downward in Takeru's general direction, he said, "Archbishop, look to your man's left hand."

Romero did just that, and noticed the apple's remaining half in Takeru's left hand.

"His is skill of singular quality, Hidalgo."

As Romero put words to what all were thinking, Takeru sheathed his blade and approached Hernan. He offered the elderly master the unbitten apple half and bowed once again.

Hernan, accepting the apple, continued Romero's thought: "And character of high quality, as well, I should think."

Takeru rose, looked at the archbishop and Hidalgo alike, and returned to the wagon.

"Tell me, Romero, do you suppose those Swiss buffoons of yours could exhibit skill of that sort?"

Romero shook his head resignedly. "I suppose not, Hernan. But I'll say this much—I shall welcome your company on the road to Rome. Between you and my man of *Nihon*, I shan't fear bandits, lest they number a hundred or more."

"Any beyond the first hundred I relegate to your Swiss apes!"

And so it was that, after a months-long journey, Archbishop Romero had successfully, and (per papal direction) in the flesh, recruited to his worthy cause the finest men in Christendom. They, along with Takeru and three Jesuit scholars sworn to the mission, numbered ten and consisted of a skilled acrobat, a Herculean strongman, a brilliant man of tongues, a heroic cavalryman, and three sword masters of immeasurable stature.

"Two sword masters in addition to myself. These orphans will certainly know their way around a sharp edge when your vision is fulfilled."

"After all, Takeru, they *are* to be Papal Blades, as even His Holiness Pope Julius, third of that name, has now taken to regarding them."

After an evening's stay in Hernan de la Vega's cozy cottage, a morning's brief preparation for the return journey, and farewells to a number of the Hidalgo's associates and relations, the party embarked for Rome.

7

SHIP

Waters of the *Yìndùyáng*, 1588

Nearly two weeks had passed since the *Ocean Castle* had last anchored in the waters of *Fēizhōu*, and the restless Jaidev had exhibited some anticipation as the vessel neared *Bhārata nū* and the vast ocean that enclosed it.

"We are almost precisely on schedule, Xavier." Jaidev's eyes were on the open sea, hands on the marvelous helm, mind on the days ahead. "The old ways, they acquit themselves nicely."

Jaidev referred often to the "old ways," the ways that had been employed when first the *Ocean Castle* had, along with many others like her, set course for lands and waters near and far.

"The *Yongle*, visionary emperor he was. Admiral Zheng He, what a sailor, what a man." Jaidev's eyes, still to the sea, looked also inward, and to a past he had not lived but cherished as closely held memory.

In the early years of the Christian calendar's fifteenth century, a great *Chinois* dynasty known as the Ming, whose descendants still reigned, had committed tremendous resources to the domination of the high seas. A fleet of enormous ships would soar across the world's oceanic frontiers, showcasing Ming magnificence and exacting from all in their path tributes of gold, silver, and treasures of every kind conceivable. This *flotte de trésor*, as Jaidev had loosely translated for Xavier, sailed proudly under the celebrated eunuch admiral Zheng He, a dear friend and trusted adviser to the *Yongle* emperor. Seven voyages in all, spread as they were across twenty years' time, would serve to showcase Ming grandeur to distant lands, some familiar to Zheng He from his knowledge of cartography and sailing precedent, others never before having been charted by civilized mariners.

A golden age it had been, this age of Ming sail. Ships like islands unto themselves, making known to peoples sophisticated and primitive alike the glory that was Ming, the glory that was *Yongle*...the glory that was Zheng He. Valuables of all kinds poured into the *Chinois* coffers and into the *Yongle*'s palaces and estates themselves, while various souls from across the seas were ferried to and fro on the mighty treasure ships, many visiting Ming lands, others simply accompanying Zheng He or his captains on voyages to the world's farthest edges, trading knowledge with the scholars, astronomers, cartographers, and poets who were to be found on each of the splendid ships.

"Would that things had continued thus," Jaidev had sadly reflected when first sharing of this marvelous history with an intrigued Xavier. "Ships like the *Ocean Castle* would have sailed unchallenged into Christian waters long before your *Kalamabasa* made his way on those three rafts to the so-called New World."

But things had not continued thus, for the *Yongle* had done his people and Ming's treasure fleets the disservice of dying, just over twenty years following the initial fleet's inaugural voyage. Men of very different vision would occupy the imperial throne for years thereafter, one of whom, the *Hongxi*, saw fit to scuttle the great treasure fleet in its entirety, stripping Zheng He of his naval authority and relegating the great man to duties on land that carried with them none of the explorer's glory...glory for which the brilliant eunuch lived.

"That great man—that godhead—knew firmly how to see beyond his time and place. He was vision itself, and that vision, Xavier, preserved the ship upon whose sacred planks your feet this very moment have purchase." Only at this moment of Jaidev's initial recounting of the tale did he deign to match eyes with Xavier, to whom some of this story was familiar. Takeru had related fractions of the saga on occasion but largely avoided the topic for reasons all his own.

"Early during the sixth voyage, a scout vessel, of which scores existed within the treasure fleet, had separated from its *qíjiàn*, its flagship, in the *Yìndùyáng*'s distant east." Jaidev read from the manuscript of legacy, cherishing these words above all others. "And after days of south-by-southeast sailing, had seen on the far horizon lands that had no end to the east, nor an end to the west."

Jaidev now studied the vast wooden map in the *Ocean Castle*'s pilot cabin. There on the map's lower right corner was a lengthy east-to-west line engraved in some detail, itself representing an island—no, a *continent* of great size.

"Perhaps as large as the great northern steppes, the scout vessel's *tokoh* would report to Zheng He himself." Emotion now took captive Jaidev's unsteady voice: "Zheng He dispatched a small detachment to journey directly southeast and to map the lands upon shores the scouting vessel's crew had lain eyes. The detachment consisted of one supply ship, two scouts, and the ship we now know as the *Ocean Castle*."

Xavier could not deny the improbable and extraordinary nature of the tale. For Zheng He, knowing the days of Ming naval supremacy were numbered, had discreetly ordered an unfailingly loyal captain, who had served in the fleet for more than a decade's time, to sail with speed and vigor on a course of interception with the *Ocean Castle*. Months later, the vessels intersected with each other and, after a period of conference between captains, parted ways forever. The loyal captain had returned to Zheng He, confirming his having conferred with the *Ocean Castle*'s senior officers, also confirming his having delivered the great eunuch admiral's final orders to the only remaining treasure ship: "Live well, and by sail."

"And with those orders, our history was born, Xavier. We have lived well, we have sailed the seas, we have honored the glory of the Ming as Zheng He knew it, and we have continued to shape ocean affairs for more than a century's time."

"That much is certain." Xavier thought back to Sesimbra, to the sunken *Anjo*. He thought also of the *Ocean Castle*'s thousand souls, the majority of whom had been born at sea, a greater majority still whose time spent on dry land was best measured in days, perhaps weeks, certainly not months, and never years.

"I cannot say with any certainty that we will see another century." Jaidev was now even in his voice. "The waterways, they grow more trafficked with vessels—Christian and otherwise—with every passing year. One day, we will…"

The thought went unspoken. But Xavier knew the *tokoh*'s meaning—one day the *Ocean Castle* would join its sister ships on the seafloor. Whether in one year or fifty, such maritime impunity would not persist in perpetuity.

"But for the present"—Jaidev was lively once more—"let us see to the safe delivery of our cargo and reshape the political terrain of your Takeru's faraway *Nihon*."

"Was Takeru himself complicit in the designing of this transaction?"

Jaidev eyed Xavier with uncertainty. "In a manner of speaking, yes."

"No matter, *Tokoh*, I'll ask him as much myself."

A polite nod and Xavier was away, leaving Jaidev at the wheel he had inherited from a century-long line of forebears.

The Training

In returning to his quarters, Xavier descended two decks into the ship and was perhaps twenty paces astern of the pilot's cabin in whose confines he had earlier stood. The descent through those decks and negotiating of those paces saw the somewhat tall man of Christendom cross paths with families, with sailors, with carpenters busy at work (almost to a one), with scholars, and with soldiers. The last of these invariably cast looks of aspersion and, to an equal degree, of trepidation Xavier's way. He had taken lives in securing his passage, and aboard the *Ocean Castle* each of those lives had been a known quantity.

There had been an episode, a violence, perhaps one month following the vessel's departure from Sesimbran waters. Predictable as it was overdue, the violence unfolded during the daily bread, and Xavier had sensed something was amiss. A small space opened up around the Frenchman, small but clearly opened by design. The well-ordered lines of patient *Castle* inhabitants had been moving along in accordance with a routine which was generations in the practicing, and while many made obvious their eyeing of the remarkable figure that was Xavier, most simply accepted the bakers' offering and returned to the duties which were their charge, to the arts they ardently pursued, to the seafaring life which was their own.

On this particular day, however, at least two among the partakers of bread sought something else entirely, something along the lines of retribution. One of the two, a young fiery man of light brown skin, dark eyes, and the wiry arms of a lifelong sailor, stepped quickly onto the cleared deck at Xavier's back and, wielding a heavy cleaver, sliced sideways in alignment with his target's neck. This transpired at once with an attack at Xavier's left side, as an older man, far larger and bulkier of build than his accomplice, swung an enormous sword in an upward slashing motion towards Xavier's abdomen.

Having been cognizant of each assailant and of their weapons some several instants prior to the dual-attack unfolding, Xavier had mapped his counteraction and placed it into motion with not so much as a heartbeat to spare. Stepping forward and to the right, the swordsman spun quickly and with precision so as to catch the armed hands of each assassin. He then thrust each arm towards the ceiling, ducked underneath and pulled both weapons into apposition with their own wielders' exposed throats. The image was as poetic in its execution as it was serious in its implication: a sharp pulling motion on part of Xavier would see each of his assailants pouring blood from opened wounds upon the deck below.

The nearly two-hundred souls who had witnessed the attempted murder were collectively uncertain as to what might follow. None dared intervene, too precarious was the safety of their shipmates. Xavier met the terrified gaze first of his younger attacker, then of the older; both exhibited fear, though neither plead for mercy. Next, Xavier turned his gaze to the crowd by which he was surrounded. In many eyes among their number, a certain sadness was profoundly evident. The loss of these lives would amount to a cruel waste, and so Xavier simply dropped the weapons whose edges had been employed in the attempting mutilation of his unarmed body.

Neither of Xavier's attackers made a move towards their intended victim, who now made his way through the parting crowd, nor did they retrieve their weapons. They simply watched the Frenchman make his way elsewhere. While Xavier did just that, his peripheral vision registered a number of nodding heads and sincere smiles. Mercy had been unexpected; mercy was deeply appreciated. Just before heading below decks, Xavier heard Jaidev's voice, "Merciful Xavier…"

Jaidev stood a few paces from the hatch Xavier was soon to enter. "You've spared their lives, and, in so doing, perhaps your own."

Xavier did not acknowledge the words which might just as well have gone unspoken. Either Jaidev had tasked those men with doing as they did in hopes that what had resulted would result, or he had tasked them doing as they did in hopes that Xavier's death would have been achieved. Regardless of his design, Jaidev had most certainly been the author of the day's discord.

That Jaidev was thereafter able to ensure peaceful transit for the conspicuous man was testament both to his supreme authority and to the knowledge on part of all that efforts at revenge would yield still further bloodshed of the sort that befell them those several months past. What had transpired between Xavier and the vengeful young men during the daily bread would prove itself an aberration, nothing more.

"Best we view those deaths as collateral losses, retribution for the lives we ended in Portuguese waters." Jaidev had diplomatically explained to his senior officers. "We've delivered death and chaos on scores of occasions since my captaincy came to be and lost virtually no lives in so doing. That our actions eventually yielded a regrettable recompense of our own blood is to be understood if not welcomed."

"But why must we also transport aboard our ship the very man responsible for this"—the speaker, a fiery deck officer, spewed forth the next word—"recompense?"

"That much is a matter between him and me. And besides, upon reaching *Owari*, Xavier may prove more useful than even he knows."

None of this had satisfied the officers or anyone else aboard the *Castle*, but the orders had been issued...and they had been followed. No violence was to be directed toward Xavier unless sanctioned by *Tokoh* Jaidev. And under those circumstances, the action would be carried out by one man.

That the particular details of this conversation were unknown to Xavier was of little consequence. He feared not for his safety and thought only of *Nihon*, home of samurai Lord Sakurai Takeru. This line of thinking populated the swordsman's mind as he stripped to only his trousers and cleared as best as he was able the confines of his quarters: sleep rack standing upright along the bow-side wall, chest and chair stacked one atop the other, all else cast tightly into corners. With perhaps two arm-lengths forward and back of him, Xavier lifted by its forge-welded chain a heavy cannon ball and began his breathtaking movements.

As the ball was whipped around by force of Xavier's muscle, it threatened to pull him violently downward, or to itself crash destructively into the planks at his feet. It was his own acrobatic leaping and torsional rotation that kept either from coming to pass. Each circumnavigation of the chain-tethered ball generated pulling force comparable to or greater than Xavier's own weight. Counteracting this force required an inhuman convergence of sheer might and expertly realized leaps and flipping motions to keep man and steel in perpetual equilibrium. The greater the force in question, the greater Xavier's investment of power and acrobatic finesse in reining in chain and ball.

The process unfolded for a longer while than what should have been sustainable for any man, swelling Xavier's long, well-formed muscles, themselves laden with power far beyond what one might have presumed existed therein. Sunlight, pouring in generously from the quarters' small aperture, visiting itself warmly upon the master swordsman's hardened physique. Had any lain eyes upon Xavier in that moment, they would have borne witness to incandescent godliness, nothing less.

This portion of the regimen completed, the sinewy warrior drew from its sheath the Solingen-forged rapier he had possessed since reaching manhood and executed a series of forms that were at once systematic and poetic; the blade moved swiftly, compromising no precision, and in accordance with a mental diagram incomprehensible to the untrained eye, and unmatchable to many a trained one. Xavier channeled forms ancient and new, obscure and common, artful and plain—they were, collectively, a language unto themselves, and no man other than Xavier spoke with anything approaching such profound fluency.

Sheathing the blade, storing the chain-tethered cannonball, and restoring his quarters to their more livable state, Xavier then rested and reflected upon the miles he had placed between himself and his native France…and of the miles he had closed with Takeru.

"I'll not keep you in any such terrestrial limbo, Takeru. The winds of sail are inexorable."

Chau Hai Fan

The "one man" to whom Jaidev had earlier made reference—the one man to whom violence against Xavier would, if necessary, fall—sat crossed of leg on the deck planks of a spacious hall, itself just above the *Castle*'s tremendous ballast, and tucked tightly against the ship's broad stern. Despite the dimensions of this space, Chau had it entirely to his sole person, and would make use of both the room and the time set aside solely for his purposes.

Rising to his feet as though pulled swiftly upward by some unseen lanyard, Chau Hai Fan withdrew from the dual sheaths that crossed diagonally upon his back the identical *jian* with which he had, throughout his years, cut short the life of many an enemy and many others still. The *jian* were perfectly straight and double-edged, the tip rather more rounded than what one might expect of such a weapon, but still the blades were capable of piercing flesh and hide alike. They were perhaps two fingers in width farthest from the hilt, and just under three where blade met guard. They were polished but did not attract light, instead appearing flat in color and hue. They were razor thin on the edges and flexed gracefully when subjected to force. They, like their wielder, were deadly and had frequently emptied bodies of their coursing blood since coming into Chau Hai Fan's skillful possession.

Swiftness and agility fell short of describing Chau Hai Fan's relationship with the mechanics of human motion. His every leap seemed to find a second life in that instant when every other body in existence would have been summoned to the ground below. These leaps were unpredictable in trajectory, in purpose, in form; they took shape precisely as their author saw fit to shape them—and he was only precise.

Also unpredictable were the angles from which a given *jian* would materialize within Chau's acrobatic essay—a biting slash here, a perfectly aimed thrust there. The most seasoned and skilled of adversaries had been reduced to clumsiness and confusion in their efforts to thwart the beautifully murderous Chau, their attempts at parrying, blocking, and counterstriking ultimately slower than needed to achieve their purpose. And in so many such instances, swordsmen who had lived years without having faced a worthy opponent would find themselves on their knees, entrails having replaced swords in their weakening grip. For his part, Chau rarely afforded his victims the dignity of a final matching of eyes, an acknowledgment of a warrior preparing to meet his god. He simply resheathed his life-ending blades and carried on, as though never having encountered those whose energies now spilled to the soil or planks.

Any who had borne witness to the display of deadly grace that routinely unfolded in the *Ocean Castle*'s vast stern chamber would have doubted not Chau's capacity for killing at will, utterly regardless of the skill possessed by those to whom such artful violence befell. He was death.

Upon completing the archangelic regimen, Chau Hai Fan returned to the cross-legged seated position from which it had commenced. This, too, was carried out as though by the delicate dexterity of an unseen and enormous puppeteer. Once at peace, Chau allowed his thoughts to venture into speculation.

Will Jaidev have me kill the Christian? he wondered.

Many aboard the *Ocean Castle* would celebrate his doing so, though their feelings were of no concern to Chau. He had known only by face (and only vaguely) each of those killed by Xavier. Their deaths had caused within him no anguish. Instead, they had created within his mind an element of curiosity.

Might I at last face an opponent worthy of my skill? Might I experience an instant of fear? Might he be a near equal?

And so the thoughts unfolded, two decks below and ten paces astern of the very quarters in which his imagined adversary now himself wandered into thought and speculation. As for the *Ocean Castle* in which these regimens and imaginings materialized, that elderly vessel moved along on winds with which it had been acquainted for days numbering in the tens of thousands.

The Conversation

Seated in his spacious cabin, *Tokoh* Jaidev had for company a number of elders and senior officers, some of whom had been aboard the *Ocean Castle* for nearly seven decades' time. These were the men, most of them, whose votes had placed Jaidev into his present station following his predecessor's somewhat unexpected death.

A cross-section of parent cultures, physical features, and favored languages were represented in the eleven faces who now looked with shared consternation to the perfectly calm Jaidev. Not one among them had voiced support for his decision to keep safe the murderous Christian who was even now a mere two decks below where they sat convened. Jaidev had made a case both cryptic and compelling that served to rationalize (and legitimize) his position on the matter.

"He would leave much death in his wake, and those we lost as he made his way aboard, though mourned, are lost to the sea forever. As for our present purpose, which I urge you to keep at the forefront of your collective mind, Xavier may be of greater use to us than any of you realize. He is familiar…perhaps even enjoys terms of friendship with a man whose objections to our *Nihon* design could create for us"—Jaidev sought to employ the perfect words—"a very real obstacle."

"Ah, yes, you mean Takeru," exclaimed Chu Xie, a lawyer and cartographer who had been aboard the *Ocean Castle* since birth, five years prior to Jaidev's own. "Another of your questionable stowaways, Jaidev."

"Do recall, Chu Xie, it was Takeru whose presence in Christendom inadvertently led to our weapons dealing with *Nihon*."

Indeed, Takeru had quite unknowingly initiated contact between Jaidev and a number of gun sellers across the Iberian coast. This had its start with the Portuguese, with whom Jaidev detested working, and ended with the Spanish, with whom Jaidev chose to work on his own terms. The Sesimbran cathedral's fantastic destruction and the sinking of that hapless caravel was in many ways owed to Jaidev's negative experiences in working, always through intermediaries, with the Portuguese.

"Precisely, Jaidev, Takeru facilitated dealings of which he was *wholly unaware*."

"To be sure. However, had he not been in communication with our *Maiḍīṭērī'ana* network, the Spanish sellers would never have known of our presence in their waters. Fortunately, they were interested in acquiring customers, as opposed to, say, attempting to sink or seize the *Castle*."

"All of this is prologue, gentlemen," interjected Khemkhaeng, an elder sail master and respected figure by all. "The fact is, Takeru was only tacitly responsible for our present undertaking and may well seek to sabotage our *Nihon* designs. We have on board a man who may be able to prevent any such sabotage on part of an old friend. Is that the measure of it, Jaidev?"

"With the possible exception of Xavier's relationship to the old samurai. They may well be enemies, I'm afraid."

"In which case"—Khemkhaeng completed the corollary—"he may still prevent any such sabotage. An enemy willing to cross unknown waters and vast distances almost certainly has death in his heart."

"And he is certainly equal to the task, as our dead can attest." Chu Xie maintained his terseness.

"Indeed," Jaidev concurred with similar terseness, "but if he is not, we've one aboard who is…one who may well also see to the Christian's demise."

Khemkhaeng posed the question all were considering: "Why not have him do so now? Kill the Christian and order that he do the same to Takeru once we have reached *Nihon*?"

"Because, Khemkhaeng"—Jaidev rose in voice and to his feet—"if the latter death can be avoided, I quite insist it be so. Takeru, unlike Xavier, I do consider a friend. Though he may not house equal sentiments upon learning of our agreement with Lord Oda."

"I see. Your Christian is a measure of peace, Chau of death."

"Death of strict necessity. I would, in truth, prefer Chau stay aboard the *Castle* throughout our time in the waters of *Nihon*, though I also recognize the impractical nature of that preference."

Jaidev allowed himself a moment to order his thoughts. He then concluded with the authority this august body demanded of all men in his position.

"But should circumstances warrant as much, Chau's swords will drip with blood Christian and *Nihon no* alike. So long as our ends are achieved, neither death will mar my conscience in the least." Jaidev very nearly believed his own words. What was of importance was the elders' trust, which he had tenuously secured.

8

NIHON

The Shogun

The shogun had inhabited his exalted station for mere months and was, by all measures, unworthy of its eminence. Nevertheless, he was largely harmless in and of himself, and Lord Sakurai Kiyoshi preferred a harmless fool to a destructive competent.

"This man can be controlled," he was heard to say on more than one occasion, "and ours is a duty to serve him, regardless."

Osamu had disdained the very sound of those words upon first hearing them spoken. "A man should be supremely worthy of his station in life," he had said to his brother Hiroshi, "and should be deserving of reverence for the man he is."

Three years had passed since the reigning shogun's cousin, Yoshifuji, had died; or rather, had committed *seppuku* in order that he not face humiliation and dishonor at the hands of Daimyo Matsunaga Hisahide and his ally Miyoshi Yoshitsugu. Lord Sakurai Kiyoshi had not overtly supported nor spoken in defiance of Matsunaga's actions against Shogun Yoshifuji; Mikawa Province was simply not in a position to influence events to any significant degree, certainly not without placing its people at risk of retribution.

But Osamu knew of his father's admiration for Shogun Yoshifuji and knew he regretted the man's tragic end. Unlike many a shogun before him, and certainly unlike his successor, the laughable puppet Ashikaga Yoshihide, Yoshifuji had studied closely the art of swordsmanship. His training had been overseen to a considerable degree by Master Tsukahara Bokuden, author of the *Kashima Shintō-ryū* techniques that Takeru himself espoused greatly.

"There are sword disciplines of equal merit in lands near and in lands distant but none superior. Master Bokuden is genius itself." Takeru had replied, when asked by Hiroshi if any men of the *Kirisutokyō no* were Bokuden's equal.

"That is not an answer, *Oji*." Hiroshi lived to rank people and objects into easily interpreted hierarchies.

Takeru smiled warmly and cast his glance to the west. "Hiroshi, I should very much hate to witness Master Bokuden in a duel with any of the *Kirisutokyō no* swordsmen I call friend. Some questions benefit from remaining unanswered."

"It's him, isn't it? The one man you've acknowledged you could never defeat. He's the one you fear could get the better of Master Bokuden."

"Come now," Takeru evaded, "let us to your own lessons."

Indeed, all men of honor throughout *Nihon* were seemingly in agreement as to the dignity that had lived within the great shogun Yoshifuji. His was a painfully endured loss and Yoshihide a painfully inadequate successor.

"Does he know of Owari Province's dealings and schemes?" Osamu asked this of his father, though the answer was irrelevant. If he did not know, no intervention could be expected. If he did know, much the same.

"It's of little consequence, my son. Takeru is familiar with those who even now make their way to our shores, carrying with them a still greater shift in the balance of power. They will arrive, Oda will issue payment, and they will onshore death."

"Then it falls to us to stop them. Make an appeal to Lord Yoshihide. As shogun, he daren't have his lands beset by *Kirisutokyō no* arms."

"We've not the time. From what he knows of their seafaring patterns, these new weapons will be upon us sooner than the shogun would be wont to act."

Osamu grasped tightly the katana hilt at his side, eyes widening in anger.

"Damn that Lord Oda! Must he disrupt the land and its peace at every turn?"

"Fault him not solely, Osamu. Owari Province has found itself pulled into and out of conflicts for much of its history. It is as much an accident of geography as anything else; Lord Oda is merely an heir to that legacy."

"And what is the Mikawa Province's legacy, my lord? Aggressive neutrality through and through?"

"Survival, my son. We must negotiate our alliances and the political landscape with a light touch. We haven't the military might of Owari, nor do we have the ear of the shogun."

"Do you suppose he would lament the introduction of several thousand muskets to the *Nihon* he is sworn to protect?"

"Western weapons have been in our midst for decades, Osamu; Oda simply seeks to usher in that which is inevitable—*superior* Western weapons. I have been far and seen much. The guns we have thus far seen in battle are few in number, and they are outdated."

"What would you have us do?"

"We wait, keep our ears to the earth. If the opportunity to upset Lord Oda's scheme presents itself, we will strike. If not, I've emissaries making their way to all allies within two days' ride. Most will surely object to Oda's methods, as they do so many of his motives."

"Brokers of power rather than wielders of it."

"There is a place in this world, my son, for both." Lord Sakurai Kiyoshi spoke sternly.

"Indeed, my lord." Osamu's grip remained tight.

"Your *oji* Takeru will be making the ride to Owari Province. There may be terms achievable with Lord Oda." Daimyo Sakurai studied his son's tense visage. "Perhaps you and Hiroshi might join him, observe diplomacy as enacted by a man who has practiced its finer points in lands quite foreign."

"It would be my honor, my lord."

"Do promise me, my son, that your katana will remain there as it is now—sheathed."

Osamu flinched somewhat, as though his father had in some way impugned his honor.

"Naturally, my lord. Unless..."

"Unless nothing! Lord Oda will direct no violence against the son of a sitting daimyo, lest he further alienate himself from the surrounding provinces. And were he to do anything of the sort, my brother is the equal of any ten Owari warriors."

"As am I, my lord, though Owari is home to more than ten warriors."

"Not one of whom will raise a hand or weapon against my blood. Now ready yourself for the embassy. Your brother will look to you and to your *oji* for examples. Disappoint neither him nor me."

A deep bow, an about-face, and Osamu had exited his father's inner chambers, leaving the great daimyo to his thoughts.

The Legacy

"Your sons, Kiyoshi, these *oi* of mine, they are treasures the likes of which few fathers will ever enjoy."

Takeru and Lord Sakurai Kiyoshi walked through a garden immediately adjacent to the daimyo's residential palace. It was a late summer day of immense beauty. Golden sunlight shimmered sweetly upon petals and leaves, danced freely atop a large pond's crystalline surface, and recast the brothers' eyes in an ethereal manner. Mornings such as this visited Mikawa Province perhaps thirty times each year, likely fewer, for which reason daimyo and vassal alike savored their every fleeting instant.

"Hiroshi has so much of his mother in him. Her eyes haunt me through his."

"Thus your considerable time and attentions with and to Osamu?"

Kiyoshi aimed an irritated glance at his taller, more youthful brother. "That time and those attentions have everything to do with his being heir to a responsibility that is surely greater than he understands."

"And did you fully understand them prior to our father joining the gods?"

Sighing resignedly, he answered, "I suppose not, Takeru. Wisdom is strictly gleaned by experience; it cannot be taught or inherited."

"Osamu has learned well in observing closely his father, an honorable man."

"Handsome words, Takeru. But Osamu is restless, more so than was I in his present year. He loves Mikawa, for it is home; he resents it, for it is vulnerable."

"Yes, he has yet to understand the potential of a cleverly governed arbiter state, which Mikawa has long been."

"He must learn, and learn soon, the limits of the sword."

Takeru laughed. "I traveled across five hundred sunsets and only at my *tabi*'s end did I come to realize such a limitation existed."

"Let us pray my sons require no such extended lesson."

"I've done my part in subduing that prospect. Each lesson of sword is followed by two of mind."

"And they are well received?"

"Osamu appears to invite the knowledge inward, grappling with it on his own terms."

"And my younger son?"

"Hiroshi yearns to know who reigns supreme in this land, a juvenile yearning, and one that he will outgrow."

"Juvenile indeed." Lord Sakurai considered the question. "But who *does* reign supreme? Does he walk the lands of *Nihon*?"

Takeru stopped to pluck a beautiful *sakura*, savoring its scent.

"Thankfully not, my brother. But possibility exists on a lengthy continuum."

Lord Kiyoshi reflected briefly upon the cryptic sentiment, then nodded in agreement as the brothers carried on with their enjoyment of the heavenly morrow.

Brotherly Love

Downward slash, upward slash, side slash, thrust. Downward slash, upward slash, side slash, thrust. *Downward slash, upward slash, side slash, thrust. DOWNWARD SLASH, UPWARD SLASH, SIDE SLASH, THRUST.*

Sakurai brothers Osamu and Hiroshi stood two paces apart, both facing the *dojo*'s northern wall, and executed in harmony an increasingly rapid succession of strikes and thrusts.

DOWNWARD SLASH, UPWARD SLASH, SIDE SLASH, THRUST

Each summoned enormous reserves of energy in performing the routine with impeccable precision, force, and grace. Though the motions performed by each brother mirrored closely the other's, a knowing eye would have quickly discerned distinctions in their respective styles.

Osamu was power. His every motion was fueled by a musculature he had invested thousands of days in hardening, an attribute that rendered him an adversary rather challenging against which to defend. He was forceful, fearless, aggressive, and strong—all of which was observable on this day, in this *dojo*, alongside his younger brother, Hiroshi…

…who was grace. His strikes were not absent strength; he was, after all, a trained swordsman. But each slash began and concluded with a certain flow, a delicate whipping motion that implied knowledge of the blade's location in time and space with every hair's breadth of its transit. Thrusts were withdrawn with the faintest turning of the blade, as if righting the katana to better align it with its wielder's precise sense of fluidness. There was rhyme and verse in Hiroshi's swordcraft, something that eluded his brother's typhoon-like force.

"You move well, brother"—none of this was lost upon Osamu—"like a true exhibitionist." The observation was meant to cut both ways.

"To say nothing for a true warrior"—Hiroshi was undaunted—"I nearly brought *Oji* Takeru to the point of yielding."

"Ah, I suspect our *oji* was engaging unarmed."

DOWNWARD SLASH, UPWARD SLASH, SIDE SLASH, THRUST

"Ha! Not at all, brother. Anyway, you might consider easing into your movements. You'll risk breaking the blade or your arms."

"Neither. The blade is well made, my arms well muscled."

"Suppose we'll be needing either in Owari?"

"Hasn't *Otōsan* spoken with you? We are forbidden from drawing our blades."

DOWNWARD SLASH, UPWARD SLASH, SIDE SLASH, THRUST

"Assuming we do not find ourselves imperiled, correct?"

"A risk Lord Sakurai Kiyoshi finds unlikely. And anyway, Takeru will be with us. He's worth a hundred warriors, apparently."

DOWNWARD SLASH, UPWARD SLASH, SIDE SLASH, THRUST

"At least half that number." Hiroshi did not imagine himself to be overstating the matter. "He is remarkable with a blade."

"And yet, *you* nearly had the best of him?"

Hiroshi grinned. "He may have been feeling charitable toward his kin in that moment."

DOWNWARD SLASH, UPWARD SLASH, SIDE SLASH, THRUST

"Almost certainly, Hiroshi, almost certainly."

Thrust, Step, Upward Slash, Step, Thrust, Step, Downward Slash, Step, Thrust

"Do you suppose we'll need to employ these movements in Owari Province?" Hiroshi now sheathed his katana.

"I should think not." Osamu continued his movements. "Lord Oda gains little in taking our lives, or in holding us hostage. No, we will observe Takeru's storied diplomacy and depart having learned something of matters mental, little of matters martial."

"I should hope. What do you know of Takeru's time in the *Kirisutokyō no* kingdoms?"

"Aside from everything you yourself know?"

"What do you know of how his time away from *Nihon* may now affect our very lands?"

Thrust, Step, Upward Slash, Step, Thrust, Step, Downward Slash, Backstep, Thrust

"Only that our father expects we may once again find ourselves at the mercy of forces beyond our ability to confront."

"But within our ability to influence?"

"That is his hope."

Thrust, Step, Upward Slash, Step, Thrust, Step, Downward Slash, Backstep, Thrust

"The Matsudaira clan has been home to honorable leadership in its time; our *Otōsan* is emblematic of that legacy." Hiroshi did revere his father so.

"Yes, Hiroshi, he is. And if honor were alone sufficient to ensure one's survival, Shogun Yoshifuji would surely still hold that exalted office."

Thrust, Step, Upward Slash, Step, Thrust, Step, Downward Slash, Backstep, Thrust

"But it is not," Osamu continued, breathing heavily, "and he does not."

"And if you were daimyo, Osamu, what then? Would we soon be in open conflict with our much stronger Owari neighbors?"

Osamu sheathed his blade and regained his wayward breath. "I cannot say, Hiroshi. However, surrendering our land's fate to devilish weapons from beyond the setting sun"—he lowered his head and gripped the sheathed katana—"that much I should find troublesome to abide."

The brothers remained for some time in the dojo, wandering away from each other in thoughts of what awaited them in neighboring Owari Province.

The Confession

"Owari Province may in and of itself imperil the stability we've only just restored, Takeru." Lord Sakurai Kiyoshi had summoned Takeru and his sons to their palace's *moya* the following sunrise. "Whatever knowledge of ambassadorial finesse you have garnered in your wandering days, employ them ardently in speaking with Lord Oda."

"Naturally, my lord"—Takeru often addressed his brother formally when in the presence of others—"though we may have still less negotiating capital at our disposal than is usual. Oda has his designs on the shogun's seat, and he may well have a means of realizing said designs."

"What is it you know, *Oji* Takeru?" Osamu's patience had not been afforded an opportunity to take root before it was supplanted by frustration. "You've withheld relevant knowledge; of that I am certain."

Adopting a pensive countenance extraordinarily uncharacteristic for the jovial man, he looked wearily to Osamu, then to the floor at his feet. After a moment's silent deliberation, Takeru began to un-ravel the truth as he knew it.

"My time in *Yōroppa* had run its course, coming to a saddening end, which left me distraught and yearning for home. But that is of little importance at the moment."

All eyes studied the handsome, somewhat wizened facial features of the revered samurai as he continued.

"Securing return passage by means swift and sure became my sole concern over two years past. Much of my journey westward had been undertaken via lengthy land routes, though much of the initial travel I completed aboard a *Chūgoku no* ship, which even now many regard as mere myth. You may even have heard mention of it from our own sailors."

"*Oji*, are you referring to the...?" Osamu was boyish in voicing his question.

"To the *Ocean Castle*, yes. After reaching *Shanhai*, I orchestrated a series of inquiries and bribes in order to secure passage aboard the vessel, which I, in fact, knew to exist long before setting out on my journey. My visit to *Pekin* during boyhood saw our vessel cross paths with that extraordinary floating relic, after which I vowed to travel aboard its decks one day. Would that I had never again seen the *Castle*."

"And it is that very ship that makes its way to our shores?" Hiroshi was far more fascinated than he was anxious.

"That is my fear. For what I know of the current *shushō*, a man very different from the one under whose leadership my initial jour-ney came to pass, the conveying of arms is a business he now ardently pursues."

"But where does *your* journey intersect with this tale?"

"The securing of my return passage required establishing com-munication with a vast tapestry of agents throughout *Yōroppa*. These are individuals sworn to secrecy and compensated for their discre-tion. It is a network that the *Ocean Castle* has maintained since early in its day."

"Are you saying one of these agents is somehow responsible for the weapons making their way to *Nihon*?" Osamu had abandoned his curious wonder for subtle accusation.

"Directly? No. But I fear one of those responsible for my second boarding of the *Ocean Castle* relied too heavily upon outside help for purposes of conveyance and the like. One of these men—and I've my suspicions as to his identity—perhaps established contact with their *shushō*; his name is *Tokoh* Jaidev. This man, of whom I am suspicious, he was himself in the arms trade, which made of him a viable partner to the *Ocean Castle*."

"And you doubtless shared of *Nihon* and of your province...and of its neighbors, Takeru, when voyaging homeward." Lord Sakurai Kiyoshi spoke not with anger, only with certainty.

"Perhaps more than I should have. Jaidev is a curious man, and given to conversation. In that way, if no other, we are alike. Our *Nihon* was not unknown to Jaidev, nor to his predecessors. But he knows far more of provincial matters than he might otherwise have, and doubtless established contact with Lord Oda shortly after my own return."

"The result being that, soon, the ship that once carried my brother home will repeat the journey as a merchant of carnage." Kiyoshi almost whispered these words.

"And may be hauling cargo of a more human but no less lethal sort."

"Something to do with the tragic circumstances that brought to an end your *Kirisutokyō no* adventures?" Hiroshi asked, always perceptive.

"Indeed, Hiroshi. Something to do with that exactly."

9

ITALY, 1554

Pope Julius III

All were now gathered. Archbishop Romero's recruiting odyssey had been undertaken, to the day, nearly five months prior. Now, here, in the heart of Rome stood his selected cadre. Only one of Romero's three Jesuits (to whom matters of administration and theological education would fall) was present, as Alexandro and Vincenzo were readying the monastery miles to the north and receiving the selected *apprendisti* as they arrived from all over Christendom.

There were the sword masters Hidalgo Hernan de la Vega, Reynier Galante, and samurai Lord Sakurai Takeru; there was the Turkish-born acrobat Ismail Öztürk; there was the Bavarian strongman Herr Samson; there was the Danish man of tongues Greve Christiern; there was the Scottish horse soldier Malcome Munro; and there was, of course, Archbishop Romero himself, who had spent most evenings throughout his months on road and sea formulating the training regimen that would produce men of immeasurable worth and papal value. His Papal Blades would one day exercise their skills of surveillance, of subterfuge, of assassination in the darkest recesses of Christendom, those hideous spider holes in which the seeds of Lutheran heresy had taken root, given rise to those misguided

Protestants, and dared impugn the sovereignty of the Church, of Rome, of the vicar of Christ himself.

Speaking of which, it was for Pope Julius himself, third of that name, that Romero's estimable corps of masters had assembled in the ancient city. Naturally, the more imaginative of their number—namely, Ismail and Munro—had envisioned this sacred occasion unfolding within the pristine Apostolic Palace itself, surrounded by the Cardinalate College, themselves surrounded protectively by ranks of Swiss Guardsmen, "Those fools!" as Hernan regarded them. Indeed, the important mission whose holy charter the bishop of Rome himself would soon endorse via spoken sacrament, thereby ensuring political legitimacy, must be witnessed by all men of standing and influence within the halls of Church power.

"I'm afraid not, my good Scot," Romero had replied in jovial tones to a visibly disappointed Munro, "for discretion is indispensable where our charter is concerned. Those aware of its conception and realization number fewer than a score, excluding, of course, the *apprendisti* themselves and the unfortunate Swiss Guardsmen who accompanied me when enlisting your services."

"Unfortunate? Are they to be…?"

"Oh, goodness, no, sir. We are men of God. They will simply be sworn to a silence each will doubtless find burdensome and threatened with the incessant fires of blazing hell itself should knowledge of our cause escape the lips of either man."

"Well, then, I suppose theirs will be lips well suited for silence on the matter."

"So, then, this blessing is to transpire under circumstances of a rather"—Reynier visually toured the duly modest trappings of what was clearly an abandoned armory—"obscure sort?"

"Necessarily so, Reynier. Necessarily so." Romero remained high of spirit. "Rest assured, the papal presence carries with it an ethereal majesty that stems not from palatial architecture but from the purity and divinity that does so inhabit the man."

Divinity to one side, the enduring wait for His Holiness's arrival yielded an element of restlessness that made itself known in the minds of all present. While several of those assembled were perfectly content maintaining a stillness of body, a number of others acted the very parts for which they had been cast in this religious–political odyssey.

Greve Christiern unrolled a parchment on which lettering and symbols of numerous linguistic extractions were artfully transliterated. Romero recognized the parchment; it consisted of a single meaning, an ancient riddle or some such, conveyed via thirteen distinctive languages, extinct and extant alike. The riddle's complexity and the various ways in which it was communicated upon the parchment invited linguistic comparison of a decidedly dedicated nature.

"Perhaps our *apprendisti* will acquaint themselves with your parchment, Greve; they will doubtless find its contents as overwhelming as do I."

"Let us begin with instructional aims of more modest scope, Romero," replied Greve, who had kept his eyes trained on a particular passage while speaking.

A few paces from where the slightly built Dane had set up shop, Hidalgo Hernan executed a number of crisp, artful sword forms with what was indeed a beautiful *espada*. A jewel-encrusted pommel capped the base of its silver-laced hilt, all of which fed upward into a glistening long blade of Toledo steel, which was purported to be the very best in Europe. Takeru had himself inspected the stunning rapier and determined its edge, flexion, and durability to be quite unlike any blade he had before encountered.

In the hand of a competent duelist, a sword of that sort was an instrument whose notes were wounds and whose song was death. And Hernan was no mere competent—he was mastery itself. Slower and stiffer of movement than Reynier and certainly than the physically gifted Takeru, Hidalgo Hernan de la Vega would nevertheless have proven a worthy opponent for either man. His form spoke of eternal practice, while his capacity for visualizing a movement instants before it came to pass was reputed to be unmatched by any blades man in Spain, in France, in the known world.

"Your forms are pleasant to behold, dear Hernan, but I might still wager a victory on part of these younger, stronger masters." Romero was coy in that familiar manner all his own.

Slash, Parry, Slash, Thrust, Thrust, Parry, Slash

"I welcome either to afford me their finest effort."

Thrust, Slash, Parry, Sheathe

Hernan turned and looked directly into Romero's kind eyes. "Or both."

Heartily laughing, Romero said, "My Hernan! Had we a thousand men of your quality, there'd not be a Protestant willing to risk in Christendom his heretical life and sinful limb!"

For his part, Reynier Galante was content in merely observing the fabled and revered Hernan as the latter displayed skills cultivated over half a century's time. Little of any of the forms, movements, and techniques at work were beyond Reynier's knowledge, certainly not beyond his ability to himself achieve. But there was a certain majesty in observing their practice embodied in the movements of a figure whose blade had carved lines into the pages of living history. At least one of Reynier's own masters, the renowned Marin Faulcon, had known as student the very man whose brilliance was now animating the space in which he stood.

"Is it Hernan channeling the forms, Reynier, or do they channel him?" asked a kind-eyed Takeru.

"I suppose," Reynier began after a brief moment of consideration, "the two no longer enjoy any such autonomy. Hidalgo Hernan is the form…the form is Hidalgo Hernan."

"Would that all of us who inhabit this way of life might one day enjoy the same such fate." Takeru then turned to the quietly seated Romero. "I would surely not have elected to fight the good Andorran in his day."

SWISH

Hernan's priceless blade had whirled whiplike, its highly sharpened point coming to a halt a mere hand's length from Takeru's throat.

"Were you as wise as you are exotic, my friend, you'd not elect to fight this good Andorran on *any* day."

"I suppose I wouldn't. The wisdom of age surely dwarfs the vigor of youth."

After a few heartbeats of thick silence, Hernan dropped his blade and burst into laughter...a laughter none had ever before observed from him.

"Oh, Lord Takeru, would that yours were words as truthful as they are humorous. My knees and hips do so disagree with that assessment. Tell me where it is I might exchange some of my hard-won wisdom for the vitality of my younger years. It is a Devil's bargain into whose arms I will wholly entrust my being."

Takeru, himself laughing, replied, "I am reminded of a saying Reynier shared with me some months past. He had asked if we in *Nihon* have a phrase of similar meaning. It is, '*C'est la vie!*' and it translates roughly as..."

"Such is life," Romero chimed in. "And Lord Takeru assures me his people have no phrase of that meaning."

Hernan was intrigued. "But there must be wording of similar sentiment in your native tongue, Lord Takeru, is there not?"

"Similar? Perhaps. A proverb did come to mind when first Reynier spoke to me those words."

Romero's eyes grew wide. "And you said nothing of it at the time?"

"It hardly carries with it the same meaning, Romero. The proverb came to mind as perhaps a distant relation rather than a sister saying."

Hernan's patience was nearing an end. "And the proverb?"

"The proverb reads, '*Nanakorobi yaoki*,' which essentially encourages that one continues rising no matter how often they might fall or be pushed to the ground."

Romero's Jesuit, Brother Andreas, looking disappointed, offered his insight: "That is hardly the same meaning at all, Lord Takeru."

Answering for his friend, Hernan replied, "No, it is not the same meaning, Brother Andreas, but its sentiment is rather good...far more worthy."

Takeru, bowing, said, "Yes, we like it. Those words have seen many a student through brutal days in the *dojo*, wherein repeated falling is a rite of passage."

"As well it should be in any gymnasium." Ismail, who had been stretching his feline-like body, contributed this at a near yell, so far was he from the conversation, so engaged in his lengthening and torqueing of muscle fiber.

Things would surely have continued thus for some time had the gathering not been interrupted by the very man for whom they had been enduring so long a wait.

Pope Julius, third of that name, was elderly in appearance, in voice, in bearing. The antiquity in those bones lent His Holiness a degree of gravitas that could surely never have inhabited the presence of a young man. Romero forced himself momentarily into the thought experiment, imagining a clergyman like, say, Andreas adorned with the papal attire and immersed in the office's pageantry.

"It would simply be laughable. High stations in life necessitate advanced years, lest all those most important of authoritative attributes be forfeit—dignity, wisdom, pain." The last of these Romero had always recognized as being most essential. Suffering, lamentable though it was, yielded knowledge of undeniable value—knowledge of oneself.

Pope Julius had known pain, had gleaned the fruit of wisdom from its grotesque tree. The *apprendisti* would likewise come to know pain and in the process come to know themselves closely.

These mental gymnastics tumbled through Romero's mind as he, along with all other Christians present, kneeled before the papal majesty, who, in the company of twenty Swiss Guardsmen, three *monsignori*, and the ever controversial Cardinal Innocenzo Ciocchi Del Monte, now walked deliberately toward a dais of clearly makeshift design.

Takeru, who had not kneeled, instead kept bowed in humble manner his samurai-tonsured head. To his credit, Pope Julius took no exception in briefly observing the standing man of *Nihon*. Romero had convened with Innocenzo days earlier, explaining Takeru's role in what was to come, emphasizing his indispensable qualities and stressing still further that, despite his being a heathen, he was indeed a good man, noble and true.

"To prostrate himself before Christ's vicar would place samurai Lord Takeru at odds with both his conscience and his gods alike," Romero had appealed. "We would never desire for any such fate to befall our Christian brethren in pagan lands. Let us not demand it of a pagan in Christian lands."

"And this...samurai lord...his is skill and knowledge both irreplaceable and necessary?" Innocenzo had inquired with genuine interest.

"Irreplaceable and necessary, indeed, Cardinal." Romero spoke in earnestness.

"Very well. I will see that my divine uncle is primed for this eventuality. Your man will not be asked to kneel."

"My thanks to you, good cardinal." Romero choked on these words, knowing Innocenzo was neither good nor a truly worthy cardinal.

"But"—there was often more to follow in such instances—"your man of *Nihon* will be asked to lower his head and to refrain from allowing his eyes to meet those of our sacred pope."

"That much needn't be requested, Cardinal, for such is the custom of Lord Takeru's people."

"See that the custom is doubly honored on the scheduled day of your cadre's formal chartering."

"Indeed, Cardinal." Romero yearned to be free of this man's presence.

"And, Romero…?" Innocenzo's voice was leading.

"Cardinal?"

"If this mission of yours should ever…" the leading voice now trailed off.

Romero waited on tenterhooks for whatever it was Innocenzo intended to say. His wait was for naught. The pope's adoptive nephew and (questionably elevated) cardinal simply gathered the surplus cloth that often imperiled the footing of so many a clergyman, turned toward a chamber door, and left.

Though he would never know just what it was Innocenzo had meant to say in that moment, Romero recalled the tone possessing a vague hint of forewarning. The words unspoken would thereafter enter his mind on rare occasion and would carry with them implications he regarded as rather unwelcome.

"*Il signorini,* do graciously make your way to the dais and stand before Christ's vicar"—Innocenzo spoke in oddly accented Italian, which Greve Christiern translated for those who required as much— "and do see that your hands remain at some distance from your weapons."

All rose and approached, Takeru included, the dais, which was too narrow for the collected cadre members to stand before in anything even vaguely approaching a straight line. A crescent shape was exigently assumed, allowing for the group to look at equidistance upon Pope Julius, who looked in turn upon the group with curiosity and evident admiration. Speaking with a voice diminished by age, the pope issued the awaited and necessary charter in his Tuscan-accented Italian (far more pleasant than Innocenzo's coarse version). There was no need for Greve's translation; all understood the meaning, the significance, the purpose.

"It is *Concilium Tridentinum* that has shaped my years in this exalted office, and it is that very same council that has given rise to the undertaking you now, in secrecy and in sacrament, assume as shared burden. Our once wayward child, that of England, is tenuously restored to our Holy fold, praise to Queen Mary and the God who grants her dominion. But that land is far from cured of its heretical plague. Elsewhere, as in England, threats of schism mount. Christendom in all its breadth must be spared the horror that King Henry, eighth of that name, did inflict upon his helpless subjects. Yours will be a charter to aid in that battle, to equip young apostles with the power and knowledge requisite in facing heretics in the manner they best understand—the manner of bloodshed."

Pope Julius, garbed heavily in the papal clothing, weighted with jeweled adornments, and beholding all before him through eyes set deeply within that wizened countenance, afforded holy licensure the training of elite warriors whose sole purpose would be the safeguarding of Church interests and the continuance of its earthly mission.

"God above casts upon you his love, his grace, his blessing; each of these upon the efforts you are soon to invest of your chosen souls. And to Archbishop Romero's *apprendisti*: give shape to their wretched lives, grow strength atop their slight frames, plant knowledge within their nascent minds, and harvest spiritual purpose from their as yet unborn energies. May their swords soon bathe in heretical blood, writing in crimson the histories of untold futures, reducing many a Protestant to that mere spiritless flesh to which they, in Christ's absence, have now reduced their beings."

Emotion swept through Reynier, Malcome, and Hernan, while Greve, Ismail, and Takeru merely allowed themselves to revel in what was clearly a momentous occasion. Romero's mind had wandered into the monastery and all that promised to unfold therein. Herr Samson and Brother Andreas betrayed little, if any, sentiment at all; the former being largely invulnerable in that regard, the latter far more a scholar than ever he was a zealot.

"And so, as any in my position might say to any in yours: go with God, my sons, and honor the charter that now renders legitimate this worthy enterprise. Papal Blades, be born!"

This last had the unusual quality of having been shouted while materializing at a volume no greater than that which His Holiness had achieved in the moments prior. Age is a penance all its own.

"Rise, gentlemen, and do please place your lips to the *Anello Piscatorio.*" Innocenzo continued to bask in his "master of ceremonies" charge.

All stood; all approached Pope Julius's outstretched arm; all pressed to the *Anello Piscatorio* their lips, including Takeru, by whom Julius was wholly intrigued.

"Far has that kiss traveled to reach this ring, my son."

"Best you not know where else this mouth has placed its gentle touch, Holiness." Whatever sense of majesty had nearly overcome Takeru moments earlier was now prologue. His wit saw fit to blossom even in the face of awesome holy authority.

Quite unexpectedly, Pope Julius, third of that name and among the most powerful men on earth, laughed. It was not a strong laugh, nor was it sustained, but laugh Christ's vicar did, leaving all else uncertain as to whether or not the moment of levity was open to all. For whatever reason, most present looked to Innocenzo for signal guidance—"Might we join in?" was the question implicit in their aggregated visage.

And "certainly not" was the perceived response. Innocenzo merely gestured to his adoptive uncle that, the Papal Blade charter having been granted, it was time for all to set about the business to come.

"His Holiness grants you each his enduring blessing—may the flowers of your shared labor blossom in perpetuity throughout the realm."

And a moment later, the cadre were left once again to their own devices. Just as his adorned frame had reached the doorway through which it had entered, Pope Julius had turned to look Archbishop

Romero directly in the eye, then shifted his sight to acknowledge Takeru with an almost childlike smile. And with that he was gone. None present would ever again see the man; only one among them would exchange words with Christ's vicar...though in the personage of a man rather unlike Pope Julius, third of that name.

Steed, Strength, and Studies, 1560

Over two centuries of martial and scholarly experience inhabited the minds and bodies of Archbishop Romero's elite cadre. Europe's battlefields and tournaments had known Malcome Munro for nearly twenty-five years while the Aegean islands, Ottoman palaces, and Adriatic coastal towns were home to Ismail's traveling acrobats for two decades. The Jesuits, though all relatively young, brought a near half century of collective scholarship to this holy charter, Greve Christiern nearly twenty as a linguistic pedagogue, and Herr Samson at least fifteen as the Christian realm's closest answer to a Hercules figure. And there were the sword masters: Reynier, who claimed to have had a rapier placed in his tiny hands immediately upon baptism; Takeru insisted a katana was placed in his shortly after birth; and Hidalgo Hernan de le Vega, dear man, who swore he was born with a blade at the ready.

"What a horrific birthing process that must surely have been," noted Brother Andreas. "I trust your mother survived?"

"And lives to this day, though in that godforsaken Cadis."

Romero always found amusing Hernan's disdain for both the Spanish and the French. "Though only in the abstract," he observed to Alexandro. "After all, Hernan is rather amiable in his dealings with Master Reynier."

The *apprendisti,* who had arrived at monastery a seemingly miserable lot, found their life-forces vitalized, their bodies and minds given precise shape, their reflexes sharpened to a razor's edge, their senses honed. For most, it did not manifest quickly; for all, it did manifest. The very men of God Archbishop Romero had sought to forge into existence were indeed forged, and by the innumerable hammer blows of his cadre smiths, each of whom played a vital role in the creation of these remarkable creatures.

Herr Samson's cannonball drills and barrel-lifting exercises built powerful, dense muscle on the skeletons of these once slight pupils. Ismail Öztürk's numerous high bars were stained with the blood of many an opened palm, as the *apprendisti* were required to swing for hours on end, slowly generating the necessary strength and technique to complete dynamic rotations and soaring dismounts. A series of cloth lines and stump-like fixtures were employed in service to balance-cultivating measures, wherein many a hapless boy had suffered thousands of stumbles and painful landings in their efforts to maintain, for instance, a one-legged standing positon atop a narrow, spinning beam.

Long horseback rides throughout the neighboring hills and forests conditioned the boys aerobically and instilled in them a well-developed sense of equine facility. Malcome nearly always followed or initiated the rides with mounted striking drills, setting up strawmen at one end of a narrow field, arming the pupils with sabers or small lances and ordering them to cut down the hapless "enemies" with ferocity and resolve.

"It is not straw but Protestant heresy inhabits those holed breeches and worn jerkins!" he often assured, or words to that effect.

Greve and the Jesuits instructed their *apprendisti* in schools of knowledge ranging from history and mathematics to philosophy and architecture. Language was the curricula fixture, with scarcely a day passing on which time with Greve was not prescribed. More important than a mere lesson in some new tongue or another, Greve taught each pupil *how* to learn.

"There are many extant languages with which I have not had the fortune of engaging. Some among you will surely encounter peoples and cultures utterly unknown to me. I would like that you possess within your minds the capacity to decode the puzzle that is any new word, be it spoken or written."

And his methods were, indeed, effective. For each successive language introduced into the *apprendisti*'s growing lexicon was quicker in the learning than had been its predecessor. Even Jakob, who often struggled to keep pace with his brethren, would eventually ascend to a level commensurate with most among their number. This was far more indicative of Greve's inspired lessoning than it was evidence of some hidden brilliance within the landscape of Jakob's often beleaguered mind. But the boy never displayed the slightest suggestion of wishing himself elsewhere, and those things for which he did possess great aptitude were not to be dismissed. To the contrary, Jakob was surely an heir to Herr Samson's own legacy, if any could be said to have existed among the *apprendisti*. Jakob, after all, was preternaturally powerful of limb and back, having outperformed most others in certain feats.

But each pupil had achieved pristine harmony in the fortifying of their given talents with extraordinary skills in disciplines similar and unrelated alike. Those *apprendisti* to whom horsemanship came easily could themselves be seen employing graceful mounting and dismounting of a gymnast's vault, which invariably saw Ismail smile when he was fortunate enough to witness as much. Others excelled in those academic trials engineered by the cerebral Jesuits and their overseer Romero, but these might also display animalistic strength feats under Herr Samson's watchful eye, thus demonstrating powerful bodies in which to house their burgeoning minds.

Indeed, not one among the *apprendisti* would conclude his training without having mastered several arts, disciplines, and tongues while coming away with high levels of proficiency in many others. The ongoing war for souls and earthly peace, perpetual duties that fell to the Church, might very well witness a tipping point in favor of papal *auctoritas*, a tipping point achieved by the presence of these Blades within the mayhem.

There could be no doubt: once unleashed upon the lands, each of these young men would be called upon to kill in papal service. And for that reason, none were spared the relentlessness of Hidalgo

Hernan de la Vega, the ferocity of Master Reynier Galante, or the exacting standards of samurai Lord Sakurai Takeru.

"The sword be your sacred," Hernan would often remind, though the translation into Italian (which had become the monastery's common tongue) was imperfect, rendering its meaning only vaguely understandable.

"Your hands," Reynier repeated endlessly, always while gripping tightly his sword's hilt, "are the ambassadors of your strength."

"Blessed is the master who is surpassed by a pupil," Takeru once quoted, "but perhaps I am not blessed." The samurai was the very spirit of cleverness.

If more than ten days passed in which the *apprendisti* were not required to hold in hand a sword of one sort or another (they used many) throughout the ten years they would ultimately spend under Romero's watch, all would have struggled to recall those specific days. The sword was life itself. While all spent many an hour with Herr Samson, with Ismail, with Malcome, and with the Jesuits and Greve Christiern, their combined time under the scrutinizing instruction of their sword masters was incalculable. Palms developed blisters that burst and bled. Gloves often adhered to dried wounds, ripping scab from skin in being removed. Wrists swelled, fingers ached, arm and shoulder muscles burned with fiery pain, eyelids grew heavy and breathing labored. The sword drills were eternal, exhausting, thorough, and fierce. Reynier, a recognized genius, contributed greatly in the instilling of dynamic and strategic thinking into each young mind, while Takeru introduced into the regime styles of swordplay the likes of which none among the *apprendisti* would otherwise have encountered had this enigmatic man of *Nihon* not traveled from more than a hundred days east to their Christian doorstep.

Between Reynier and Takeru alone, the protégés would have grown into fine and brilliant and deadly swordsmen, of that much nobody was in doubt. But it was the grinding, brutal, repetitious, unforgiving drills of Hidalgo Hernan de la Vega that would transform the boys into warriors of discipline, resolve, and positively reflexive skillfulness. Again and again the *apprendisti* would negotiate the various footwork patterns of Hernan's ever-changing design, doing so while also carrying out striking and parrying commands as the Andorran master called them out. Often the boys would, blindfolded, be faced with a human-shaped striking target, during which Hernan would indicate on which section of the target the pupil's blade should strike. The task was one of both precision and of endurance, as Hernan was known to keep such exercises under way for several hours' time, the sun having been at its apex when a pupil began and nearing its nightly exit when the pupil, bone weary, was permitted to sheathe his sword.

In what were the most charming and remarkable of instances, Hernan de la Vega would allow for multiple *apprendisti* to engage him at once, all the while offering spoken suggestions and form corrections while effectively parrying and side-stepping the plurality of attacks. Such scenarios typically concluded once Hernan had methodically disarmed each assailant one by one. This practice was abandoned as the pupils' skill and might grew and the Andorran's endurance began (ever so slightly) to wane, though the practice of correction and ritual disarming of his fledgling opponents would carry on for years to come.

And on this regimen continued—minds becoming repositories of vast knowledge and countless languages, muscle fibers reformed into cords of flexible steel, and swordsmanship elevated to heights the likes of which perhaps only a handful of Christendom's renowned masters could themselves equal. If Archbishop Romero had erred in any way at all where the regimen's design was concerned, it was in its duration. As all cadre and the three Jesuits were forced to admit around the charter's eighth year of being, the *apprendisti* had achieved mental and physiological supremacy well ahead of Romero's schedule, yet they were still, by and large, adolescence itself.

"A curious incongruity, that," Brother Vincenzo observed, "abilities and mental cognition on par with many a man, but their maturation yet unfulfilled."

"I suppose we will need to adjust the regimen in certain respects," Alexandro suggested, "author some sort of revision that allows for their treatment as peers until such a time as their minds are steeled for the dreadful taskings they are destined to fulfill."

"Nonsense!" Romero, to whom Alexandro had subsequently posed this suggestion tended toward stubbornness, or resolve as he deemed it. "They are but children, still very much in need of guidance both spiritual and academic."

Alexandro had relented, forced to acknowledge a certain truth in Romero's words. Though the monastery's charter had been met with success beyond any and all cadre imaginings, the *apprendisti* were largely adolescents in many respects. Further guidance, spiritual and academic, they did receive, and for several years after they attained masteries in the physical arts to which their early lives had been dedicated.

Largely granted the courtesy of autonomous training in gymnasia and upon riding fields alike, the youthful warriors were nevertheless subservient to those sword masters against whom they occasionally found themselves lacking. For no amount of time spent enduring Ismail's rigorous drilling, nor under the yoke of Samson's various weighted apparatuses, nor in the saddles of Malcome's war mounts would instill within the *apprendisti* a sense of parity with the magnificent Reynier Galante, the wise and subtly skilled Takeru, and certainly not the inestimable Hidalgo Hernan de la Vega, who generally regarded the ancillary training requirements to be of little use.

"Certainly little use to a true swordsman," he occasionally chided, "this flying around and stone-lifting nonsense, what use is any of that to a man of steel and honor?"

But the acrobatics and strengthening exercises had indeed proven themselves worth their spent whiles. Hernan, and Reynier to a lesser extent, were often disinclined to acknowledge the truth therein, even if Takeru routinely argued the validity of such an interpretation. Of course, a realization impossible to dismiss would visit itself upon the monastery in its entirety, more than a decade after Pope Julius, third of that name, had granted Archbishop Romero his charter via sacrament. It was an unusually warm morning when Hidalgo Hernan de la Vega elected to engage in final duels with his every pupil.

"A rite of passage, if you will," he had explained to Romero. "The *apprendisti* will engage with me to the very best of their hard-earned abilities. In proving themselves capable of matching me strike-and-parry for strike-and-parry, prior to my bringing each to yield, you may be wholly confident of their capacity for violence and for the defending of oneself in dispatching them throughout the lands."

"Bringing e*ach* to yield, de la Vega?" Romero was incredulous. "A number of them have developed a fine mastery of the sword. Courtesy, to be sure, of your teachings and those of your fellow cadre."

"Yes, Romero, bring *each* to yield. Not one has bested me in their ten years under my instruction. The master doth shine." Hernan held high his gray head, which had Romero wondering if the old genius had taken inventory of his aged state in recent years.

"You've also done little other than spar with many of the *apprendisti*, all of whom have either continued their studies under Reynier and Takeru, or…"

"Or…?" Hernan was intrigued.

"Developed styles and techniques all their own. They have been trained to think in ways dynamic and unorthodox, my good Hernan."

"Ha! Let the very best of them try his own techniques against those that I have spent sixty years' time perfecting."

So the man has taken inventory of his years, Romero silently mused. *Let us hope modesty within brings to heel hubris without.*

The archbishop then placed a hand endearingly atop the Andorran master's shoulder and spoke lovingly.

"I should be honored to witness this proverbial torch passing unfold, my old friend, very honored indeed."

Dueling, 1566

"Good, Simon, very good." Hernan worked closely with each *apprendista*, often for hours at a stretch, sometimes for no more than a matter of minutes. If any among the cadre had a better sense for precisely what a given protégé needed at a given time, Romero had not witnessed as much. Under Hernan de la Vega's inspired tutelage, the *apprendisti* had indeed become the best swordsmen Christendom had ever produced.

"Certainly more than a match for any three of Swiss Foolsmen, under whose protection we entrust Christ's vicar!" Hernan had once proclaimed, upon overhearing the Jesuits speak admiringly of his pupils' sword skill.

Hernan now allowed for the truth of those words to reveal itself, as he engaged in official *graduació* duels with each protégé, all having trained under his guidance for ten years' time.

Cut, Cut, Lunge, Parry, Thrust, Parry, Parry, Parry, Cut,
Aerial Wheel, Cut

"Very good, indeed." Hernan more and more found his breath escaping his aging lungs when drilling his students. "The aerial wheel was an inspired incorporation of Ismail's teachings into my own." Hidalgo Hernan reluctantly admitted.

For the *wheel* in that series of strikes and parries had been a midair cartwheeling motion that Ismail Öztürk had drilled into the boys via brutal repetition. Early in their monastic tenure, the *apprendisti* had been conditioned to perform the maneuver again, again, and again still more, some having executed upward of one hundred wheels in the space of a morning, a splendid action to observe when done well. The more graceful of Ismail's students had found occasion to enrich their budding swordsmanship with its careful inclusion.

Hernan's subsequent challenge came from Judah, the soft-spoken Portuguese soul whose own style matched that of Hernan de le Vega more closely than was the case with any of his peers. Indeed, as the duel unfolded, Romero could not help but imagine each duelist essentially parrying with a mirror image. Judah matched his master, Christendom's *greatest* master, nearly strike and deflection for strike and deflection. It was, to be sure, a sight of beauty and of perfection. And the glistening in Hernan's eyes upon reluctantly forcing to a yielding state the now seventeen-year-old Judah was not attributable to perspiration, as he might have attempted to argue. No, tears born of pride found purchase in the stony Hidalgo Hernan's eyes, for in Judah a worthy heir to his own legacy did live and breathe.

The final duel to which Hernan was committed amounted to as much an unnecessary contest if ever there was one. Mathieu entered the master's enclosure, a diagrammed and ordered patch of monastery floor in which the *apprendisti* had spent infinite hours perfecting the *ciència* of swordsmanship, of dueling, of blade-to-blade discourse. Hernan studied the finest pupil he (all cadre) had ever known and exhibited a most fleeting glimpse of apprehension before steeling his resolve for the task at hand.

Master and protégé positioned themselves one across from the other and raised their respective weapons in an outstretched form—the swords overlapping by perhaps a finger's length. As the tension mounted, Romero noted that Hernan's fellow cadre, the *apprendisti* themselves, and the three Jesuits were in attendance whereas only he, Andreas, and Reynier had observed Hernan's preceding lessons. This would be no ordinary duel nor a gracious passing of any torch, thus the interest.

Hernan, after having made a commendable effort to instill a degree of uncertainty into Mathieu's unblinking eyes, cocked his sword arm and thrust forth with a precision few could ever hope to equal. Mathieu, however, could equal it and did. What ensued thereafter was simply remarkable.

Blades crossed and deflected each other with frightful speed while Hernan's footwork resembled that of a spritely dancer—it was all that preserved the contest beyond its initial exchange of strikes. To the trained eye, meaning those of Reynier, Takeru, Malcome, and the *apprendisti*, the duel was a study in patiently accumulated skill and God-given ability.

He is, after all, a demigod, the blasphemous Romero thought.

To the unknowing eye, two men of inordinate capacity for sword-craft dueled like archangels, the outcome impossible to determine, unless, of course, it was possible.

"Mathieu surpasses Hernan this day." Reynier had spoken these words to nobody in particular while extracting from its handsome scabbard his long rapier, itself forged in the fires of a Solingen smithy, and kneeling before it in open-eyed prayer.

The duel continued, Hernan tired, and Mathieu readied his blade for the very sort of threatening placement intended to exact from its target a word of submission.

Slash, Parry, Parry, Parry, Slash, Thrust, Seize

In a single motion, Mathieu had deflected his master's sword tip to the ground, seized the sword by its hilt with supreme strength, and hurled his own body in a flipping motion over the head of a stunned Hernan de la Vega, whose sword was wrenched from its grip well before Mathieu achieved a gracile landing at his back. By turning himself 'round to face the boy who had disarmed and humbled him, Hernan had positioned his throat within a hair's breadth of Mathieu's sword tip. The duel was over. Hernan, for the first time in recent and distant memory alike, had lost.

TING!

Before anyone, Hernan included, could fully process the enormity of what had just unfolded in plain view of all, Reynier had soundly struck away from Hernan's throat the sword tip by which it was nominally threatened.

"Your duel with Hidalgo Hernan de la Vega is done, Mathieu. You will now face me."

This was in at least one other sense unprecedented, for Master Reynier had never before engaged his *apprendisti* on Hernan's dueling grounds, having his own somewhat distinctive patch partitioned for the same purpose.

For all of Hidalgo Hernan de la Vega's prestige and instruction instincts, he had long departed from his physical prime. Reynier had experienced no such departure. Mathieu exhibited not the vaguest element of concern over having been so brashly challenged by a master of Reynier's standing and reputation.

A breathless, dazed Hernan joined Romero at the training grounds' edge, sheathing the sword that Mathieu had graciously returned while positioning himself opposite a stern-eyed Reynier.

As had been the case moments earlier when Hernan faced Mathieu for the final time as a master faces his student, all attention was keenly paid to the impending duel...

...which, like Hernan before him, Reynier initiated.

Clang, Clang, Clang, Clang, Swoosh, Clang, Clang,
Clang, Clang, Swoosh, Clang

The swords crossed powerfully, creating a steel maelstrom in their doing so. Every step advanced belonged to the thick-armed Reynier; every backstep belonged to the lithe Mathieu.

"But that's no retreat," Malcome quietly (and correctly) observed. "It's a flanking maneuver in the making."

The lifelong cavalryman astutely applied his own discipline to the battle he now observed. Mathieu, who absorbed a whirlwind of forceful, skilled attacks from Master Reynier, was not backstepping in a liner manner; rather, there was a long circular trajectory along which Reynier was unwittingly being pulled.

To his great credit, Reynier had not allowed the prodigious Mathieu so much as an instant's reprieve since having first administered a ringing blow to his protégé's blade.

Ting, Swoosh, Swoosh, Ting, Ting, Ting, Swoosh, Clang,
Swoosh, Clang

Duels had on occasion claimed the life of even a well-made sword, and this might certainly have been such an occasion had Mathieu not long ago been educated (by the very man he now faced) in the proper deflection of a powerful strike, parrying at angles intended to preserve one's blade integrity.

But the parrying had been under way for quite long enough. Mathieu, who in the space of mere seconds had achieved the semicircular repositioning of his exigent design spun and wheeled, driving his pommel down hard upon Reynier's lowered sword hand then upward into the man's lower jaw, roundly fazing his fellow Frenchman.

Firmly in the talons of a seething rage, Reynier unleashed a sword-mauling of such fury as to have all present wondering whether or not an intervening effort might prove necessary—all save Malcome, who expected the outcome would be soon in the realizing...would be conclusive...would require nothing in the way of intervention.

CRACK, TING, CRACK-CRACK-CRACK, TING,
SWOOSH, SWOOSH, CRACK

Romero, the Jesuit brothers, and Greve shared in their fear for Mathieu's life at this point, the latter turning to Herr Samson (with whom he had developed an abiding bond) with a look that pleaded, "You should stop this!" Samson seemed prepared to enter the dueling ground for that very purpose, until his doing so became unquestionably unnecessary.

Another moment of monstrous attacks from the masterful Reynier, another moment of uncertainty on part of the gathered cadre and *apprendisti*—until Mathieu identified the opening he had sought from the outset. As Reynier's arm brought down his heavy blade in a right-to-left diagonal slash, Mathieu moved inward, only just clear of the attack's path, and rotated his torso exactly as much as was necessary to avoid the wounding or death that would certainly have befallen him. He then knelt, threw his sword hilt first between Reynier's feet, turned the sword so as to have its breadth run flat against Reynier's heels, grasped the blade at the center, then hurled himself backward with enormous might. His design took shape as intended, for the force of his backward leap had pressed the flat of his sword against Reynier's heels in such a way as to take them out from under the now falling sword master.

As Reynier's back struck the ground below with a gruesome cracking sound, Mathieu had already recovered both his stance and his blade, the latter of which he held to his master's heart.

"Seems your influence has empowered our *apprendisti* in ways rather devilish, Ismail." Hernan spoke these words aloud, but all shared the thought in one way or another. Was it Samson's training that so elevated these once frightened orphans? Or was Hernan correct? Had Ismail's acrobatics merged to dreadfully potent effect with the lessons of Hernan, Reynier, and...

"Takeru?" Romero noticed his friend of many years discard one layer of outermost clothing before drawing his katana and entering onto the dueling ground. Reynier had, by this point, risen to his feet, sheathed his sword, nodded curtly to Mathieu, and taken a place at Hidalgo Hernan's side.

"Worry not, Romero—a victory will secure pride in my swordsmanship, a defeat pride in my teachings." Takeru spoke the latter words while smiling at Reynier and Hernan, both of whom smiled in response. Mathieu was, among other things, a testament to their worthy tutelage.

The image was poetry. Takeru, after taking up position two arms' length from his student of over ten years, turned perpendicularly to Mathieu; bent slightly his knees. thereby lowering himself into a crouching stance; and raised his katana overhead, the point aimed in close alignment with his line of sight.

Standing perfectly upright and dead still with sword extended outward, its tip nearly reaching the ground, Mathieu faced his master directly...and waited.

What was it about this boy, Hernan wondered, *that inevitably drew the first strike? One is unable to meet his eyes for any stretch of time; we attack to avert the gaze, it would seem.*

But while Hidaldo Hernan de la Vega and Master Reynier Galante had sought to avert that gaze within mere heartbeats of facing the demigod Mathieu, Takeru was inclined to draw out the moment. The ensuing wait contributed to the face-off's poetic quality, as Takeru and Mathieu kept their bodies serenely still, poised, rigid—until, that is, Takeru struck forth with a tightly controlled cross-torso slash, a slash that Mathieu had shrewdly anticipated, deftly deflected, and coolly answered with a straight thrust, flexing his forward knee deeply and in harmony with the striking forth of his sword arm.

Takeru managed to avoid the impossibly forceful straight thrust—*the gods this boy is strong*, he noted—but the avoidance had placed him off balance momentarily. Mathieu pressed.

Thrust, Thrust, Slash, Slash, Thrust, Thrust, Thrust, Wide Cut, Thrust, Thrust, Slash

Each of these Takeru had managed to deflect, though only just, and he now found himself in a defensive posture from which he had little hope of escape.

Planting his rear foot firmly while sharply turning inward the fore, Takeru let loose a horizontal slash of sheer ferocity, letting out a loud cry in so doing. Mathieu leaped straight backward, flipping his body in order to place swift distance between himself and the trajectory of that wind-like slash. Landing in a crouch, Mathieu cocked his forefoot in a manner nearly identical to that of Takeru, who was himself doing so again. In perfect synchronicity, master and pupil unleashed directly opposing slashes, which saw their blades strike with ear-splitting strength.

The two pressed their blades one against the other with some force. Takeru, very much in danger of succumbing to the lean Mathieu's inhuman strength, noted that his katana, a fairly heavy blade, had chipped deeply into the lighter rapier. As the struggle continued and Mathieu betrayed no sign whatsoever of fatigue, Takeru took desperate action: sliding his katana downward into the compromised section of Mathieu's sword, which was confirmed with a *Ktch* sound, he then wrenched his blade with as much force as his sinewy wrists could produce. And as he had presumed would happen, the rapier broke cleanly, allowing Takeru to slash unopposed toward the unfailingly serene Mathieu.

What happened next happened at once. Takeru's katana continued its forward path toward Mathieu, whose speed was equal to the task of averting serious injury, though not injury outright. For the very point of Takeru's blade, its slightest and almost invisible of cutting edges, had found its mark on Mathieu's face, leaving a thin opening of skin well below his right eye. None of this could Takeru fully realize in that instant, for Mathieu's face had merely been passing by the blade that had authored the first such harm he had ever before experienced. Mathieu, broken rapier still in hand, had lowered his stance and rotated 'round, ultimately bringing the ruined weapon's pommel upward from under Takeru's dual grip. The force of this strike had the desired effect of disarming Takeru while sending his katana into the air overhead. Though the katana's fate was of little concern at the moment, for Mathieu now held the remains of his rapier cleanly against his quarry's neck. The duel was over; Mathieu bled, Takeru yielded, and the katana landed in rattling and clanging manner at their feet.

"Wear the scar well, Mathieu; you are unlikely to know another." Takeru then bowed, retrieved his katana, and walked away from the scene entirely.

Mathieu examined his broken blade, looked to Romero, to Hernan, to Reynier, to his brethren. All looked to him with wonder, with reverence.

"To the chapel, my sons." Romero could not bear the silence. "Let us pray for peace in our ranks."

As all followed the archbishop and his Jesuits to the monastery's chapel hall, Mathieu knelt to the earth below. He recovered the length of broken blade and held it to the lower section of which he had kept hold since Takeru had yielded.

A shadow loomed over the still kneeling Mathieu; a sword was drawn from its long scabbard; a voice spoke.

"This one will suffer no such fate."

Mathieu looked up at an expressionless Reynier, upon whose outstretched arms rested the sword whose edges, hilt, and weight he had wielded since prior to the birth of even the eldest of *apprendisti*.

"That sword is a part of you, Master Reynier. It was forged in Solingen, the *Épée Ville* you once termed it." Mathieu spoke in a voice so very calm.

"It is part of me to a lesser extent than are you, my boy. Never in my years did I envision myself being surpassed by a protégé, nor by any other man. Surpass me you have. Now do me the honor of accepting as acknowledgement of that fact this, my cherished sword—may it serve you well."

Neither man was given to ceremony, but the passing of weapon from master to pupil was not without an element of gravitas. Reynier certainly felt as much and imagined the same was true for Mathieu.

Though I will surely never know, not if my knowing requires his telling. Reynier silently mused.

The two then nodded one to the other and made their way to the chapel.

The Attack

"And you will simply walk to Rome?" Archbishop Romero was perplexed as samurai Lord Sakurai Takeru rolled gently a number of parchments that he in turn placed into a well-worn satchel.

"It is but a few days' journey, and I took note of those highway houses when last we made our visit by wagon."

"This is rather sudden, my friend. You overwhelm me."

"Which I can surely understand, Romero, but I have spent now more than ten years' time from my lands, from my brother, from his sons. The teachings I have imparted upon your, no, upon *our apprendisti* I might still impart upon my own blood."

Romero relented somewhat. "They will be how old by now, your nephews?"

"Assuming my return journey is of similar duration to that which brought me here, Osamu will have entered his twentieth year when next I see him; Hiroshi his fifteenth." Takeru's face was alight with sentiment.

"How ecstatic they will be in seeing their long-absent uncle Takeru."

"Their *oji* Takeru."

"Ah, yes—*Oji*. I regret having learned so little of your words this past decade."

"Take heart in knowing I taught Greve much of my language, as well as our pupils. The seeds of my tongue are now planted firmly in your Christian lands."

"And the seeds of your marvelous swordsmanship. How the *apprendisti* did so benefit from your teachings, my friend. They'll not soon meet an equal."

"Only among themselves. May their swords never cross with one another."

"Speaking of which, Cardinal Innocenzo sent correspondence some days past. Seems he would like to bestow upon the Papal Blades rapiers of special quality and meaning, blessed by the bishop of Rome's own hand."

"A high honor, that." Takeru had returned to his assembling of documents and materials. He would be traveling rather lightly.

"You'll not miss the imparting ceremony, now will you, my friend?"

"Barring Innocenzo's arrival by high noon, I am certain to miss it. Though I do intend to voice a farewell to protégé and peer alike."

Romero's eyes shone. "I should hope as much."

An hour's time thereafter, all had assembled in the monastery's sprawling garden. Brothers Andreas, Vincenzo, and Alexandro had found ample time in which to see to its tending; thus it flourished. Whether by accident or design (Takeru could not tell), the cadre had lined up on one side of the garden's wide central walkway, the *apprendisti* on the other. Two wives (those of Greve and Reynier) and a number of small children stood at some distance from the cadre whose families they comprised.

Moving patiently from one cadre peer to the next, samurai Lord Sakurai Takeru held firmly the hand of each. To some he spoke knowing words that channeled years of cherished friendship, to others a mere nod of respect conveyed the same meaning.

To Romero he simply said, "Ours are paths fated to once again cross, whether here or in heaven above, my friend."

Romero had been nearly overcome by the statement's warm sentiment and said nothing in response. Nothing needed be said.

To the *apprendisti* Takeru then turned, observing them as one and reflecting with great pride upon the thousands of days they and he spent in training, in conversation, and eventually in friendship. Each of these carried within himself elements of Takeru's teachings, most had learned well his beautiful language, and all held him in the highest esteem. Few expected ever again to see this man of *Nihon* who had shared so much of his knowledge and skill in support of a cause not his own.

A moment's silence was brought to an end when Takeru brought his feet together, placed a hand on his katana hilt, and bowed deeply to the largely misty-eyed *apprendisti*, who bowed deeply in return.

Takeru then approached the sublime Mathieu, whose eyes, naturally, were devoid of tears, and proffered him a short, beautifully sheathed knife of appearance similar to his katana. Not a word was exchanged between the men, though each held one end of the bequeathed weapon for some time. Takeru then bowed (less deeply this time), placed a hand on Mathieu's shoulder, turned away, and was gone. All eyes watched the extraordinary samurai depart their monastery, knowing he would never return. Jakob, though far closer to Greve and Herr Samson than was he to Takeru or any others, fell to one knee, tears streaming down his fair cheeks.

The day had grown warmer as Takeru set forth on his walk, a walk of several days' time southward to Rome, from which he would then make his way either east to Istanbul or west to the Iberian Peninsula. As had been the case on most days during his time with the monastery, Takeru was clad in a dark, somewhat worn *haori*, which he wore loose around the shoulders, tightly around the chest and abdomen, and long at the waist. His *hakama*, similarly dark and worn, clung closely to the samurai's narrow hips. To be sure, the warrior's attire set him firmly apart from any and all he might encounter in the Italian countryside, *unless*, the ever imaginative samurai thought, *I was to encounter one of my countrymen here on this patch of earth so distant from my beloved* Nihon.

Had any curiosity or concerns been voiced as to the nature of Takeru's travel or his purpose in Christendom, official documentation had been prepared by Archbishop Romero in order that his passage would be recognized as legitimate by any who burdened themselves with asking. This document Takeru kept handily at his side, immediately adjacent to a more visceral form of protection: his well-traveled katana.

"I suspect you'll need not draw it while on Italian soil, my friend." Romero had sought only to provide comforting words for a man he regarded as brother and comrade alike. "Papal roads tend to be clear of bandits and thieves, as they are frequented by papal soldiers."

This was true enough and would explain the absence of any alarm on Takeru's part upon, two days into his journey, catching sight of what appeared to be a mercenary contingent (in papal employ?) making their way north via the very same road he now took south. They were mounted and moving at something of a trot.

"Fifty, perhaps even sixty soldiers. Does Pius himself accompany Innocenzo?"

Pope Pius, fourth of that name, now held the office that Julius, third of that name, had occupied when Takeru and his colleagues had been granted their sacramental charter. Three bishops of Rome had been elected since Julius's death shortly after the monastery began its work, two of whom had joined Julius in the Christian heaven and one of whom, Pius, now stood vigil over Christendom. It was Takeru's understanding that Innocenzo had shared with Julius's successors very little of the monastery, fearing they might misunderstand (or understand all too well) the charter's purpose. Takeru also understood that Innocenzo had been in poor favor with papal and cardinalate authority since shortly after his adoptive uncle's death a decade past.

"That much seems certain," Romero had confirmed in conversation with the cadre. "Nevertheless, Innocenzo continues to find means of funding our enterprise, an enterprise that remains worthy of our combined energies."

And all concurred, fervent group that they were, continuing with the charter's fulfillment as though Pope Julius had never escaped his mortal coil. Innocenzo routinely sent money and corresponded with Romero often enough to keep alive a suitable sense of legitimacy. Discretion nevertheless remained the monastery's watchword, and those rare occasions during which cadre were absent for purposes of family visits and the like meant sharing little in the way of detail with said family.

"We know our cause to be pure," Alexandro had once said to Reynier. "We answer only to God."

"And to Innocenzo, it would seem," responded Reynier, a "Doubting Thomas" at times.

"Well, perhaps to his coffers," said Alexandro, equal parts zealot and pragmatist.

But it was Innocenzo alone who represented Church *auctoritas* at the head of this martial company that now blocked Takeru's southward route.

"Cardinal Innocenzo," Takeru said in civil, still heavily accented Italian, "it has been years."

"Greater than ten, in fact, Lord Takeru." Innocenzo was terse in speech and in demeanor. "You make your way from the monastery... alone?"

"I do, yes. My time in your lands is at an end." Takeru had instinctively gripped his katana hilt, of which Innocenzo took notice.

"No need for caution, Takeru. I speak to you as a friend."

"The need for caution never abates, Cardinal." Takeru extracted his blade by a thumb's width, just enough for the steel to be made visible. "Your men number high and come well armed."

Innocenzo made a vulgar show of turning to examine his company, exhibiting mock dismay in confirming Takeru's observation.

"Indeed they do, Takeru."

"What is your purpose, Cardinal?"

A thick, heavy, tense silence befell the men, a silence broken by the synchronized shouting of Innocenzo, "Take him alive!" and blade-drawing on the part of Takeru.

Seems you were wrong, Romero, Takeru said to himself, *the katana has indeed been unsheathed.*

Four well-placed musket shots landed just before Takeru's feet, another six to his left and right. He had planted his rear foot and cocked inward the fore in a manner resembling his technique when dueling Mathieu. Innocenzo was well out of striking range, though Takeru could easily have closed the distance at the price of absorbing into his chest and abdomen a dozen musket balls. Relaxing his stance, the deadly samurai began to sheathe his katana as four guardsmen approached for purposes of disarming and restraining him. They stopped just short of where he stood. After silently agreeing on how best the man should be subdued, they closed...

Slice, Slice, Swoosh, Slice, Slice,

With a speed all present deemed incomprehensible to the naked eye, Takeru had sliced through the hands of two mercenaries, through the throat of another, and through the abdomen of the last. He then tossed the sheathed blade over his right shoulder, holding it only by a silk lanyard, and ran quickly into the forest that lined the road's eastern side. Musket balls peppered tree and soil alike as the fleet-footed warrior ran at a pace he had not employed since adolescence.

"Cease your fire!" Innocenzo ordered. "He's more than a day on foot from the monastery. We'll reach it ourselves this very afternoon."

Innocenzo's men had placed the dead and wounded atop their horses and sent them with two others back to Rome. Just before setting off at a gallop, Innocenzo noticed a parchment not far from the wood's edge, precisely where Takeru had vanished.

"Retrieve that parchment," he ordered a guardsman. "Now, bring it here."

Upon taking inventory of the parchment's contents, Innocenzo could not help but grin wolfishly.

"Our exotic friend will find travel throughout papal lands a less than hospitable experience."

And with that, the vile Cardinal Innocenzo and his undiscerning mercenaries made their way with mounted haste to the monastery from which Takeru, who observed the departure from a hiding place near the wood's perimeter, had set out on foot two days prior.

"Damn that Innocenzo!" he exclaimed, aloud. "Damn him mightily!"

The samurai then watched the road for another moment or so, ensuring no others followed Cardinal Innocenzo in support of whatever foul deed that villain had in store for the monastery.

They number six fewer than did they an hour past, he noted. *Hopefully, that counts for something when the cardinal's machinations are put in motion.*

And then, alone on the road, Takeru began to run. He ran not northward, for catching Innocenzo's galloping company was an impossibility on foot. Takeru instead continued southward, where six horses trotted toward Rome, carrying only two uninjured men along with two dead and another two wounded. But he needed to make haste, for every moment spent racing south placed him farther behind the deceitful Innocenzo, whose was riding at a near gallop.

Running as swiftly as ever his sword had flown, Takeru felt firmly every pound of his racing heart, registered every burning breath of his laboring lungs, and thought only of driving a blade into Innocenzo's throat with every step of his relentless race to intercept the south-ward-bound party. But they had covered some distance while Takeru was scanning the surrounding area, and his reaching them was a somewhat lengthier process than he had anticipated.

Hearing the unmistakable *clip-clop* of trotting horses just ahead, Takeru halted to both determine his next course of action and to re-gain a breath that had abandoned him several hundred paces back. An ambush was the only viable tactic under these circumstances, Takeru concluded.

"And an ambush it shall be," he said in a thin whisper through heavy gasps, "strength and speed by my allies."

Knowing what needed doing, Takeru sprinted with sword drawn 'round a bend his quarry had an instant earlier themselves rounded. The first to enter his visual field was a wounded soldier who leaned in pain over his saddle—a sword sliced through his neck rendering head separate from body. The pain was no more.

The man's living comrades all turned upon hearing the sound of a head falling to the ground, itself followed by the body. Nearest the now decapitated mercenary was one of the unwounded whose last sight, curi-ously enough, was of the same fate he himself ultimately suffered, as his own head was immediately severed from its perch of a neck. This left two soldiers—one whose hands had been sliced through by Takeru a short while earlier and one uninjured. While the latter drew his ornate blade from its long scabbard, the former struggled to load a short musket that had been suspended from his saddle.

Though the man inclined toward musketry had been dealt deep cuts across his hands, Takeru took no chances. Leaping upward, he touched one foot to the man's mount, drove his blade into the man's back, and landed heavily on the soil at the man's side...just before the man slid helplessly from the saddle.

Takeru now faced an enemy swordsman, the first since those ear-liest days of his journey from *Nihon*. Many Italian mercenaries were reputed for their bravery and had cultivated an element of mystique that stemmed from their purported mastery of weapons both bladed and ballistic. Thus Takeru knew he was not facing, by any measure, a novice duelist. The man was tall, much taller than Takeru, and was clearly very strong, possessing neck musculature not unlike Herr Samson's.

Nevertheless, Takeru noted, *he's no Reynier.*

Clang, Swoosh, Clang, Slash, Cut

And it was indeed over. The man defended cleanly and precisely Takeru's initial attack (a feint), agilely dodged the next (a legitimate strike), firmly blocked a third, but proved unable to anticipate the following two moves, one of which cut through his sword arm, the other through his inner leg. Looking in shock at the man of *Nihon* at whose mercy he now stood, the man expected his head, too, would be leaving its shoulders. But Takeru's bloodlust had waned; at heart, he was not heartless. He struck the guardsman unconscious, quickly bound his wounds with thick cloth strips, of which there were plenty lying about, and...

KTCH-BOOM!

Takeru had taken for granted the death of his third ambush victim. A sword thrust through the back may not be *as* reliable as a behead-ing in ensuring the death of one's enemy, but it is at least *somewhat* reliable. However, in this case, the soldier of fortune had proven re-silient, enough so to fire the musket that he had, while Takeru was tending to his fourth victim's wounds, finished loading.

Fortunately, the man lacked the strength to position himself for an accurate firing of his weapon. Unfortunately, his firing had achieved its likely intention. That of frightening the horses, all of which now ran, five southward and one, *Thank the gods...*north. As he set out for yet another race, Takeru observed that the stubborn mercenary had indeed succumbed to what had, after all, been a deep thrust of a long blade into his broad back.

"Enjoy your heavenly reward, you troublesome soul." Takeru muttered while beginning his pursuit. With any luck, the steed would arrest its frantic fleeing within a moment or so. That still meant a long stretch at a rapid pace for the tiring Takeru, but he had little choice in the matter. Innocenzo had evil in his heart and death at his disposal.

And so samurai Lord Sakurai Takeru ran.

Monastery...Tragedy

When Archbishop Romero recovered consciousness, he could make out a vaguely familiar face...a similarly familiar voice. Both of these belonged to a blood-covered and distraught looking Takeru.

"Takeru, my friend"—the voice was weak, smoky—"you've returned to us."

Tears now streamed forth from the samurai's eyes. "Romero," he sobbed, "there is no 'us' of whom to speak. Only you survive. And me, my loathsome life intact."

And then it struck Romero with hellish force. "God in heaven!" he exclaimed, lifting his head from Takeru's lap, then sitting upright with some difficulty and much pain. He was wounded, a musket shot had struck his lower stomach, but he lived.

"Innocenzo, that treacherous demon!" Romero clutched his side, but the anguish was one of the soul, not of the body.

"I encountered him going southward and knew there was something foul in store. He tried to detain me. I killed several and made my way here."

"Something foul, yes. We knew not what until so many shots had been fired—killing master and pupil alike."

"But why, Romero, why?" Takeru pleaded through tears.

"He arrived just before dusk, fifty men at his back. There had been talk of ceremony and what have you. I imagined the soldiers an honor guard...not murderers." Romero parted ways with composure, childlike sobs crippling temporarily his capacity for speech. With some difficulty he continued, "Those perfect men, master and pupil alike, perfect to a man."

"Innocenzo said nothing of his motives, not a word?"

"No, there were words. God *damn him* and his words." Romero attempted to stand, and failed. "He had indeed run afoul of Pius, to say nothing for his predecessors."

"But what had that to do with the monastery; why the order to lay it waste?" Takeru's visage was pain itself; the man was living grief.

"Only everything. Our cause had been unknown to every of Julius's successors. Innocenzo's latest transgression—a rape—had led to inquiries as to his various dealings and schemes. The monastery and its purpose were laid bare, a sacrificial lamb through which Innocenzo's cardinalship was preserved."

"Pius ordered this?"

"Don't you see? Innocenzo framed our cause as operating outside papal authority, a threat whose being he would himself extinguish, thereby preserving order."

"But surely Pius knew…"

"Pius knew what Innocenzo *wanted* him to know. We were but a relic of Julius's papal tenure, an unknowable quantity whose very existence suggested the possibility of insurrection…perhaps even of assassination."

Takeru took his mind from these poisonous thoughts of political treachery, of evil betrayal, and surveyed the carnage that enclosed the earth on which he and Romero now sat…defeated.

There were thirty dead mercenaries, no fewer, perhaps nearer forty. Strewn throughout their corpses were faces so painfully familiar to Takeru as to reduce him once more to cries of unbridled anguish.

Hernan had died sword in hand. His body lay on its back, right arm bloodied from the elbow down. He had run through at least one hapless soldier. "Hopefully a dozen, my old friend," Takeru whispered.

"Herr Samson's mighty torso had become a repository for enough musket shot to decimate a regiment. At his side were the mangled remains of two soldiers, one of whom had suffered the fate of having his head rotated fully until it faced precisely backward. The other had experienced the terrible death of a wholly collapsed jaw, likely by Samson's grip.

Ismail had not given fight but had apparently attempted to protect the defenseless Greve, who had never so much as held in hand a blade larger than a small knife. Both had died by musket shot. At their side was Jakob, dear Jakob, who had adored Greve since childhood, the latter having recognized in the former a poor sense of language but a wonderful heart. He had worked so selflessly with the boy throughout the years, so selflessly indeed. Jakob had taken one mercenary with him in death; Romero had observed the act in a moment of chaos.

"The man who shot Greve"—Romero coughed—"Jakob fell upon that man with murder in his palms, crushing his skull between them and hurling the body downward before being run through by Innocenzo himself. He crawled to Greve and Ismail, breathing his last upon the Dane's body."

Reynier Galante was the center of a killing wheel, for around his own lifeless, blood-drenched body were those of soldiers who had foolishly closed with Christendom's fiercest blade. He, too, had died sword in hand.

"But he was no longer the fiercest blade, was he?" Takeru imagined the events of two mornings prior.

"The *apprendisti*," Romero went on, "how well they acquitted themselves. Many a soldier of fortune found himself surprised then dead at the hand of a mere adolescent."

What Takeru had observed in at last reaching the monastery suggested Romero was correct.

"But so many were killed in that first round of fire, Takeru"—Romero again coughed—"had Innocenzo any honor he'd not have his life. But, then, had he any honor…things would not be thus. It was the unexpected volley of fire that doomed us. Seven of them died there and then, Innocenzo having asked that they be assembled for his"—at this Romero spit hatefully—"papal gift."

"And those who did not die then?" Takeru thought of Mathieu.

"They are responsible for as many of the enemy dead as are any of the cadre. More."

Innocenzo had not been foolish—not when approaching the monastery, not when leaving. Takeru did catch the northward horse, not far from where his encounter with Innocenzo had come to pass. By then there was little chance of gaining on the company, too long had they been moving at a gallop. But he would ride his horse into a premature grave in attempting as much.

Covering as much distance in mere hours as he had moved in two days of patiently strolling, Takeru was, by dusk, within sight of those familiar landscape features that surrounded the monastery. There was musket fire and murder on the horizon. He rode harder…

…and into a trap, of sorts. For Innocenzo was evil, not stupid. The vile cardinal had anticipated Takeru (or perhaps some oblivious witness) might make his way up the road while his wickedness was unfolding. Thus he had stationed men some distance south of the monastery.

"Just enough to slow and perhaps kill me," Takeru observed, seething.

Charging the detachment, Takeru closed with them well before any could bring their muskets to bear. One beheading, a throat slit, and there were then only *two to kill*, Takeru noted.

The two attacked a breathless Takeru with greater effort and force than had he anticipated, one even managing to open the samurai's upper leg with a skillful slash, though at the expense of his own life. Within heartbeats, both were eviscerated. Takeru worked hastily to halt the loss of blood from his wounded leg, then limped over to his now recalcitrant horse. The exhausted horse refused to gallop and eventually suspended its locomotion entirely, forcing Takeru to limp in agony a remaining half mile to the training grounds.

There, too, Innocenzo had taken no chances. Having killed every cadre member and, he believed, their every *apprendista*, he had fled on one of Malcome Munro's beautiful mounts, which was fresh, flanked by six mercenaries who had been spared the death so many of their countrymen had suffered. "Even if a pupil or two had survived, their world has been destroyed around them," Innocenzo reasoned. "Our work here is done. The monastery is no more."

Takeru had not taken full account of his own dead before coming across the surviving Romero. He had counted eight *apprendisti* and the cadre in its entirety...himself excluded. Malcome was the first of his peers whose lifeless body he encountered. They had not been close, he and Malcome, but a mutual respect was, of course, extant between them. Munro, too, had died fighting; a soldier lay dead at his side, the Scot's heavy sabre buried to the hilt in that man's chest.

"Romero"—Takeru was now largely in control of his emotions, though grief saturated his every syllable—"I count only eight of them."

"Eight of who, Takeru?" Romero surveyed the field.

"Where are Thomas and Judah? Where is Thaddaeus?" he paused, tears again laid siege to his helpless eyes. "Where is Mathieu?"

Romero sat up fully, enlivened by the prospect of some mercy having made itself known on this hateful day.

"I cannot say. All resisted Innocenzo's attack; I imagined all had died in the effort. So numerous had the soldiers been, so dishonorable their means."

"Romero, those who escaped death when subjected to Innocenzo's cowardly salvo..."

"Yes, what of them?"

"They may live. To a man, they may well live."

10

ARRIVAL

The Bocho

"Lord Sakurai," said a voice that belonged to a longtime Sakurai vassal, "a ship passed through our waters early this morning. It was thought to be of *Chūgoku no* origin."

Daimyo Lord Sakurai Kiyoshi had been tending to provincial matters of agriculture when the vassal had entered, bowed, and delivered this frantic message. Rising to his feet, the daimyo directed his eyes to the Mikawa Bay waters. "Any further description beyond its origin? Was it large in size?"

"No, my lord, it was the length of a normal *Wakō* vessel, perhaps smaller."

"Summon Lord Takeru. He is to join me in the *moya* immediately." Lord Kiyoshi spoke calmly.

Some minutes later, Lord Takeru, who had been composing poetry in the palace garden, joined his brother and several retainers in the *moya*. Lord Sakurai was speaking in measured tones.

"*Nihon* has exported its share of piracy in recent years. We have been naïve in imagining ourselves invulnerable to similar trespasses."

"These are not pirates, my lord," Vassal Hirate contended, "but purveyors of still more foreign weapons."

"Yes, Lord Oda has been incorporating musketry into his warfare tactics for years." Lord Sakurai's rejoinder was oddly inconclusive.

Takeru compensated for his brother's partial absence, the reason for which had everything to do with Osamu and Hiroshi being, at present, in the Owari Province for which the *Chūgoku no* ship was headed. They had joined him for a well-intentioned but ultimately fruitless embassy to Lord Oda's court, electing to return some weeks later for hunting and a tour of Owari's countryside upon their host's rather insistent invitation. Lord Sakurai had not approved, but Takeru argued that the experience would prove worthwhile in more respects than one. Furthermore, "Lord Oda may warm to them, perhaps come to regard them as kin. We should be so smiled upon by the gods."

Of course, this had all preceded the *Chūgoku no* ship's arrival. Takeru fully suspected this was the *Bocho*, vassal ship of the *Ocean Castle*.

"Indeed, Lord Oda's employment of exotic weapons is well attested. He furthermore has been experimenting with clever means of enhancing their battlefield efficacy."

"What is your meaning, Takeru?" Hirate sensed something of still greater relevance was yet to be voiced.

"The muskets Oda has thus far implemented have differed in no significant way from those first introduced into his province more than ten years past." Takeru made eye contact with his brother, who was once again fully present. "The muskets soon to be offloaded in Owari Province are of better design and will combine nicely with the training measures to which Lord Oda's men have been subjected these past months."

"It could spell doom for the shogun, for Mikawa, for *Nihon*." Lord Sakurai Kiyoshi betrayed no fear, merely stated the facts of the matter at hand: "Lord Oda is ambition itself, and he knows no limits. These weapons, they…"

"They are the future, my brother, a future to which I have borne close witness," said Takeru, recalling the hideous fate of his pupils, "but if interrupting the future for a time means doing the same to Lord Oda, then we must pursue that end ardently."

"And what of Osamu and Hiroshi?" asked a genuinely curious Hirate. "What part will they play in this pursuit?"

"My sons, Hirate, are of their father's blood, and their *oji*'s" replied Lord Sakurai. "When the time comes, I trust their instincts will guide them well and true."

"Under the circumstances, brother, perhaps a retainer might be sent to retrieve them. Best have the family consolidated should matters, shall we say, deteriorate."

Lord Sakurai weighed carefully his brother's words, then responded amenably.

"Indeed, Lord Takeru, please do see to their safe return. Lord Oda trusts you to some degree, as do so many others. Perhaps your return visit aligning so closely with that of their anticipated shipment will not strike him as being in any way suspicious."

"Surely not, though I may be inclined to inquire as to the shipment's nature. The veracity of his response, or lack thereof, will tell us much as to where Mikawa Province stands in relation to his larger plot."

"And if he responds untruthfully," Hirate inquired, "what should we infer from his doing so?"

"Only that he expects to employ the element of surprise in unleashing these improved weapons upon *Nihon*."

"Beginning with Mikawa Province?" Hirate was pensive.

"Or ending. Does that really much matter, Hirate?"

"Perhaps not."

"Let us see to the safe return of Lord Sakurai's sons, of my *oi*, then turn our attentions to the fate of our lands." Takeru spoke directly to his brother: "Neither of whose outcome may be entirely within our power to determine."

Lord Sakurai's face was of granite; his eyes grim. This remained the case until somewhat later that afternoon, only a very short while after Takeru had set out by small caravan for Owari Province.

As the weary daimyo considered all that was under way in and around Mikawa, he afforded himself a brief moment of prayer for his sons, for his brother, for his province. The prayer had only just reached its natural end when a rustling of foliage or some such visited Kiyoshi's keen ears.

"Who is there?" demanded the daimyo, very much wishing he had kept a sword in hand.

The question was met with darkness.

Darkness.

The Owari Terms

The *Bocho* had anchored rather near the Owari Province shore and was in plain view of Lord Oda, his various retainers, and the sons of Lord Sakurai, Osamu and Hiroshi, both of whom found themselves marveling at the exotic ship's aesthetically pleasing construction.

"It's a handsome craft, this *Bocho*," Hiroshi observed, though the observation went unacknowledged.

"The winds of progress, Osamu, they are upon us." Lord Oda had taken to addressing only Lord Sakurai's eldest son despite Hiroshi's consistent presence.

"Perhaps the title of 'heir apparent' is worth even more than I've always imagined it to be," reasoned the irritated Hiroshi.

"And this progress, Lord Oda, is aboard that ship?"

"Aboard the *Bocho*? Probably not." Lord Oda's was a matter-of-fact tone: "*Tokoh* Jaidev has perhaps sent a proxy, someone charged with rendering official those terms he seeks to realize."

"Those terms being?" Hiroshi would make himself heard.

Lord Oda turned in mild amusement to face the younger son of Lord Sakurai, his occasional rival. "Those terms being of concern to me and to the people of Owari, my boy." It was then clear that Lord Oda would brook no prying inquiry, certainly not from a boy of the Matsudaira Clan, Sakurai or otherwise.

"But you *are* paying him for the arms, Lord Oda"—Osamu now aided his brother's probe—"we knew that much from our spies, and you've tacitly confirmed as much since our being in Owari."

"Of course we are paying *Tokoh* Jaidev, Osamu; the man has sailed a week of weeks, more, in transporting weapons of marvelous design across endless waters." Lord Oda was condescending: "Do you suppose his to be a charitable endeavor?"

"Naturally not, Lord Oda, but if payment is to be made, then what further terms..."

Lord Oda sharply interjected, "Come, let us ready ourselves to receive this proxy of the sea."

Osamu and Hiroshi exchanged a knowing glance, looked once more to the *Bocho*, then followed Lord Oda down a pathway that itself led to a sturdy jetty. A small barge had been lowered down from the *Bocho*'s stern, which made its way by oar to the jetty, on which stood Lord Oda and his entourage, numbering over thirty.

"Not many aboard the barge," Osamu observed. He was correct, for only five figures were visible upon the barge's top deck, aside from the sixteen oarsmen who were making short work of their rowing.

"Not many at all," Lord Oda concurred, "but among them is *Tokoh* Jaidev. Which, I must say, is surprising."

"But you have met before, Lord Oda, have you not?"

"We have, yes, but aboard his vessel. Those aboard the *Ocean Castle* rarely step foot on dry land."

Osamu and Hiroshi now looked upon the approaching barge with still greater fascination. *Who is this man,* Hiroshi wondered, *who has, by Lord Oda's account, lived his entire life at sea, aboard some mammoth vessel that traverses the oceans like a sailed province unto itself?*

"Well, he comes to land this day," Osamu supplied, "though for what reason I should be interested to know."

"You will know what *Tokoh* Jaidev and I desire you to know, Osamu," Lord Oda snapped, "nothing more. Do not forget your place, nor mistake for weakness my now waning kindness."

Osamu bowed. "Of course, my lord. Forgive my impudence."

Lord Oda was generally assuaged by overt acts of subservience or, at a minimum, sincere respect. While Osamu certainly felt neither, his bowing and choice of words suggested otherwise.

"Very well." Oda's calm had been restored. "Do see that your words find no purchase on your tongue during our time with *Tokoh* Jaidev or any among his away party."

Recovering from his deep bow, Osamu responded agreeably. "To be sure, Lord Oda."

Lord Oda, his retainers, and the Sakurai brothers reached the jetty's end as the barge docked at its edge. A well-crafted ladder, thick in its rungs, sturdy in its wide stiles, was hooked to the barge's larboard side and angled so as to have its base rest perfectly atop the jetty.

It was Jaidev who first descended the ladder, followed by two warriors of nondescript size, clothing, and appearance. These were followed by an elderly man who appeared to be of *Kankoku-go* origin, though his attire, like that of his companions, was simply impossible to place.

Last to descend the ladder, though with far more speed and agility than was exhibited among the four by whom he was preceded, was a dark-clad man of decidedly *Chūgoku no* origin. He was hawkish of eye, somewhat short of stature, but moved with a grace and a sureness neither Osamu nor Hiroshi had ever before observed in man or beast. On his back were twin *jian*, swords whose construction both recognized from their visit to *Pekin* years earlier. His age was difficult to place. *He is either fifteen or fifty,* noted Hiroshi, who was generally astute in the assessing of such things.

Prior to a single word having been exchanged between the embassy and its hosts, the twin-bladed, dark-clad figure had taken visual assessment of all by which he and those under his protection were surrounded. His eyes fell last upon Osamu and Hiroshi, exporting an element of menace that both found unsettling. *This man,* Osamu determined, *he is death.*

"Lord Oda!" Jaidev was seemingly oblivious to his protector's inherent menace, or all too aware, as he was rather at ease for a man notoriously more at home aboard his ship than upon dry land, a ship that had been left curiously from sight. "How uplifting to again lay eyes on your noble features."

Jaidev's *Nihongo* was fluent, the accent detectable but unobtrusive. He made himself very well understood by word, by tone, by bearing; he was plainly a communicative spirit.

"Likewise, *Tokoh* Jaidev. Much has come to pass since last we shared each other's company." Lord Oda allowed a thin smile to vitalize his serious countenance. "Your timing is perhaps more to our advantage than I could have anticipated."

"Ah, yes—word of the new shogun reached me some weeks past."

This did, in fact, have the effect of invoking from Lord Oda a laughing spell quite at odds with his character. "Jaidev, your capacity for keeping apprised of goings on in our *Nihon* is for me a source of endless fascination."

"We've had generations' time in which to produce and expand our lines of knowledge, both landward and seafaring, dear Oda. Shall we to business?"

"Indeed, Jaidev." Hiroshi took note of the formalities having been abandoned, the great men were now merely "Oda" and "Jaidev" for all to hear. "I have arranged for comfortable transport to *Kiyosu-jō* and for a brief tour of Owari Province as we make our way to the palace."

As all readied themselves for the brief trip to Lord Oda's palace, which sat in Kiyosu, Osamu and Hiroshi kept their eyes trained closely on the killer in Jaidev's midst, who was in no way unwise to having captured their attention.

Walking the length of the jetty back toward shore and to Lord Oda's awaiting caravan, the Sakurai brothers kept their hands at their hilts and their ears attuned, for Jaidev's protector walked at some distance behind the party, *All the better to eye his prey*, Hiroshi gloomily concluded. *What was it* Oji *Takeru had said about having encountered only one man more skilled in swordcraft than himself? Had he indeed crossed paths with this...?*

"Chau Hai Fan!" Jaidev beckoned. "Do close some distance with our group. You keep rather far for my liking."

"Chau Hai Fan?" so he was *Chūgoku no*, Hiroshi confirmed. Not that it was of any great matter; killers are loyal only to themselves.

Lord Oda's planned tour was very much worth the while of all who took part. It ran through large population centers, through a farming community, through a small woodland, and ended with Lord Oda's pristine palace coming into sudden view—a sight it was for all.

Upon making their entrance, a number of servants saw to the care of Lord Oda's guests, with garments being removed, refreshment provided, and the showing of Jaidev and his companions to the great hall in which their dealings were to unfold.

The Conference

"The *Ocean Castle* is a rather massive collection of planks and sails to be kept hidden in the way you've managed, Jaidev." Lord Oda's tone was a near perfect blend of admiration and accusation. "Do you fear for the safety of your cargo?"

All were now seated within the magnificent *Kiyosu-jō* great hall whose northern wall had been opened to reveal a beautiful late summer's day.

"For the cargo, yes; for my citizens, more." Jaidev's was a manner open and trustworthy.

Does the man keep no secrets? Osamu wondered.

"Your waters are replete with piracy, Lord Oda," continued Jaidev. "I trust the shogun is aware of this menace?"

"Perhaps. Though he is impotent, a puppet ruler." The disdain in Oda's voice was weighted with animus. "The man is powerless to act."

"I see." Jaidev seemed to find incomplete this angry response.

"In any event, the raiding tends to occur elsewhere; it is simply the harbors and coves of *Nihon* in which these pirates take refuge."

"Of that I am perfectly aware, Oda. But it was a risk to which I could not subject the *Castle*." Jaidev sighed. "However, once a suitable passageway has been identified, my vessel will make its way to your harbor for an offloading of the long-awaited cargo."

"Indeed, Jaidev. Long-awaited indeed."

"I trust your men's musketry has improved?"

"They are limited only by the flaws in these *tanegashima*, these 'matchlocks.'" Oda spoke the translated term with a distinctive pronouncing of each syllable.

"Yes. You will find the snap lock mechanism far more commensurate with your vision. And *these* muskets, Lord Oda, will fire more accurately. The barrels, they are spiraled to give the ball a guiding spin."

"What welcome news! I shall put my smiths to work in matching these spiraled barrels." Lord Oda then paused, as though uncertain about continuing with Sakurai heirs in his presence. "As for the diagram parch...?"

"Yes, Lord Oda. That is firmly in hand and will soon be yours." It was Jaidev who now paused. "But there are matters of still greater consequence, which are perhaps best discussed as *tokoh* to daimyo."

"Agreed." Oda then turned to his retainers. "Leave us."

"And us, Lord Oda?" Osamu was sincerely uncertain as to whether or not his continued presence might be requested.

"You and your brother had best return to your chambers. I will call for you prior to the evening's feast."

All made their way to the *moya*'s eastern door, which Jaidev's men then closed behind them. Chau Hai Fan, too, had left his master and Lord Oda to their secret dealings but maintained close watch over the sole entryway through which any potential threat might enter. Hiroshi had cast a parting glance upon the only man in whose presence he had ever before experienced such fear. The glance was returned but suggested only indifference on part of its caster.

The Fates Beckon Home

"We must ready ourselves for a return to Mikawa Province." Osamu was rolling his sparse traveling wares and clothing into a stretch of cloth that would then rest atop his broad shoulders. He and Hiroshi had returned to their chambers a short while earlier.

"A sudden departure would invoke suspicion, Osamu." Hiroshi was preparing for a departure not at all. "Lord Oda is untrusting of us as it is."

"Lord Oda's trust is no concern to me at the moment, Hiroshi, only Matsudaira and our province's survival. Father was right—ours must be a middle way." Osamu had finished his preparations and now looked his brother dead in the eye. "We must share with him what we have learned here."

"Which is what, Osamu? Lord Oda's penchant for musketry is well understood, and we have known for months of his plans to receive new weapons."

"Then we must tell him of Lord Oda's secrecy. Jaidev has something planned, something that may well affect our own lands."

"We've only our suspicions, Osamu, nothing more."

"But those suspicions are grounded in"—Osamu's intensity was dampened; he exhaled quietly—"in our instincts, which I trust. Do please ready yourself, all the same; we may find ourselves needing to make a hasty departure from Owari Province."

"Very well, brother." Hiroshi *did* suspect foul motive on Lord Oda's part. "That much I will do."

But Hiroshi's preparations were interrupted almost immediately. Lord Oda had sent a retainer to retrieve the Sakurai brothers, requesting their presence in his private chambers.

"Well, now, this is a more sudden summons than was expected." Hiroshi had now joined in his brother's suspicion.

As they made their way to Lord Oda's chambers, the brothers were suddenly joined by an additional retainer, followed by two more and another two as they neared the chambers' entryway.

Three-to-one, Osamu silently noted. *I know greater odds have been overcome.*

"Ah, the Sakurai heir and his brother." Lord Oda smiled falsely as he dismissed the escort party. "Please do enter. We've matters of legacy to discuss and of feasting."

"Your business with *Tokoh* Jaidev is concluded?" Hiroshi's was a reflexive inquiry; he was genuinely curious.

"For the time being, yes." Lord Oda then gestured for the brothers to take their positions on either side of where he was himself seated. "What do you know, Osamu, of sacrifice? Of rendering forfeit something...or someone...in service of a higher cause?"

"Very little, I suppose." Osamu's heart pounded, his grip tightened around a hilt he imagined might crack from the pressure. "But I know your question unsettles me."

Lord Oda merely chuckled. "Which is understandable; your instincts are sharp. But you will learn of sacrifice soon, Osamu. And, when that lesson has taken painful root, you will learn of causes higher than the protecting of any one province: Mikawa, Owari, or otherwise."

Osamu, correctly sensing a veiled threat, could no longer contain whatever inside him had threatened to boil over. "What have you done?" he demanded, katana drawn and directed at the still seated, still perfectly calm Lord Oda.

Hiroshi, too, had drawn his blade, though in fear rather than anger. "Brother, what is this?"

The question went unanswered, for at that moment, four soldiers, none of them retainers from what the Sakurai brothers could tell, burst into the chambers from behind Lord Oda, all armed with muskets, themselves aimed at Osamu and Hiroshi.

"There will be a shift, Osamu, in regional politics, soon, followed by another in shogunate authority soon thereafter. And tonight..." Lord Oda suspended his speech with a chuckle. "Oh, Hiroshi, Osamu, do please drop your swords. Only two of my men need strike their target to end your lives, and there are four here capable of doing so."

After a heartbeat or two of rage-inhabited hesitation, Osamu, with teeth gritted, dropped his katana; Hiroshi did the same.

"They are unarmed, Jaidev." Oda beckoned over his shoulder. "You are safe here."

Jaidev then entered, flanked once again by his two soldiers and followed by the eerily silent Chau Hai Fan.

"I don't expect you will understand our means, Osamu; nor you, Hiroshi," said Jaidev, "but you will appreciate the motives that have rendered them necessary."

Osamu and Hiroshi listened reluctantly to their captors as Chau Hai Fan retrieved from the floor their respective swords. Eyeing one in curiosity, he seemed to disapprove of something in its form...or perhaps in its weight, then laid them both at Lord Oda's side—*was this rehearsed?* wondered Hiroshi—who merely acknowledged them with a brief glance before rising to his full, not inconsiderable height.

"You will be restricted to your chambers until the hour of our feast." Oda addressed only Osamu. "Leading figures from neighboring provinces will be in attendance. Your own is necessary to suggest a degree of stability on our eastern border."

"Which would otherwise have been the case, had you not held us against our will." Osamu was anger itself.

Oda adopted an oddly sympathetic tone. "No, Osamu, we would have had no such image of peace, not from you, nor from your brother. Not after learning of..."

"Oda." Jaidev softly interrupted, prompting the Owari daimyo to meet his eye.

Turning back to Osamu, he said, "Not after news of Lord Sakurai's death was made known during the feast."

Osamu now saw only red, lunging to the floor at Oda's feet; he had felt firmly the grip of his hilt, just before he saw only black.

For Chau Hai Fan had anticipated Osamu's action and expertly intercepted with the pommel of a *jian* to the man's head, rendering him unconscious. He then whipped the blade around to meet Hiroshi's pulsating throat, suggesting with a flicker of his eyes that the boy should fall to his knees, which Hiroshi then did. Staring up at Chau, Hiroshi imagined running the man through with his katana, *though he'd need to be fast asleep or miles away from his jian for me to render that fate*, Hiroshi miserably accepted. *The man is death.*

"You two," Jaidev said to the nearest musketeers, "help Lord Osamu to his chambers. And treat him well: he is a daimyo of the Matsudaira clan as of this night."

With Hiroshi shouldering the burden of his brother's weight, the four exited Lord Oda's chambers, which left only Jaidev once Chau Hai Fan and the remaining musketeers had followed suit.

"And Chau"—Jaidev stopped the killer just before the latter had made an exit—"do keep your eyes watchful for anything...for anything deserving of being watched."

Chau Hai Fan had probably nodded in understanding, though if so, it had not registered with Lord Oda.

"The brothers," Jaidev asked, "we are certain nothing in the way of a disruption will hinder the evening's festivities?"

"They will be under tight control. A single outburst and our collateral will be, let us say, rendered active."

"Ah." Jaidev understood completely. "Osamu parts way with his composure and Hiroshi parts ways with his life?"

"We are so very much of one mind, Jaidev." Oda's was a menacing grin.

"And Lord Takeru?"

"Was not in the palace when the act was carried out."

Jaidev was now pensive. "That man *does* worry me. True—were it not for his time aboard the *Ocean Castle*, this partnership would not be under way. Takeru inadvertently opened Owari to still greater firepower than did it already wield. But the unwitting nature of his involvement—complications could surface for that reason."

"Because of his having the shogun's ear?"

"And because he is Lord Sakurai Takeru—a resourceful man, and proud."

"Worry not about his shogunate influence; that office will soon be held by a man worthy of it."

"Indeed. And we are certain of the daimyo's having met his end?"

"Most certain, yes." Lord Oda's gaze pointed firmly east. "Most certain indeed. His death was known to me a short time before our return to the palace. The Owari Province tour provided me with good reason to be on the westward roads this day. You will recall the messenger who approached as we turned to the east?"

"I do, yes. He confirmed the act?"

"He did."

"And the man who carried out this assassination?"

"What of him, Jaidev?"

"He has your trust?"

"He is an assassin, Jaidev, and therefore not deserving of trust. But he did prove worth his price—Lord Sakurai lay dead this day."

"Very good. Then let us discuss the shogunate as envisioned by you, Lord Oda Nobunaga, and of the *Ocean Castle*'s place in that envisioning." Jaidev spoke in light tones of serious matters, which sat perfectly well with Lord Oda.

11

COVERT

The Feast

Lord Sakurai Kiyoshi, who had only two years past reunited with a long-absent brother, father of two strong sons, beloved daimyo of the Matsudaira clan, and an irrefutably good-hearted man, was dead.

The realization continually thrust itself upon Osamu's broken heart as he and his equally distraught brother sat nearly motion-less alongside Lord Oda, whose feast had drawn senior figures from throughout Owari Province, from its neighbors, and from lands sym-pathetic to the ambitious man's poorly kept secret of a desired *coup d'état*, as *Oji* Takeru had taken to terming it.

Prior to having been shown into the banquet hall, Osamu and Hiroshi were assured of the latter's death should Osamu attempt to harm Lord Oda, any of his guests, or even himself for that matter.

"Is the anguish over your father truly worth still greater heart-ache, *Daimyo* Osamu?" Lord Oda had hoped the emphasis upon his captive's newly realized title would be sufficient to ease lingering ten-sions. "Your father was a past Mikawa Province can no longer endure; you are a future of which it is deserving. You will not see the truth of those words this night, nor any other for some time to come." Oda now leaned in with menace on his breath. "But do see the truth in these: Your brother's corpse will serve as a mere practice target until nothing but red mist remains of its once strong sinews. This I promise, Osamu, should any I host this night regard you as anything other than a loyal vassal in service of Owari...of me!"

Hatred threatened to burn from the sockets of Osamu's reddened eyes; love for his brother restrained him.

"Yes, Lord Oda. I am at one with you."

Lord Oda now composed himself, fangs withdrawn. "See that you are, Daimyo Osamu, for Hiroshi...for the Matsudaira."

Now all were seated in the hall and had been for some time. The Sakurai did their best in pantomiming both enjoyment and the act of eating, though the former was impossible, and the latter amounted to nothing at all.

Tokoh Jaidev was not in attendance. *Perhaps he returned to his ship to oversee the cargo transfer?* Hiroshi wondered. *Would that we could keep from reaching Owari Province a single crate.*

Lord Oda now stood to address those in attendance. Here he was, as much as on any battlefield, very much at ease. Comfortable in his command of soldiers and audiences alike.

"My friends, my brothers, my *Nihon no* kin!" The room was Oda's. "Turmoil has beset our lands in years past, with peace having come at the price of strong and worthy and noble leadership. It is, therefore, a peace not of stones and mortar but of paper and air, threatening to blow away when met with the faintest of winds. That which comes cheaply is cast aside freely! And I say, let us cast aside the yoke of reprehensible rule, reclaiming the dignity that is our people's right. A right by birth!"

All present, save the Sakurai, affirmed their agreement to varying degrees. There were cries of unity with Lord Oda, there was the beating of empty bowls against one another, and there were fists raised in imagined triumph. Clearly the shogun would soon face insurrection, Mikawa Province's position on the matter aside.

"Some distance from our shores sits a powerful man whose alliance I have cultivated for more than two years' time. Aboard his vessel are housed thousands of weapons that promise to reshape *Nihon no* fields of war forever. The initiative is ours for the seizing, and seize it I intend to do. By this time tomorrow, my every crack conscript will be armed with a musket still more advanced than those we have well employed these ten years past. And victory within those struggles yet to come will be a foregone conclusion—the days ahead will amount to an inheritance of prosperity that we shall bequeath unto ourselves! Ready yourselves, gentlemen, for Owari Province shall usher in an era of greatness never before imaginable."

Lord Oda Nobunaga, a man somewhere in his fourth decade, spoke with an elder's dignity, a clear authority that was undeniably compelling. Were it not for the man's evil act in making an example of Lord Sakurai, Hiroshi's father, *perhaps I would have fallen in behind this charismatic creature*, the mourning boy reflected.

Some hours following Lord Oda's rousing words, the feast was adjourned. Osamu imagined most of those in attendance would be overcome with drunkenness and thus remain in the palace until morning. Whether or not that was the case remained uncertain to the brothers, both of whom were escorted to their chambers under an "Honor guard for the Matsudaira clan's heir and his loyal brother!" Lord Oda had explained to his apparently oblivious guests.

The guard, which Osamu found less than honorable, would remain in place outside the chambers until such a time as Lord Oda deemed them unnecessary. What Osamu wouldn't have given to simply hold a sword in hand; being disarmed left the natural warrior feeling miserable, powerless.

Once settled into their imprisonment, of a sort, Osamu and Hiroshi looked to each other in sadness, then settled themselves in for a dark night. Neither intended to sleep, though both were worn down from the day's demands both physical and mental.

"Osamu?" Hiroshi was not sure if his brother had managed to sleep.

"Yes?" He was not asleep.

Beginning to sob, Hiroshi fought past the wall of tears that might otherwise have imprisoned his speech: "You will be a fine daimyo; I will serve you well." At this, the tears found purchase in his eyes.

Rushing to his brother's side to provide comfort, a rarity, Osamu replied, "Hiroshi, let us first honor Father in doing right by Mikawa... by the Matsudaira." Osamu himself then felt the tears, repressed for hours, begin their flow. "My responsibility is to them, not to myself."

As the brothers wept, a nearly full moon filled the sky visible through their chamber's small window. Illuminating and beautiful though it was, Hiroshi could not help but resent the moon its indifference over human affairs...over his father's death. "I hate Oda," he wept, "and would see him killed had I the means."

The weeping continued.

The Rescue

Slice, Swoosh, Ting, Slice, Swoosh, Swoosh, Ting, Slice, Slice

Hiroshi, who had succumbed to a wounded slumber around midnight, when the moon was nearing its apex, was awoken by the distinctive sound of violence, of swords. Whatever had pulled him from his sleeping state, it was deadly.

"Osamu! Osamu!"

Having fallen into a deeper sleep than had his brother, Osamu came to only at the sound of Hiroshi's pleading voice.

"What is it? What?" he whispered forcefully.

"Outside, I heard something."

"Was it a...?"

But the question needn't have been asked, for the chamber door was then opened from the outside, allowing for Lord Sakurai Takeru to make a violent entrance.

"Your father is dead. We leave immediately."

Takeru's sword was drawn, it was bloodied, and it still rang with the clashes it had suffered a mere instant prior to his entering the room.

"*Oji*! You live!" Hiroshi was reduced briefly to the boyhood he longed to escape.

Osamu was reduced to nothing of the sort. "Where were you when father was killed, Takeru? Where?"

Grasping Osamu by the shoulder, Takeru spoke with thick sincerity. "I was on my way to Owari Province, on my way to retrieve you. My absence was either a blessing or a curse for his killer. We'll know soon enough, but at the moment we must be on our way to Mikawa."

A moment of hesitation staid Osamu's feet, as though hearing from his *oji* a more satisfactory response might, in fact, reverse his father's fate.

Reluctantly, Osamu joined Takeru and his brother in the palace corridor, where both crouched and readied for a covert departure.

"Take their swords." Takeru gestured to the dead sentries. "They'll be put to better use in your hands than ever they were in theirs."

The brothers did as they were told, each retrieving a katana and rotating it around for a sense of weight and balance, then followed their uncle to a servants' entryway, which led them to a wholly open patch of land at whose far edge were waiting three mounts.

"I had scarcely placed the palace at my back when news of your father's death reached me. Messengers had been sent to encourage my returning." Osamu spoke as they made their way in patience and silence to the field's edge, to the waiting horses who would return them to Mikawa by sunrise.

"And why didn't you return?" Hiroshi had his own supposition as to why that might have been but wanted to know with certainty.

"I knew Oda was responsible; I knew my *oi* would need me. I wish this were all of a less foreseeable nature, but, in truth, much of this I should have anticipated. I'm sorry."

"What are you saying, *Oji*?" Osamu's was a vulnerable state of mind. Damning revelation would further unsteady his compromised spirit.

"My return passage via the *Ocean Castle* inadvertently brought Lord Oda into Jaidev's orbit, or the reverse." The three had now reached their horses, which Takeru had quietly appropriated from the palace's adjacent stables. "Jaidev was also aware of the enmity that has historically characterized Owari/Mikawa relations. He is playing one against the other in hopes of benefiting from the ensuing chaos. He seeks political sanctuary under our shogunate—preferably a shogunate whose office he is instrumental in securing."

The three had stopped at the field's edge, horses mere paces away. What was being said needed saying; a delay would not do.

"And our father," Osamu realized aloud, "was mere fodder in service of this foul design?"

"Nobility occasionally exacts a price from its wearer, Osamu, particularly when the nobleman in question is indeed noble. Your father would never have supported Oda's insurrection."

"But he surely could not have stopped it, either." Hiroshi was invariably rational. "What difference was his life in this terrible business?"

"Grudges and examples, Hiroshi. Oda harbored the former against your father and would therefore render him the latter. It is not his having been able to achieve the murderous design that is of importance but his doing so free of repercussion."

"There will be repercussion," Osamu said through gritted teeth. "I will see to it mys—*Oji*, look!"

But Takeru moved too slowly, or his assailant too swiftly, for Chau Hai Fan had already sliced through the samurai's lower right leg by the time he had turned around. This he followed with another deep slice through Takeru's left forearm before bring both *jian* round for a dual slash at neck height. Takeru, though injured and certainly stunned, was nevertheless among the finest of swordsmen and would not prove so easy a kill as that to which Chau Hai Fan was accustomed.

A fraction of an instant prior to the *jian* having ended his life, Takeru had pulled from its scabbard his katana in an underhand manner, ensuring the base of its blade would intercept Chau's attack. He then drove his head hard into that of his assailant, forcing the smaller Chau Hai Fan to step back, brace himself, and reevaluate the contest.

"Leave us, *Oi*, this instant—leave us!" Takeru's was not a voice but a roar. "You must ready Mikawa for whatever awaits. Now go!"

"*Oji...*" Hiroshi, like his brother, was nervously holding his borrowed katana, pointing its end toward the indifferent Chau Hai Fan.

"Go!" Takeru had by now assumed a flawless stance, as though he were not cut deeply on arm and leg alike.

The brothers each mounted a horse, then looked back to the two warriors, both of whom now stood in a stance unique to their respective sword disciplines. Wearing a visage of regret, Osamu urged his horse forward, as did Hiroshi. They were mere steps into the ride when Hiroshi's horse dropped to its knees in agony, for a *jian* had found its way into the horse's broad neck, Chau Hai Fan having thrown the blade some five body lengths in order to arrest the brothers' escape.

Making matters worse still, Hiroshi's own leg was trapped beneath the horse's massive weight; too suddenly had the animal's weight rolled over.

"On my horse, Hiroshi, now!" Osamu channeled Takeru's roar but to no effect, for Hiroshi was indeed unable to extricate himself from the position in which he found himself. Osamu now set himself to the task of liberating his brother's captive limb.

While the brothers struggled, Takeru and Chau locked eyes, little more than a sword's length separated them. When at last movement disrupted their stillness, not even the keenest of observers could have stated with certainty whose blade struck forth first. The masters moved in perfect unison.

The Duels

TING! Slash, Slash, Swoosh, TING! Slash, Swoosh, Swoosh,
Swoosh, Swoosh, TING! SWOOSH!

Gods above, he's quick, Takeru thought. *He* is *quick*.

Takeru's injuries were crippling. Both footing and grip had been compromised in Chau's ambush, and he needed both now perhaps more than ever before.

I wonder how old Hernan would have handled this little terror. Even under such circumstances did Takeru's nimble mind wander to such questions.

TING! Slash, Swoosh, Swoosh, TING! TING! TING!
Swoosh, TING!

This last meeting of blades drove Takeru's katana into the soil at his feet, a move that was followed by Chau bringing his heel to bear on the samurai's head, dazing him to a dangerous extent. Had he not fallen prey to Chau's vicious sneak attack, Takeru was quite certain he might have proven a match for the vicious and awesomely gifted sword artist.

Now, however, suffering from the effects of blood loss and concussive force, Takeru resigned himself to an end for which he had effectively been preparing since childhood.

His wounded leg an anchor, wounded arm unable to grip the katana hilt, and vision blurred, samurai Lord Sakurai Takeru, hand shaking, extended forth the full length of his blade, single-handed, and invited Chau to render his killing blow, an action toward which the killer was inclined.

But at that moment, of all moments, a horse reared up, a "Hyah!" made itself heard, and hooves beat the ground in haste. The brothers had mounted Osamu's horse and rode east at the fastest gallop their burdened beast could deliver.

Clearly unwilling to abide the brothers' escape, Chau took swift action, deftly knocking aside Takeru's katana, administering a jumping kick to the samurai's chest, then mounting the third horse, which the masters' duel had blocked the brothers from reaching.

Riding in pursuit, Chau Hai Fan leaned down along the animal's flank to pluck his thrown *jian* from the skewered horse, then forced his mount into a full sprint. Gaining on the brothers would take little time, as their single horse rode with too great a weight to maintain any real speed.

Within moments, Chau had gained on the Sakurai brothers, the younger of whom had heard their pursuer.

"Osamu, he'll be upon us soon," Hiroshi shouted. "We can't outrun him."

"What would you have us do?"

"We are two; he is one," Hiroshi yelled with a surety he did not feel. "Let us make proud our *oji*...our father!"

Osamu needed hear nothing else. He brought the horse to a sudden halt and dismounted. Hiroshi, too, dismounted, though his leg was injured and his favoring of it betrayed the impairment.

As both drew their respective swords, they realized Chau Hai Fan was already upon them, his *jian* drawn, his legs flexed for a pounce.

The short man then spoke in broken *Nihon no*: "I am not to kill you."

From what they could tell, Chau's words, spoken at an oddly flat pitch, were directed solely to Osamu.

He continued, pitch still flat: "Come to the palace."

"You move right, Hiroshi," Osamu whispered. "I will attack from the left."

The boys fanned themselves out, attempting to come at Chau from two directly opposite sides, forcing him to turn his back on one or the other.

They attacked. He turned his back on neither.

Instead, Chau simply leaped backward, striking away each katana as they, in turn, flailed harmlessly in the air before him. What he did next was beyond either brother's ability to answer, at least initially. Chau unleashed a deluge of artful sword strokes, kicks, and pommel thrusts, which collectively kept Osamu and Hiroshi, well trained though they were, at his mercy. Dodging and deflecting unpredictable and multidirectional attacks was all they could hope to achieve at the moment, too swift and precise was their opponent.

Ting! Swoosh, Swoosh, Ting! Ting! Slash, Cut, Thrust,
Kick, Thrust, Kick, Ting! Ting! TING!

This final strike had sent Osamu's sword flying from his grip, after which he suffered a cruel kick to his forehead that saw him tumble into a dry creek bed that ran parallel to the road they had been traveling. Osamu's fall was halted with a sickening thud, as his back cracked brutally against a thick stump, taking momentarily from the young samurai his wind, his senses, his strength.

"Hiroshi..." he gasped weakly, gripping the air as though he might will into being yet another sword.

Some distance away, a wounded and nearly helpless Takeru attempted to stand but crumpled to the dirt for his effort. He had managed to drag himself to a nearby tree, hoping it might serve as a brace against which he could regain his footing.

"I'm coming for you, my *oi*," he struggled to say. "I'm coming for..."

Just then, a figure blocked from his sight the moon overhead. It was a man who held in his hand Takeru's katana. He knelt in deliberate fashion, handed the weapon to a calm Takeru, then stood and made his way down the very road the brothers and Chau Hai Fan had just ridden.

With a knowing smile, Takeru gripped his sword and used it in a cane-like manner to indeed stand. "Good to have this back in hand."

For its part, Hiroshi's sword was presently occupied, as twin *jian* crossed its length, edge, and hilt with such relentlessness as to have him wondering, *Will those* jian *soon break? Will* my *sword do so?*

Ting! Ting! Ting! Ting! Ting! Ting! Swoosh! Swoosh! Ting!
Swoosh!

Osamu watched helplessly as his brother, very clearly overmatched, fought with valiant resolve a man who would surely author his death with another stroke of those *jian*.

"I love you, my brother." Osamu clung in agony to the dirt at his fingertips. Still unable to will his body into motion, he simply looked on as Hiroshi, a brother of singular quality and a good person by any measure, was maneuvered into a death blow he lacked the skill to avert. Chau Hai Fan would kill Hiroshi, and Osamu would be forced to bear witness. He had failed his father, had failed Takeru, and now had failed his brother. The agony threatened to overcome Sakurai Osamu, the proud heir who had only a day earlier felt himself endlessly strong and capable of protecting all he loved.

Ting! Ting! Ting! TING! Swoosh! Swoosh! Ting! TING! TING!

I can't beat him, the brave Hiroshi accepted. *He'll have me any moment.* Hiroshi fought on. It had been a solely defensive project since Osamu had been disarmed, but Hiroshi had to extend the duel as long as was possible…if he did so, his father's heir just might make an escape.

Swoosh, Crack! Thwack!

He would extend this duel no further, nor any other ever again, for Chau Hai Fan, exhibiting no signs of having tired himself at all, had disarmed yet another member of the Sakurai family. Hiroshi backed up quickly until he found himself pressed squarely against the trunk of a sturdy tree.

Chau Hai Fan moved forward slowly, looking to savor this kill. His *jian* crossed over his chest, his backhanded swinging of each would see their cutting through either side of the boy's neck. Cocking back each wrist to augment the coming dual slash, Chau let loose…

Swip, Crack! TING!

When Hiroshi, who had reflexively squeezed closed his eyes, opened them at last, he was at a loss to fully comprehend what…and who… he now saw. It appeared one of the *jian* had been sent flying skyward, only to land tip-first into the ground some distance from where he and Chau Hai Fan still stood, while the other had simply found itself deflected from its trajectory, the very trajectory that would have seen Hiroshi's head removed from his shoulders.

Chau Hai Fan's back was now wholly turned to Hiroshi. He had adopted a deeply crouched stance and now held his remaining *jian* directly before him, arm fully extended so as to place maximal distance between himself and...

"Who was this man?" Hiroshi wondered at the tall, fair-complexioned, darkly clad man who had—what other explanation was there?—spared Hiroshi a certain beheading. He was lean but sturdy and held in his right hand a sword not unlike those *Oji* Takeru had described when sharing of his time spent in *Kirisutokyō no* lands—long, flexible, pointed, and with an elaborate basket hilt. A *reipia* Takeru had called the bizarre sword. Hiroshi preferred his own, or, rather, his borrowed katana but was grateful for this *reipia* having interfered with Chau Hai Fan's lethal design.

Having been spared for the moment, Hiroshi ran to his brother's side and helped him to an upright seated position facing the warriors, foreign and exotic, as they, naturally, faced one another.

"Who is he?" Osamu asked with a wheezing voice, his body still unresponsive to his insistence that it rise.

"I've no idea, but he would seem to be a friend." Hiroshi looked on in fascination, for the "friend" stood utterly undaunted before the very man who had killed Takeru. "Curious sword, that."

Death

Xavier stood before Chau Hai Fan, betraying nothing in face or bearing. Chau Hai Fan's was a near mirror image, though he now moved with some delicateness toward his misplaced *jian*. Once both blades were firmly in hand, he again adopted his crouched stance and faced the still Xavier. The standoff endured sufficiently long for Hiroshi to have counted at least ten labored breaths escaping Osamu's damaged body, with at least that number having elapsed before he began the count. Steam rose from both bodies, which veneered the moon in a poetic mist.

Finally, as movement was of course inevitable, Chau Hai Fan launched himself with an enormous fervor he had not troubled himself with channeling when in battle with Osamu and Hiroshi. The *jian* moved as though on the winds of a hurricane, Xavier being the eye of this particular storm. The duel was one of gods, not mere mortals, too fast and expert were Chau's attacks, too precise and effortless Xavier's parries and counterstrikes; neither duelist seemed capable of anything less than perfection, which is what led to Hiroshi's revelation: "The one man whose swordsmanship *Oji* Takeru could never equal," he whispered in awe.

And indeed, what Xavier produced in those moments was a skill and dueling brilliance the likes of which neither Hiroshi nor his brother had ever before seen, nor even imagined. He was grace and might, the best aspects of each: he was force; he was strategy; he was talent. And he was under attack by a man who, to his own great credit, was forcing all of these attributes to the manifest surface.

Swoosh, Swoosh, ting-ting-ting-ting-ting-ting-ling-ting,
Swoosh, Cut, TING! TING! Swoosh

This last attack, though wide of its mark, had seen Chau's *jian* soar with imperceptible speed over Xavier's then-lowered head, leaving the Frenchman in a partially crouched state, his right arm gripping the rapier that was wrapped around his left side, ready for a muscular cross-body draw. The draw materialized across its wielder's torso, driving the rapier to collide hard with Chau's nearest *jian*.

Chau then moved to drive his latter blade into Xavier's largely exposed abdomen. But Xavier stepped aside and seized Chau's arm in midthrust. One arm of each duelist was locked via Xavier's grip, the remaining arms pressed blades one against the other; the duelists had now become a sole bundle of sinew, of will, of struggle.

Chau attempted to break free of the grip with a torsional leap, but Xavier simply mirrored the motion, now bringing both of Chau's wrists together in his left hand while doing so. This maneuver seemingly locked Xavier's rapier (which was now pointed downward) in a sort of jigsaw trap between the *jian*. As Chau made sense of the odd entrapment, he attempted first to kick and then head-strike Xavier, though neither assault met its target. He then labored to part ways from the puzzle but could not break Xavier's powerful grip. As the struggle continued, Hiroshi noticed a slight shifting of the lean, fair man's long blade. "Was that by design?" he wondered.

A few more torsional leaps, Chau leading and Xavier following, and an extrication was imminent. Chau placed a foot up on Xavier's flexed thigh and from that exigent perch leaped over his opponent. Xavier leaped as well, keeping himself even with Chau up until the instant just before their respective feet again touched the earth below, an instant in which Xavier pulled hard to the side and landed some two body lengths from Chau.

Now free of the binding entanglement, Chau again assumed his crouching stance and readied himself to unleash his signature whirlwind attack. But Xavier, standing perfectly upright and perfectly still, simply sheathed his sword and stared with frightfully icy eyes, visible in this brilliant moonlight, at the fiery Chau Hai Fan…

…from whose mouth blood now seeped. The deadly warrior then fell to his knees and allowed both swords to slip from his hands, which he then placed upon his fully opened abdomen. His evisceration was, like most such wounds, fatal. Chau Hai Fan had lost the duel, and with it his life.

12

FINALE

Reunion

Samurai Lord Sakurai Takeru had drifted into and out of a fitful state of thin slumber after having had his katana restored to his weakened grip. And though consciousness was again steadily escaping him, he had summoned sufficient energy to look upon the moon...to look upon the moon and to smile.

"Osamu will live," he had said softly, head resting against the tree. "Hiroshi, sweet Hiroshi, will live."

The moon, in predictable manner, did not respond but merely glowed upon its smiling audience, as that man bled onto the soil of Owari to which he had traveled in hopes of saving his brother's sons.

He had failed, but fate had anticipated the failure and had sent from faraway lands...

"Mathieu"—Takeru's faint grin had wrenched itself into a wide smile—"you are here, and my *oi*, they live."

Cl-Clank!

Xavier had dropped at Takeru's feet Chau Hai Fan's twin *jian*.

"I've not gone by that name since last we saw each other."

Takeru nodded knowingly. "You restored yourself to Xavier?"

"You remember my given name." Were Xavier one to smile, he would this moment have smiled. But he was not one to smile.

"Of course, yours and all the others. 'Mathieu' never suited you, at least not to my foreign ears. I expect you found passage aboard the *Castle?*"

THUD

"Osamu!" Hiroshi had been supporting his brother's weight as Takeru spoke with this strange man but was himself exhausted and succumbed to the burden. He now helped Osamu to his *oji*'s side.

"And these young men, my brother's sons, they live by your hand because another died by it."

"We were likely destined for such a duel, one way or the other."

"Yes, but tonight your dueling saved my kin from an early grave, if not me." Takeru had forfeited much of his blood to the ground below and spoke with hollowness in his voice.

"I'm afraid yours is a death I cannot abide this night, Takeru." Xavier's was a response to be taken most seriously. "Your doing so would make of my months at sea an exercise in the futile."

"Which poses an interesting question, Xavier—why *did* you follow me to *Nihon?*"

"We haven't the time. You and Osamu must take the remaining steed to your province. Hiroshi will remain with me."

"What are you...?"

Xavier interrupted. "I spent enough time in conversation with Jaidev to know you did not intend your passage to see the importing of still more muskets by the thousands into *Nihon.*"

"But what are we to do now?" Takeru seemed to be strengthening, the spirit of hope restoring power to his limbs, to his heart. "Jaidev is here, now; the *Ocean Castle* will be delivering its cargo by morning."

"Return to Mikawa, see to your wounds, and await word from Hiroshi, or from me." Xavier had remembered Takeru's nephews by name from his days speaking with the samurai at the monastery and learned one from the other after having spared them from Chau Hai Fan's *jian*.

"If Romero had any notion as to where it was his prized *apprendista* would find himself…"

"He'd have abandoned the enterprise straightaway." Xavier finished the thought for Takeru. "Your horse awaits, as does Mikawa."

Osamu, whose injury had proven itself debilitating, leaned heavily against Takeru, his own wounds now tightly bandaged, atop the horse. Both nodded in encouragement to Hiroshi, who stood with the stance of a warrior resigned to some dreadful task ahead. Xavier kept his eyes trained on *Kiyosu-jō* wherein Lord Oda, his retainers, and their many visiting nobles slept off the drink and feasting of several hours prior.

"Why don't we kill Oda ourselves?" asked Hiroshi, quite uncharacteristically, once Osamu and Takeru were on their way. The violent death of the man's father had exacted a toll.

"Because I am not an assassin, Hiroshi," replied Xavier in his tone of frost. "Nor are you."

"Then what is it we are to do? Why did I remain?"

"To begin with, we've a message to deliver."

Hiroshi's anger was momentarily displaced by curiosity: "And how are we to go about delivering this message?"

Xavier turned to Hiroshi with a response quite unlike what the young samurai had anticipated. "Let us, for our purposes, find an ox."

Beast of Burden

"Missing!" Lord Oda had not asked a question but hurled one at the hapless retainer.

"Yes, Lord Oda"—the retainer remained in a deep bow—"both guards lay dead, their weapons gone."

Though Lord Oda had been modest in his imbibing the night prior, he had also not expected to be awoken an hour prior to sunrise with news of his captives having escaped.

"And you have searched the palace, the grounds, the armory?" he dressed quickly while hastily interrogating the still bowing retainer.

"Yes, Lord Oda. Three horses were found to be missing from the stables, and…" He paused, seemingly uncertain as to the relevance of his subsequent words.

"And"—Lord Oda's face was forming an inquisitive scowl—"and *what* besides the missing horses?"

"And one of the nearby growers, he approached *Kiyosu-jō* shortly before we learned of the escape. His ox"—another brief lapse in communication—"it was, um, missing."

"Which has, I trust, something at all to do with our missing Sakurai?" Lord Oda afforded himself a moment of bemusement. After all, Osamu and his brother having escaped would ultimately have little effect on his greater design; their eventual submission to his regional rule would simply have served to render Matsudaira a still greater puppet clan than already it was.

"Perhaps not, Lord Oda, but the beast having been stolen the very night of Osamu's escape"—the retainer had slowly, cautiously recovered his posture—"there may have been some relevance."

"Indeed. Perhaps the brothers and their rescuer—Takeru, I expect—saw fit to slaughter and dine upon the ox before making their way eastward." Oda was now suitably clothed to allow for his exiting the chambers. Sword at his side, he turned to matters of far grander scale.

"*Tokoh* Jaidev has signaled?"

"Indeed, he has, Lord Oda. The *Bocho* gave signal of the shipment being en route for our shores."

"It will be good to see that marvelous vessel once more. Mighty were the Ming fleets in their day; mighty is their sole surviving ship still."

Jaidev had dispatched the *Bocho* in a perimeter-sweeping route shortly after its having returned him to the *Ocean Castle*. Once a passage clear of potential interference had been identified, the *Bocho* would first signal Jaidev, then return to within sight of Owari's shores and convey the same.

As the *Ocean Castle* had been fairly near, perhaps an hour's sail from Mikawa Bay, it would reach the same waters in which the *Bocho* was now anchored shortly after sunrise. Unlike the regrettable Sesimbra business, unwitting participants in the pan-global transaction that they had been, no cannon fire would prove necessary this day. Nor would there be any such elaborate transferring of cargo.

How favorable it is, reflected Jaidev, *conducting business with willing recipients of one's goods and wares.*

For the thousands of snap lock and rifled muskets would simply be ferried directly to the very jetty on which Jaidev had himself only the day prior stood. There would they be welcomed by a grateful Lord Oda whose resultant battlefield success would reshape the *Nihon no* landscape—its nobility, its wealth, its identity.

Tokoh Jaidev was nothing if not farseeing. The *Ocean Castle*'s days of seafaring autonomy were nearing a natural end. Legitimacy under a shogunate, under one of the world's *great* governing entities, would create for his people a legitimacy the growing European navies would elsewise soon have denied them, by sheer crowding of the waterways, if not by endless pursuit...endless attack. What had begun under the *Yongle,* that marvelous emperor of a truly wonderful people, the Ming, would continue under a Lord Oda shogunate many miles to the east.

But these are thoughts for the days to come, Jaidev concluded upon his mental scroll. *This day we must see to that cargo for which our journey was undertaken.*

"*Tokoh!*" A sail master had made himself present at Jaidev's cabin door.

"Ah, I take it land is within sight."

"It is, *Tokoh.* We will arrive as planned, just after the sun has risen."

"Very good, see to our steady passage." Jaidev then nodded and dismissed the sail master. *Now, would that Xavier might make known his whereabouts.* For Xavier had not been seen since Jaidev had boarded the *Bocho* the day prior. *He is not a man I should like to have at my back.*

As the sun was climbing from behind its concealing horizon, a great deal of pandemonium was materializing throughout the palace grounds. News of two competing tales had served their combined confusion to all those in and around *Kiyosu-jō*: first, a ship enormous of size and marvelous appearance had made itself known in Owari waters; it looked to be a legendary treasure ship from those glorious days of Ming supremacy more than a century past. There was no mystery as to the nature of this relic's appearance, for in its cargo holds was housed the very future of warfare itself, a future Lord Oda aimed to seize by force.

Second, and wholly unrelated, an ox had wandered its way up to the *Kiyosu-jō* walls, just east of the palace's main gate. The appearance of any unclaimed livestock would have been enough to generate some degree of confusion among villager and sentry alike. What elevated this particular incident to one of alarm was the burden borne by this beast of burden: atop its back was slumped the corpse of a man Lord Oda would recognize as Chau Hai Fan. Indeed, the ox had served as unknowing messenger. *But from whom?* Oda wondered to himself. *From Takeru?*

"Not a word of this to *Tokoh* Jaidev," Lord Oda barked to his nearest vassals. "I will tell him of this loss myself." Turning his back to the macabre sight, Oda scanned the lands about *Kiyosu-jō*. "I would not have thought you this man's equal, Takeru, though perhaps those *oi* of yours played some part in this foul deed."

This terrible incident combined with the earlier news of Osamu's escape might have distracted a lesser man from the business at hand. Lord Oda, all would acknowledge, was not a lesser man.

"Come"—this was directed at his accompanying vassals—"let us to the jetty."

And with that, Lord Oda made his way to the shore, where soon his dealings with Jaidev would reach their long-awaited zenith.

Aboard

From a wooded vantage point, perhaps two hundred paces from the jetty where Lord Oda now awaited, for the second consecutive day, the arrival of *Tokoh* Jaidev, a concealed Xavier and Hiroshi looked on. Oda was surrounded by armed retainers, as well as by several of the visiting lords who had attended his feast the day prior. Perhaps a quarter mile from the long jetty's farthest end was anchored the *Ocean Castle*. Xavier had been aboard the vessel for so long a time as to render its appearance from this distance once again remarkable.

Hiroshi had expressed astonishment of a muted sort: grief, exhaustion, and the general tumult of the preceding day diminishing what might otherwise have manifested as childlike wonder. He was clearly kind of heart, imaginative as well. *There is a bit of Jakob in this one*, observed Xavier, *though his mind is stronger, strategic.*

The *Ocean Castle* had lowered two floating anchors to provide stability during the activity presently under way—a large-scale disembarking of literally hundreds from the decks below. Lord Oda had encouraged Jaidev to send ashore all those who would, within a few months' time, enjoy sovereign legitimacy under the banner of his own shogunate. "Let them taste the air and kiss the soil," Oda had declared. "We welcome our kin of the oceans to these, our cherished Owari lands."

Jaidev had embraced the gesture with considerable enthusiasm and had spent the preceding evening overseeing a readying of long boats that would ferry his people to their second home of Owari. It was these ferrying long boats and a number of smaller paddle-propelled boats that now populated the short stretch of water between the *Ocean Castle* and the Owari shores. "Half of the souls aboard," Xavier estimated, "have made for the shore. More are doing so even now."

"Does the promise of land beneath their feet carry with it so much appeal for these seafarers?" Hiroshi wondered. "Will it not seem an alien surface to their sea legs?"

"We will allow that process to unfold awhile longer. I welcome fewer being aboard while our purpose is realized." Xavier seemed to be counting, perhaps calculating some headcount or the like. He then resumed his speaking to Hiroshi: "Breathe as I instructed you, Hiroshi, and control closely your every movement. We will be submerged for some time." Xavier spoke evenly to a clearly anxious young warrior.

"I will breathe as you instructed," replied an obedient Hiroshi, "and will control closely my every movement."

"The moving of cargo will be under way soon and with it our most favorable opportunity in which to board."

Hiroshi looked with equal parts fascination and trepidation at the odd length of tubing, like a thick reed composed of dried flesh, which Xavier had handed him as the two made their way to the concealed ground in which they now crouched. It had been fashioned from the partially tanned hide tissue of a large swine, and it was actually of *Nihon no* design. One of the lessons Takeru had imparted his *apprendisti* while in the employ of the *Kirisutokyō no* holy men.

"Why did *Oji* Takeru not see fit to provide me with such lessons?" Hiroshi was at least somewhat hurt by having been forbidden this remarkable knowledge.

"Because your *oji* was grooming you for statecraft and leadership," replied Xavier, "not for espionage and assassinations."

"But you're not an assassin." Hiroshi reminded Xavier of his earlier words.

"No, I am not. The cargo is making its way to the *Castle*'s top deck, readying for its conveyance."

"Are we to…?"

"Yes, to the water—slowly." Xavier had wrapped tightly his rapier, the very weapon given him by Master Reynier mere days prior to that great man's death, in tight-fibered cloth, securing both ends of the bundle with a length of strong twine. This bundle he then tied closely to his back via the scabbard's long lanyard. He had done the same for Hiroshi's borrowed katana. "Though you'll have your choice of blades once we are aboard," he assured the wide-eyed and increasingly fraught Hiroshi.

"On your back, allowing the tube a hand's length above the surface. Breathe rhythmically and paddle your feet in much the same way. These tubes respond to the drawing and expelling of air; they will expand as needed. Trust in them, in me, in yourself. Now let us to the ship."

They reached the shore some moments later, entirely unnoticed by the distant Oda and his entourage, all of whom kept their eyes excitedly upon the Ming relic that carried in its hold, ironically enough, weapons of a dawning age. Xavier, whose trousers had been tied off at their ends, walked into the bay waters until they reached his neck. He then rotated onto his back and allowed himself to submerge just beneath the surface, with only one finger's length of breathing tube visible. *It will surely be impossible to see from any reasonable distance,* Hiroshi deduced, ostensibly convincing himself of the truth in those words, *or we should hope.*

The sensation was, for Hiroshi, unexpectedly relaxing, perhaps even meditative, at least once he had achieved the at-first elusive rhythm of breath and paddle, observing Xavier's technique momentarily before himself entering the water. A strong swimmer from early childhood, Hiroshi had nevertheless not commuted beneath the surface of any stretch of water while paddling and drawing breath from a tube; how exhilarating was the act!

Xavier had wisely tethered the young samurai to himself with a lanyard of perhaps five sword lengths. It was enough to ensure neither would subject the other to irksome tugging but also enough to allow for Xavier to signal Hiroshi once he had reached the *Castle*'s hull.

They paddled for some time, making fairly slow progress in order that their efforts would remain unknown to those ashore and onboard alike. Eventually, and much to Hiroshi's relief, the samurai felt a sharp, guiding tug—he was being pulled those final paddles toward the hull, where, he then saw, Xavier had planted a hand-claw into a dense plank.

"You'll need the tube no further." Xavier now indicated his own clawed palms. "Clad your hands thusly."

Xavier had secured the *tekko-kagi* from aboard the *Ocean Castle* prior to leaving the vessel, as Jaidev's own soldiers occasionally employed their usage. They had, for instance, been used by a number of the warriors who met their end at Xavier's hand aboard the *Arcanjo* more than three months past. Hiroshi now donned a pair and followed Xavier up the vessel's corner where starboard planks made a more or less right angle with their counterparts at the stern. This corner was completely obscured from the jetty and, in any event, a man's figure might not prove visible against the dark ship planks from any great distance.

A climb of perhaps five men's height above the water's surface brought Xavier and Hiroshi to a small aperture that the former had come to know rather well during the preceding months. Xavier stopped and removed the iron claw from his right hand, placing the majority of his weight on the left alone.

"We'll not fit through there, Xavier." Hiroshi had strained to keep pace with the experienced Xavier, which his erratic breathing confirmed. "We'll need to find another opening."

Creak, Crack, Split

Xavier had removed from just beneath the aperture a large section of plank that, Hiroshi reasoned, must have been partially sawn through prior to their having reached it this day. With only just enough of an opening through which a reasonably lean man might enter, Xavier, being more than reasonably lean, entered. "Make haste, Hiroshi," he then said in his accented *Nihon no*. "Time works only against us."

Once having secured his clawed right hand within the aperture, Hiroshi found his body pulled forcefully through it. *The strength of this man...*he found himself thinking upon rising to his feet.

"I'd offer you tea, but I'm only just returning to these chambers myself." Xavier unfurled the cloth in which his rapier had managed to remain utterly untouched by the waters in which it had been moments earlier immersed.

"These were your chambers?" Hiroshi's was a rhetorical question, which Xavier ignored.

"Laborers and soldiers alike will be assisting with moving the crates to their loading docks," he said while gloving both hands and placing his exceptionally wide-brimmed hat atop his head, a sharp whipping of which had served to dry it considerably.

"We will move unchallenged?" Hiroshi's question here was anything but rhetorical.

Xavier's response was oddly perfunctory in its voicing: "No. There will be killings this day."

"I understand." Hiroshi's tone did not suggest any such understanding.

"I should hope so." Xavier was now at the chambers' door, which he prepared to open. "Dozens of lives ended aboard may save thousands of your countrymen. Or not, but we'd be foolish to absolve ourselves of the effort."

Hiroshi then nodded and, having unfurled his own blade, held it before him with some degree of resolve.

"Sheathe the weapon, Hiroshi. Nobody aboard has reason to believe me an enemy, nor you. When we do give them reason, draw your sword."

Xavier then opened the door, kneeled in exiting the chamber, looked to both ends of the corridor, which was empty, then signaled Hiroshi to follow.

Hiroshi had traveled in his day; his father had desired he do so. Ports and harbors throughout *Nihon* and well beyond. But he had never before seen a vessel of such size and magnificence. The *Ocean Castle* was exactly that: a castle. But he warned himself against becoming enamored of its marvelous properties at present—there was work to be done.

His knowledge of the ship's layout equal to that of any who had lived their lives in full aboard it, Xavier guided Hiroshi through corridors and stairwells without so much as a moment's hesitation, even acknowledging with a nod here and there inhabitants who recognized the tall, fair Frenchman. He may have killed in coming aboard in Portuguese waters, but familiarity had a way of diminishing resentment, and this man had also secured for himself passage endorsed by *Tokoh* Jaidev himself. And so, many an *Ocean Castle* citizen nodded with timid smiles to Xavier…

…who would end his time aboard with killing. A quick look in upon that very space wherein Xavier had made his inaugural entrance at the start of that summer revealed that Jaidev was overseeing the activity. *Only ten crates have made their way to the loading dock at ship's stern,* Xavier noted. *The remaining thirty would be on their way soon enough.* Or so the crewmen and their master had every reason to believe.

Jaidev observed the crates as they were carried to the dock one by one, where they would then be loaded onto the *tokoh's* personal barge, itself having been lowered to loading-dock level from two decks higher. There was no particular urgency in this case, not as there had been when the cargo was first acquired.

"Do be delicate in your handling of the crates, men." Jaidev correctly estimated the fragility of the wheel lock mechanisms housed within. "Lord Oda's men will subject the muskets to sufficient hardship as it is."

Since entering manhood, Jaidev had kept careful record of his every day spent on dry land, a number that had grown only incrementally since that time. *One hundred seventy as of yesterday,* he noted. *I wonder what that number will amount to within a year or two of our* Nihon no *alliance?*

What had prompted this line of questioning was the fact that so very many of the *Ocean Castle's* citizens had taken it upon themselves to step foot on the dry land of Owari Province. Much of Jaidev's plans for imperial legitimacy had been made known to elder and lower folk alike, with the result being that Owari afforded Jaidev's people an opportunity to step foot in a civilized province, a first for many among their number. Nearly every instance of the vessel's citizenry departing the ship for time on land took place in lands scarcely known by kings or emperors. They were often the untamed lands of those vast continents so very far east from *Nihon* or west from Portugal. Certain areas in and around the coasts of *Fēizhōu* had proven themselves hospitable, but those waters were soon to be flush in Christian merchantmen and, naturally, warships.

"The world grows smaller, our vessel too crowded." Indeed, even the population-control measures and the occasional decision on part of some citizens to try their luck as wanderers in lands unknown, the *Ocean Castle* was home to far more souls than ever its designers had imagined would be the case. Recruitment of the sort Xavier once witnessed had long ago been limited to the adding of heavy laborers and their wives, and even theirs was often a temporary presence aboard. "Across so many generations we have grown in number, in mystery, in wonder." Jaidev was nothing if not poetic.

"Fire!" a voice bellowed. "Fire on the gundeck!" a voice cried out, followed by numerous others who in their collective panic joined in that alarming chorus.

And Jaidev leashed his inner poetry.

Owari, Ashore

At the jetty's farthest edge, Lord Oda noticed something unusual. "There appears to be smoke."

"Is that unusual?" asked a retainer. "You have suggested they smith and bake aboard."

"Indeed so, but that looks to be something else entirely."

Moments earlier, Lord Oda had been waxing eloquent about the sea change to which these thousands of advanced weapons would contribute greatly. "There is now and there will continue to be a place in our ancestral lands for the samurai ways"—he then held outward, as though acquiring an invisible target, a wheel lock pistol he had received from Jaidev two years past—"but mine is leadership and vision both sentimental and pragmatic. We will restore the shogunate to an office of power, of dignity, and we will do so with weapons against which our enemies will prove themselves no match!

Nods and noises of approval had ensued, which had Oda smiling in sincere appreciation of the support his plans had garnered. "Now if only the Sakurai matter were better in hand. And would that a corpse-bearing ox had not approached my palace this day. And, further, would that the corpse had not belonged to Jaidev's trusted (and ostensibly undefeatable) killer."

It was then that smoke from somewhere below decks had begun billowing out a number of portholes and various apertures. Oda knew little of sailing, but he had difficulty imagining this to be anything other than a threat to the day's plans.

Guns Blazing

Xavier, having made his way to the *Ocean Castle*'s largest holding bay, Hiroshi in tow, had subtly poured several vials of a sulfur/lime concoction—*my thanks to you, Brother Andreas*, he thought—generously upon a pile of kindling neighboring the remaining thirty crates, all around which lay dead laborers and soldiers.

Hiroshi, arms blood-covered, sword held out before him, breathing heavily, stood off to one side surrounded by the four who had fallen to his death blows. The other nine, poor souls, had died by Xavier's hand, after which he had closed the overhead hatch through which this particular bay was accessible, using a number of sword blades (their wielders no longer having need of them) to bar it from being opened...or opened with any degree of ease.

As a rule, most powder kegs and dangerous supplies of that sort were stored separately from the muskets and cannon to which they gave projectile life. But the two Xavier found on hand would be more than sufficient.

"We're going one deck down. I expect the diving port is open."

"The what?" Hiroshi had been more or less lost since following Xavier aboard.

"Follow me. And roll that barrel ahead of you."

"Why?"

"Seeds of his own destruction," was all Xavier said in reply as he rolled his own keg.

After rolling the keg into a neighboring bay, which was unoccupied, Xavier pointed to a number of large linen crates. "Stack two of those right"—he paced out six steps then looked at the ceiling directly overhead—"here."

Once that was done, Hiroshi watched as Xavier maneuvered one of the kegs atop the stacked crates. Procuring a matchlock fuse, fittingly enough, which he then lit using a length of flint on his scabbard, Xavier placed the fuse into the keg and pointed to another bay door. The bay they had left behind was now fully aflame, and a concerted effort was being made by frantic crewmen and sailors to break open the barred entryway.

"To the next hatch, and move that keg with you." Xavier was eerily calm throughout these trials. Death lay in his wake, more was to follow, and he spoke as though reading the soothing verses of a lover's poem.

They reached the neighboring bay, the door of which Xavier closed firmly, just before covering himself and Hiroshi with his cloak. "Do cover your ears, Hiroshi."

BOOM!

The powder keg, Hiroshi observed upon reentering the bay, had blown both upward and downward with enough force to severely damage the ceiling above while destroying the empty crates below and similarly damaging the floor upon which they had been stacked. Hiroshi could clearly see the deck above, and the feet of panicked people running back and forth, few stopped to look below, as all were racing to the now opened hatch in the crate-laden bay. Man-high flames prevented a swift entry into that room, while an initial salvo of bucketed water had merely spread farther the all-consuming fire. Any serviceable snap lock muskets once the fire was contained would number in the scores, perhaps fewer, nothing approaching two thousand.

Xavier began tearing with brute force at the damaged planks below, indicating to Hiroshi that he should take his sword to those overhead. "I'll be needing both opened to a body's width."

"You? What about me?"

"You'll need only"—wrenching a complete plank from the floor—"this one. Join me once your work is done." Xavier then dropped into the deck below, where Hiroshi heard a chaos of steel and blood unfold.

"Would that such a sound was not so familiar a cacophony to my ears," he said quietly while hacking at the board above.

Precisely as the hole reached a man's width, a harpoon was thrust from above, narrowly missing the startled Hiroshi, who fell backward and landed in thudding manner in the deck below, wherein Xavier had allowed his solo swordsman act to unfold in brutally bloody fashion. Three lay dead around what looked to be a massive iron bell, itself dangling from several chains over what Hiroshi deduced was the previously mentioned diving port...which was open.

"Luck is with us. They hadn't yet lowered the bell." Xavier looked above, noting that ropes were being lowered into the higher of the two blasted holes while flames still devoured crate and musket alike one bay up and over.

"Keep your reed?"

"What? No, it's in your chambers. I thought we might go out that way."

"Take this one. My exit will be less clandestine."

"Your exit? We're not going together?"

"Afraid not. And time, as has been the case this morn, trespasses upon our efforts. Dive in and get yourself to safety. Keep clear of the jetty. Oda will be summoning soldiers to the shore."

"But I..."

"You haven't a moment to spare."

"Whatever happens, thank y—"

But Xavier then gave Hiroshi a light push, sending the startled samurai three men's height into the waters below. Fortunately, the overwhelmed samurai had held tight his breathing tube and quickly resumed the very same paddling-breathing rhythm taught him that very morning.

Whatever does Xavier now have in mind...? Hiroshi managed to inquire of his own mind while making his way to shore...*with the cargo gone and our purpose fulfilled?*

Tokoh's Quarters

The fires raging below punctuated with two horrific explosions had led to panic among those four hundred or so souls who had not gone ashore, many of whom now worked to contain the blaze while readying the main deck's remaining long boats for a hasty escape, should that prove necessary.

Tears of rage washed down Jaidev's otherwise unreadable face. *Damn you, Xavier. Were we not in league? Were you not aboard to kill or tame Takeru, to do me that kindness as I showed you the kindness of ignoring your killing of my men? Damn you!*

"*Tokoh*, the crates are lost. We have contained the fire to one deck, two bays, but it does rage." The sail master was flanked by two crewmen and a taskmaster.

"See the women and children still aboard to my barge, as many as can safely board, the rest to the long boats."

"All are nearly ready to depart the ship, *Tokoh*. Many of our stronger souls lowered themselves down by rope and now swim to the jetty."

"Then cast off the others via boat to the Owari shores with my blessing and an assurance that they will board the *Ocean Castle* once again."

"And what of you, *Tokoh*, and of the crew?"

"We pull anchor immediately and head east, for the Mikawa shore. We've a palace to raze."

The sail master and his men nodded knowingly. Even a skeleton crew of sixty could effectively maneuver the *Ocean Castle* to so near a bay, while a mere ten were capable of readying the great cannon for its destructive business. These well-trained and highly capable men then saw to the quick off-boarding of the hundred or so women and children who sat uneasily in longboats and Jaidev's barge. "May Lord Oda take pity on them," Jaidev solemnly prayed, "he'll surely afford me nothing of the sort."

"*Jungsa!*" Jaidev spotted the very soldier Xavier had wounded when coming aboard several months past. "Our enemy is still aboard. See that he is found; see that he is killed."

With apparent uneasiness, the *jungsa* nodded his understanding and went below decks.

Shortly thereafter, Jaidev heard the distinctive sound of anchors being withdrawn from some distance beneath the water's surface, saw the crew unfurling sails, the sail masters overseeing the mast positioning. He then gave the verbal order to cast off, leaving at his back a confused Lord Oda, who was, to say the least, manically confused as to just what had gone awry with his brilliant design.

"Takeru imagines his islands will enjoy reprieve from the peril of firepower. Let us prove to him otherwise."

And ashore, perhaps a half mile from the jetty where Lord Oda watched impotently the *Ocean Castle* make sail, without so much as a single crate of snap locks having reached Owari shores, Hiroshi rested against a bush-enclosed tree trunk.

"Whatever it is you have in mind, Xavier, I hope we'll see one another again. I owe you my life…and hope to repay the debt."

Sink

The winds were favorable; the waters calm; the crew competent—the *Ocean Castle* entered Mikawa Bay unchallenged within the shortest of whiles after having set sail. Jaidev had ordered the cannon readied for its firing once his target, the coastal palace in which the Sakurai family had lived and thrived for three generations, was in sight. It was well known to Jaidev, who, having lain eyes upon it twice and heard much about it from Takeru himself, would surely revel in seeing its fine architecture reduced to splinters.

"Whatever foul pact you forged with Xavier, Takeru, a pact that saw the man travel thousands of miles in its service, that pact will be your home's destruction." Jaidev's was a mind operating at some distance from a balanced state.

Below decks, the loyal *jungsa* and his three recruits sought out the man they feared responsible for their vessel's damage. The bay fire had been extinguished, though not before devouring all save one of the musket-laden crates, its flames then spreading to the neighboring bay whose floor and ceiling had been blasted cleanly through.

Their faces covered in soaked cloths, the hunting party moved below decks systematically seeking out the elusive Xavier.

"Mikawa Palace in sight!" the voice belonged to the sail master whom Jaidev had charged with the oversight of this hastily conceived deed. "Ready the cannon!"

And indeed, after having rounded a small peninsular patch of Mikawa's gorgeous land, that province's coastal palace was in clear sight of the *Ocean Castle*, which need now only wheel its stern into position for a firing of its ferocious cannon, whose projectiles, as Sesimbra well knew, carried a demonically explosive charge to the recipient of their impact.

As the vessel began its wheeling about, one of the *jungsa*'s men heard a faint *swish*, like smoke and air billowing in response to quick motion. The four were now nearing the deck immediately below their cannon and nearing the chamber corridor just above the ceiling-blasted bay. It was dim, the air fumed with lingering wood smoke, and the *jungsa* noticed a small powder keg tied to the ceiling above, itself immediately above the two earlier blasted holes, down through which the *Ocean Castle*'s diving bell was visible.

"That keg," the *jungsa* realized, "it's immediately below the cann—"

Slash, Swoosh, Slash, Slash, Cut, Slash, Cut, Swoosh, Cut,
Swoosh, Cut, Slash

The *jungsa* lay dead, alongside the bodies of his three men. Not a one had fully registered an enemy sword nor the swordsman whose skill had taken their lives. Xavier then placed a fuse in the tiny powder keg that was, indeed, immediately below the cannon's chariot-size wheel carriage.

Mikawa

"*Oji!* Look!" the heavily limping Osamu stood weakly in the palace *moya.*

"The gods above." Takeru realized immediately what evil was rearing its head. "We must away. I will see to the others; you are too weak to be of help."

"But, *Oji...*"

"Listen to me—you are now daimyo and must survive this. I'll not lose you and your father on successive days. Now go."

As Osamu hobbled away, Takeru looked in utter dread at the wheeling *Ocean Castle.*

"If you are aboard, Xavier, now is the time."

Final Shot

"Is the target acquired?" Jaidev asked from the main deck, his sail master maintaining a visual line of communication with the gunners below.

After receiving his response, he replied, "It is, sir, and the cannon is readied for firing."

"In that case, my good man"—Jaidev smiled with some madness—"fire."

Xavier waited for the telling series of sounds, lighting the fuse at just the precise moment.

Jaidev was on tenterhooks. "You will pay, Takeru, you and your kin will pay."

BOOM!

SSWW—BOOM!

The familiar sound of the *Castle*'s cannon fire had indeed made itself heard, but it was preceded by a smaller, entirely unfamiliar blast.

"What was that?" a concerned Jaidev asked.

"*Tokoh,* look!" the sail master pointed toward the palace, which, he now saw, would not be struck by cannon fire at all, certainly not by the initial shot.

For the cannon ball had shot high, very high, clearing the palace roof by what must have been a man's height in full. It crashed into neighboring trees with awesome force, severing their tops and casting flames all about.

"What is the meaning of this?" Jaidev demanded while racing below decks, where he saw his great gun angled hideously into a crater where once its wheel carriage had been planted.

"The gods in heaven!" Jaidev exclaimed, only then noticing a number of dead gunners and crewmen around the cannon and none other than Xavier himself standing at the crater's edge. Around his shoulders was a heavy chain, one end of which led to a porthole. It had been wrapped thrice 'round the cannon's girth and was prevented from sliding off by pressing against the rear section's fused and bolted lip.

"Xavier! What have you done?" Jaidev was plainly wounded of heart.

"You've said as much yourself, *Tokoh.*" Xavier then wrapped the chain once more around his shoulders. "The *Castle*'s days were at an end." He then dropped, with chain following, through those man's width holes his blasts, prying, and hacking had created throughout the confusion aboard.

Coming to a wrenching halt, the chain now suspended Xavier just above the diving bell. He quickly unfurled his shoulders from the links and dropped down onto the bell, which was normally lowered very slowly through the port below via a powerful gear-and-pulley network...which Xavier had disabled while tethering the bell to an anchor that was situated in an adjacent bay.

Running and looping the heavy chain through the bell's sturdy top ring, Xavier then drew his rapier and severed a sole length of heavy rope that had prevented the gear-and-pulley from releasing the diving bell. It now released the bell, but in a crashing rather than steady manner—taking with it Xavier, the neighboring anchor, and the cannon three decks above that had been vulnerably angled into the crater by the blast of a few moments prior. The combined weight of the anchor and the diving bell, not to mention Xavier's ferocious grip, pulled Jaidev's tilted cannon through the decks below, crashing through each with ship-rocking force.

Those crewmen, who, along with Jaidev, looked on in horror as their storied and powerful cannon was dragged unstoppably deck through deck until finally crashing into the diving port below, crushing the raised enclosures whose presence prevented waterlogging within that bay and those adjacent to it. Water, naturally, was now pouring into that bay and into those adjacent.

"All men below decks!" Jaidev spoke not as a man in control, but as a man enraged. "Please, hurry. Buckets, men, we need buck—m..."

BOOM!

Xavier had, it seemed, left nothing to chance. Prior to descending with cannon, diving bell, and stern anchor, he had lit a lengthy fuse within the *Ocean Castle*'s primary powder-storage bay. The resultant explosion had blown through the stern planks, through every deck above, and through the ballast and keel itself.

Flames touched all, as Xavier's sulfur and lime concoction (*thank you, Brother Andreas*) had been strategically administered so as to ensure a rapid spreading of fiery death, which Xavier knew to count on. What Xavier could not have counted on was the mass exodus of souls to Owari Province soil that very morning. The sanctuary Lord Oda had promised was simply more than Jaidev's people could overlook, though most had imagined returning to their seaborne home at some point. Either way, their absence had ensured the only deaths on board belonged to soldiers and a few hapless crewmen who, to their own discredit, would have been party to mass destruction in Mikawa Province had Xavier not intervened.

"We are lost," Jaidev conceded, walking catatonically to the pilot's cabin. "We are lost." Placing his hands aboard the wheel for what was, he knew, the final time, he exhaled in sadness and simply watched as his remaining crewmen leaped overboard or dropped ropes in order to climb down the flame-engulfed *Ocean Castle*'s submerging hull. The vessel, having only a dozen moons past marked half a century at sea beyond the first hundred years since it was born under the blessed *Yongle*, now surrendered itself, plank, sail, and spirit, to the waves it had for so many generations commanded.

But my people will live on, which was I suppose the aim of all this. Jaidev, mere moments from a watery death he had, on occasion, dreamt would be his fate, took genuine solace in that knowledge. *Oda will have them. Perhaps reluctantly...but he will have them.*

From in and around the palace grounds, Takeru, Osamu, and scores of retainers, servants, and local villagers watched the massive ship, which had threateningly entered their bay, succumb to fire and to the waters flooding its vast decks. A short time later, the *Ocean Castle*, whose massive cannon had nearly obliterated the Sakurai palace, was gone. Takeru, having voyaged twice upon the Ming relic, experienced a curious sensation of melancholy in watching the page of history disappear beneath indifferent waters.

"*Oji*, it is him!" Osamu pointed toward the shore, where a soaking wet Xavier walked toward the congregation.

He was cloaked; wore his floppy, wide-brimmed hat in such a way as to conceal his eyes; had at his side the very rapier Reynier had wielded when first dueling Takeru so many years earlier; and moved with that same gracile litheness that had beguiled every stranger he had encountered since having left the monastery.

"I didn't expect Jaidev had simply elected to sink his own ship." Takeru's voice was hoarse, but he looked stronger now than he had early that same morning. "Pleased you engineered for yourself a clever escape."

"Hiroshi lives." Xavier spoke these words to Takeru and Osamu both: "If he can evade capture, he may well return by nightfall."

"He was with you aboard the *Castle*?"

"For a time, yes."

Osamu was stunned by all that had happened in so short a time. "But how did you—"

"Brother Vincenzo." Xavier now spoke directly to Takeru.

"Ah, yes, an argumentative soul, that Vincenzo."

"Aside from you, he was the only cadre member absent when Innocenzo laid waste our number."

"Is that why...?"

"I ruled out your complicity immediately, though the others needed convincing."

"The others?" Takeru's smile nearly ruptured his visage. "So they do live."

"They suspected your involvement; I convinced them otherwise. Once they had recovered from their injuries, each returned to his own homeland." Xavier now spoke to the horizon. "But I sought out Vincenzo, and confirmed what my instincts had compelled me to presume—Innocenzo was not the puppeteer but himself a puppet."

"Gods above, Xavier, what are you saying?" Takeru no longer smiled.

"That we—you and me—are going to *Les Amériques*...to the New World. We've vengeance to carry out, justice to fulfill."

"But I've only just returned, and..." Takeru stopped himself, then righted his still commanding posture. "When do we leave? And how are we to reach these Americas?"

"The *Bocho* floats and is sailed by friendly hands." Xavier looked to the east. "As for when, once you have said what needs saying to your *oi*. To both of them."

Takeru pointed to a bag some distance from his feet. "I've also a message that needs delivering."

"For Oda?"

"For Oda," Takeru confirmed. "The head of my brother's treacherous assassin. Oda dispatched a particularly craven retainer for the killing of my brother. His name was Hayato, a guest in our home while the *oi* were in Owari."

"An assassin from within, not unlike our own Innocenzo." Xavier looked with neat contempt upon the bag. "If it is of any concern to you, I left Vincenzo's head atop his narrow shoulders. His heart, however..."

Takeru's notorious smile emerged from hiding. "Ha! Traitors within, revenge carried out. For some reason, one of Reynier's favorite sayings just came to mind, though it seems a bit out of place."

Xavier's eyes narrowed a bit. "You know Reynier's daughter lives, do you not?"

Takeru's eyes glistened in joy. "Until this moment, no—I was wholly unaware of as much. Now the saying is particularly out of place!"

"I'd wager you mean..."

Takeru intercepted his former protégé and exclaimed, *"C'est la vie."*

AFTERWORD

There were indeed fifteenth-century Ming fleets consisting of enormous treasure ships, and these did, in fact, sail the Indian Ocean (and perhaps well beyond) the better part of a century before Columbus's famous expedition of 1492. Under the inspired admiralty of that great seafaring eunuch Zheng He, the Ming treasure fleets extended Chinese prestige, diplomacy, and military power across stretches of ocean that could have swallowed whole the landmass of two Europes and still had room for a Mediterranean Sea or three. This was a glorious period for the Ming and, had they so chosen, would doubtless have marked the beginning of an enduring Chinese Age of Exploration that no European kingdom could nearly have equaled at the time. But for reasons as unclear as they are seemingly simple, the Ming withdrew from the stage of international maritime affairs and turned their attentions inward. This self-imposed hermetic sealing of Chinese culture would persist for centuries thereafter, only coming to an end when the enterprising sea powers of Western Europe came knocking. If only *they* could have seen the treasure fleets in their prime.

And the likelihood of a sole treasure ship having survived the great purging of Zheng He's fleet shortly after the *Yongle*'s death? It is, to the say the least, unlikely—but it is possible. And had such a vessel outlasted the era in which it was born, who is to say it could not then have continued for decades thereafter? Well, almost anyone knowledgeable on the topic of wooden sailing vessels, for one. Such vessels could certainly have enjoyed years and, with proper maintenance, even decades at sea. But hulls and keels and planks and masts inevitably succumb to wind, to water, to time itself; thus, for the *Ocean Castle* to have been afloat for well over a century would have required circumstances of a rather fantastical nature. It does, however, make for a decent yarn, and with a reasonably thorough overhaul halfway through its lifespan, perhaps such a vessel *could* have, perhaps...

Firearms were introduced into Japan in 1543, or around two decades prior to Lord Oda's imagined dealings with the seafaring Jaidev. These would have been matchlock muskets, or *tanegashima*, which, though fairly effective in *very* well-trained hands, were largely improved upon by their snap lock successors, which would have been welcomed by many a Japanese daimyo for the battlefield efficacy they provided their wielders. License has been taken on the matter of rifling, which does have its origins in the sixteenth century but would probably not have found itself applied to so large a shipment of muskets in the 1560s. This is not to rule it out entirely, only to acknowledge that the rifling of barrels would not become commonplace for more than a century thereafter. In this case, we needed to make the weapons worthy of Jaidev's retrieving them personally and also worthy of Lord Oda's interest.

On to Europe and to papal power/politics in the mid-sixteenth century. The Council of Trent (to which this fictionalized rendering of Pope Julius III makes reference when chartering the Papal Blades undertaking) was a doctrinal-political response to a burgeoning Protestant threat, which had yielded considerable instability throughout Western Europe in the decades prior to our story's beginning. Though nominally a peaceable approach to addressing the matter of religious insurrection, the council's very existence was owed to a sense of crisis that had for years gripped the Catholic Church in general and the papacy more specifically. Would any pope, but *especially* one whose entire papacy had existed under the shadow of Trent, have provided such a project with official sacrament? Possibly. However, we've no reason to think that any such undertaking ever took shape.

But the remaining Blades do exist in our story, and their work is not yet finished. Though many of the *apprendisti* died on that horrible day in 1566, four do live, three of whom have been putting to good use their skills in Christendom and elsewhere, while Xavier...well, Xavier is off to the New World accompanied by Takeru, the latter of whom hopes to see you there.

Thank you and be well,
Mark Joseph Mongilutz